CGW 11/26/99

HIGHEST PRAISE FOR
JOVE HOMESPUN ROMANCES

We at Jove Books are thrilled by the enthusiastic critical
acclaim that the Homespun Romances are receiving. We
would like to thank you, the readers and fans of this wonderful series, for making it the success that it is. It is our
pleasure to bring you the highest quality of romance writing in these breathtaking tales of love and family in the
heartland of America.

And now, sit back and enjoy this delightful new Homespun Romance . . .

LADY'S CHOICE
by Karen Lockwood

Lady's Choice is a wonderful American romance novel.
Morna is a great character who readers will take into their
hearts. However, what makes Karen Lockwood's historical
romance so exquisite is the authentic interrelationships of
people residing in a company town. Whatever era this
author would choose to write about, one thing is a lock, Ms.
Lockwood always writes a great story. *Lady's Choice* is
another winner by one of the most talented Americana
writers of our time.

—*Affaire de Coeur*

Lady's Choice

Karen Lockwood

JOVE BOOKS, NEW YORK

LADY'S CHOICE

A Jove Book / published by arrangement with
the author

PRINTING HISTORY
Jove edition / November 1996

All rights reserved.
Copyright © 1996 by Karen Finnigan.
This book may not be reproduced in whole or in part,
by mimeograph or any other means, without permission.
For information address: The Berkley Publishing Group,
200 Madison Avenue, New York, New York 10016.

The Putnam Berkley World Wide Web site address is
http://www.berkley.com/berkley

ISBN: 0-515-11959-8

A JOVE BOOK®
Jove Books are published by The Berkley Publishing Group,
200 Madison Avenue, New York, New York 10016.
JOVE and the "J" design are trademarks
belonging to Jove Publications, Inc.

PRINTED IN THE UNITED STATES OF AMERICA

10 9 8 7 6 5 4 3 2 1

For my sister-in-law Diana Wattum,
who insisted I could do this

and

for my brother Tom, who had the wisdom to marry her

Prologue

MORNA PATTERSON'S CONSCIENCE struggled. Some might call her plan wicked; others would say a solution born of desperation. But what else should she do about the sobbing little boy?

She'd always been an honest lass, but once this ship docked, she needed a town of her own, a destination. Surely, God would forgive a touch of deception on her part.

Of course, with Conor's mother dead just hours, the boy might need a wee longer to see God's hand in this. One by one, the other passengers had gathered their bundles and disembarked, but still she sat with him in the smelly hold. Conor clung to her.

"I won't leave you, Conor," she promised over and over. "I won't." And she was not speaking false.

He sobbed anew. "But Ma said she'd come to Papa. She br-broke her pr-promise."

Morna ran a hand over the sandy curls. "Well, now, maybe heaven looked better than what she'd seen down in this dark hole of a ship."

"W-we were almost there."

"Aye, sometimes God has a peculiar sense of timing."

Conor sniffled. "Why did she leave me?" He slumped against her.

She held the six-year-old boy, tiny and inconsolable elf that he was, and carefully draped her shawl about him. It was white and of the finest Irish lace. That and the fancy glass buttons on her dress had both drawn resentful glances down here in steerage, where coarse black shawls were more common sights. She'd finally had to knot the lace about her waist to keep it from getting stolen. The snipes about her fine airs let up some, but she'd still kept to herself.

Only little Conor—attracted by the shiny buttons she wore—had befriended her, and proudly shared with her his own little blue button, stored like a treasure in his pocket. It was plain and humble, not fancy cut glass like hers, but it gave them one thing in common. Now grief bound them.

"Conor, God decides these matters. What He does usually has a reason."

Another sniffle was all the reply God received.

"Conor, you have to go on to your papa . . . your ma wanted it. . . . Can you do it for her?"

"For M-ma? Aye." Small and vulnerable, he pressed his entire body close to Morna. His rib cage heaved in and out as he trembled in her arms.

"Shall we look at the letter?" she asked briskly, trying not to sound too anxious.

After a pause, Conor dug into the pocket of his frayed coat and held up an envelope of wafer-thin paper. Inside would be train tickets to Conor's town. She longed to reach out and grab it, assume Mary O'Brien's identity, and vanish into America. . . . If God disapproved he could strike her dead with lightning.

Not that she really wanted to die. She'd only told

Horace Westerhaus she'd rather die than have his hand sliding around her maid's backside and bosoms; hearing which accusation, he'd thrown her against the family portrait of her dear late mother. The unprincipled cad.

But perhaps in that God revealed His plan as well. For sure and it was clear to her for the first time that Horace only wanted her money, not her, and all of County Kilkenny knew it. Her father had once advised her: no man wanted a woman with a business head when he could have one with a bedroom back, but she'd called him wrong. In that advice her father was right, after all. But he was wrong in allowing her brother—a complete idiot when it came to business—to inherit the lace factory.

Sure and men were unjust creatures, rarely thinking with their heads when it came to women, she decided. She certainly hoped this America would be different.

Here, she could find her own lace factory to run. Which required a town, of course. Yes, first the town.

"Please, give me the letter, Conor."

Still sniffling, Conor handed over the letter. Out of his frayed pocket fell another packet—the hanky in which he stored his blue button. Shyly, he unwrapped it. "My pa likes blue buttons," he confided, and held it up with obvious pride. Morna, touched by his confidence, admired the homely little bit of bone. After a shy glance up at her, Conor spun the thing like a top.

"Tell me, Conor, what does your papa say in his letters? I mean, about his town . . . his job? Do they make lace?"

He rubbed his nose and then took the handkerchief Morna offered and blew. "Of course not. He cuts trees into boards—with the biggest saw in the world." He handed back the hanky.

Morna took the damp thing and sat immobile.

A factory town. "I came from a factory town, you know. It was my da's factory, and I used to tour it with him, watching the workers make the lace. . . . I expect you'll want to see your da at work."

"No, miss. Ma said a mill's no place for a lad, and then, too, Da's gone deaf from the noise, and so she feared I'll go deaf, too." He lowered his voice to a whisper. "She didn't want to come, you know. But I did. Do you think it's my fault she—"

"Of course not. You'll have a fresh start in America. We all will. There's nothing to be sorry for in facing the unknown. Not braving the unknown, there's the pity."

Secretly, Morna's heart sank. Mercy. A lumber town. Not at all as refined a thing as lacemaking. More in a league with coal mines and shipbuilding, she guessed. Probably full of drunks and reprobates and foul language. Not a lace tablecloth in the entire place. And her not knowing how to even chop kindling for the fireplace, let alone split logs. But there was always the hope she could sew something. Perhaps canvas for covered wagons. Or circus tents. Or ladies' corsets. It didn't really matter, as long as it paid.

A steward from the deck above poked his head into the hold. "Everybody's to disembark now." He moved past them to gather his own knapsack.

Conor flung his arms more tightly about her. "Don't leave me, Morna. Stay with me."

"Now, now," she soothed, stroking his curls while unfolding and smoothing out the envelope he'd thrust at her. "I'd never leave you. But, Conor, if I came with you, because you need a friend for company, well . . ." She lowered her voice to a mere whisper. "I might have to pretend to be your mama for a few minutes . . . just to pass through the government men . . . not that I could ever be as beautiful as your ma. . . ."

He opened and shut one palm, staring at his little blue button.

"Conor, we have to go ashore."

Conor seemed uncertain, but tiny arms pressed closely about her again, and she could feel a tiny heart beat inside the fragile rib cage.

"Shall I borrow your ma's ticket, then?" He still had not said anything. "May I?"

Her heart sank at his long silence. But at last Conor nodded his head and stood. Tears stained his grimy face, lines of them trailing down toward his heart.

"Ma says—said that Papa wrote about how it's a—a company town. Ma read me how the whistles at the mill tell the time exactly in Bunyan, every day except Sunday, and the owner takes care of everything just like God. Better, maybe."

She bit back a smile. "Indeed, and a man owns this place?"

"Men own everything in America. Pa wrote that, too."

"Men own everything, Conor. Everywhere." But not once she got there, they wouldn't. A lady landowner, that was her dream of America. Never again would a man decide her fate.

She put on a brave smile for Conor's sake and reached for the little boy's hand.

So this Bunyan had an owner who allowed himself to be called God. Not once Morna arrived and set him down a peg or two.

"Hang on tight to that button, Conor, and say a prayer to the good fairies. Then let's go find this little town."

1

BUNYAN, MICHIGAN—PROPERTY OF
MONTGOMERY LUMBER COMPANY
NO TRESPASSING

*Q*UINN MONTGOMERY STEPPED off the train, planted himself on the platform, and stared at the view. Nothing about the scenery warmed his heart.

It didn't help that Theodore wasn't here to meet him. Cousin Theodore, who was supposed to keep things running in an orderly fashion, had no right to do this to him. Not when it meant dragging him across Lake Huron in a boat and then miles and miles by railway.

Quinn crossed his arms. He squinted down over the rows and rows of straight-lined streets, platted like a checkerboard, and filled with identical houses of wood, each painted the exact same color. He looked at the stark silhouette of young elms, not yet warmed enough by the thin spring sun to have leaves. Like soldiers, they stood in a precise line, exactly the same distance from each other. Even the street numbers were predictable. Streets going east and west had numbers, and those going north and south bore names of trees.

Well planned. Boring. Monotonous. Quinn had designed it all out of a deep-seated need for order in his life. Yet, to his consternation, he never found any peace in it. Just chaotic memories, and a desperate need to leave, as if by leaving town, he could also leave his emotions behind. Now he had a few tricks for keeping emotion at bay. Early in life, to his mortification, tears and joy showed equally easily on his face. His father had laughed, calling it a womanly trait. Sarah had laughed. The result had been his beard. The beard was as much to camouflage emotion as anything. Now he distanced himself from all but the impersonal, and he avoided coming back to Bunyan if possible.

At the edge of town, the sawmill whined. He turned his gaze. The mill stood at the edge of the Rome River, flanked by a calm river inlet that served as the millpond and holding pen for logs. Logs glutted the water. Logs clawed their way up a band saw into the mill. Stacks of logs, end to end, glided into the mill, where the piercing teeth of a razor-sharp saw whined.

This—this was the heart of Quinn's fortune, and the very smell of sawdust in the air meant money in his pocket.

His gaze roved to the woods stretching north and south—well, at the edge of town was the only break in the town's square predictable plan. Alone amid the tree stumps perched an old-fashioned log house. The bachelor boardinghouse. Two stories. The back half boarded up. The front half divided into dining room and sleeping quarters. A separate kitchen. An attic—long shut up. In its day it had been quite a house.

Now . . . well, Quinn never went near it anymore. If it weren't for the bachelors needing somewhere to bunk, he might have torched the place to be rid of it. Nothing about it fit in with the precise painted square symmetry of his town.

If he looked in the other direction, he could forget about the place. Out of sight, out of mind, which is how he liked it. He swung away, squinting through the trees for signs of Theodore. Damn his cousin. Theodore knew he detested waiting in this place longer than necessary.

But he owned it—the sledges, the wedges, and six kinds of saws. Sixty kinds of lubricating tins. Heck, he even owned the whistle and so decreed when entire families went to bed at night and awoke each morning. Best of all, he owned the profits. Yes, he reminded himself, that's what made a visit here bearable.

And Theodore, who managed the whole ugly little place, had better get here soon.

As if someone had read Quinn's dark thoughts, the sound of horses galloping and wheels turning came to him from the direction of Sixth Street. The town called it Main Street. Quinn focused. Theodore Montgomery appeared then, riding hell-bent-for-leather in a wagon.

He reined in, got out, and hurried over, wiping his hands on a handkerchief. Red smeared the white linen.

Theodore pulled out his watch. "The train was early."

Quinn didn't blink. "When I ride it, it's on time. Tell me why you've dragged me here. You said you could manage everything yourself, and I'd have no more to worry about besides investing the profits."

Theodore looked nervous. Even as a boy, Quinn had distanced himself from the foppish Theodore. Painful events in the past had only served to alienate Quinn even further from Theodore. Only when Theodore had obtained a law degree did Quinn see his usefulness.

"So what is it? Another mill accident? You didn't need me here just to clean that up, did you?" Accidents were full of blood and sometimes dismembered fingers. He should have known Theodore would be squeamish. He rued the bed he'd left back on Emerald Island. The languid female form, lush with curves, was his sole consuming interest—until the telegram pulled him away.

Theodore pocketed the handkerchief, withering under his cousin's gaze.

"I pay you a good salary, Theodore. I give you a house here rent free, and allow you to take care of these cogs in the workings. So now you call me to come here every time there's a problem. For what? Some mill accident?"

Theodore gulped. "It was not precisely what I'd term an accident."

Quinn pulled out a cigar and unwrapped it. "What then? Did one of our competitors sabotage the mill?"

"A few mill hands got into a scuffle."

"A death?"

"Two."

Quinn looked up, eyes narrowing. A town's reputation could be hurt by things like this. "Bachelors?"

Theodore hesitated, then nodded while mopping his brow.

The wind, raw and biting, picked up. Bachelors. To a company town, they were a liability. "Why, Theodore, do you have so much trouble with bachelors?"

"Quinn, it's obvious. They have no women to occupy them at nights, and so all they do is brawl."

"For once, you got to the point."

At Quinn's raised brow, Theodore rushed on. "But it wasn't your ordinary fight in the mill. Someone didn't understand the sign language—you know that's how they talk in the mill with all the saws so loud—"

"And?"

"And so a married man thought his daughter was

slurred . . . a misunderstanding. You know how men get when there's a fight, how a brawl can turn into a free-for-all in a blink of an eye. Maybe if they were allowed to mingle and—"

"No." Quinn made a quick decision. "From now on, I want only family men here. That's the only way to keep the town running smoothly."

"But the mill's working overtime," Theodore said. "I—I haven't got enough family men answering the advertisements, Quinn."

Quinn spun round, impatient. "Advertise back east with a company that brings in family men."

The irony of his edict was not lost on Quinn, himself a single man. But these rules did not apply to him. Quinn was above the rules.

He glared at Theodore. "Now, what was so difficult about solving the problem? Hire more family men and then evict the bachelors. And stop acting like you're afraid of me."

Theodore's mouth opened and shut. His face drained of color. "Yes, Quinn."

They were all afraid of him, especially Theodore who had more reason than anyone to fear Quinn. He watched Theodore tug at his collar, uncertain of what to do next. Quinn took charge.

"As for the deaths, do what you always do. Make certain the families receive letters on company stationery. Condolences and all. Signed by me, and send the last paycheck on to the family."

Theodore, clearly uncomfortable, again ran a finger around the neck of his shirt. His collar was askew, his tie off center.

"Is this a problem?"

"The family part is why I sent for you . . . One was

a bachelor, but the other one, Mick O'Brien, he had a wife back in the old country. A young'un, too. And well . . . they were—are, on the way."

"Why does this concern me?"

"There's no rule for disposing of women—and their youngsters—whose husbands die before they arrive."

Hellfire. If Theodore had any imagination he could handle this, too. Theodore was just like the town. If it didn't fit into a prescribed rule, he simply couldn't think.

"Shall I evict them as soon as they arrive?"

Despite his reputation, Quinn wasn't quite that heartless. "What's the name?"

"O'Brien. Mick O'Brien. Son and wife out of Ireland."

Quinn took his time lighting his cigar.

Widows had no business in a company town and were sent packing, but a few days wouldn't hurt. A decent interval to demonstrate the decency of the company town.

"Quinn, Mick had no house. I can't put a woman in the boardinghouse. The rules say—"

"I know what the damn rules say. I wrote half of them. . . . Loan her a tent. Dammit, do I have to do all the thinking?"

Quinn didn't feel exactly proud of this discussion between owner and manager, but rules were rules. Subject closed.

The train was ready to pull out. By the time Quinn returned to the comfort of his bed, the lovely Louise would be out socializing with her snobbish friends. But tonight he'd make up for it. Women, he'd found, unlike trees, were the one commodity of which there would always be an endless supply, especially for men who owned companies.

He decided he might have been too curt about the matter. He turned back for a parting word, tone softer.

"If there's a funeral, let me know. I might return and put in an appearance to remind the workers who's in charge." He headed for the railcar and hoisted himself up onto the first step. Funerals and Christmas parties. They were the only times he ever came closer to Bunyan than the depot.

He gave his monotonous little town one last look. From high up here on the train, it looked tranquil, perfectly ordered. Controlled. He wanted it to stay that way.

Theodore cleared his throat for attention. "Quinn, I'll take care of things better from now on. I won't bother you again."

The trouble with Theodore was the man couldn't see the forest for the trees. Any lumberman worth his salt knew the truth. One day soon, the forests would be cut down and it'd be time to move on to another forest farther west. Quinn knew this but was too comfortable to do anything about it—until this morning. Maybe it was time to start selling, before the prices fell. If he waited too long, until a boom turned into a bust, then his company could sit holding the bag.

"Theodore!" By now, the train was moving, and Quinn had to stick his head out the window. "I've got another idea. Sell that boardinghouse. Then you'll have to try harder to find family men. Understood?"

"Sell?" Theodore was trotting along to keep up with the chugging train, and steam was billowing about his pants legs. "Sell? Sell part of the town?"

"One building, that's all. Sell the boardinghouse. Then the bothersome bachelors have no choice but to take their stake and move on. Sell first before you mention evicting. I don't want to lose any rent. Understood, Theodore?"

By now, Theodore was lost in a swirl of steam, and green pines were rushing by Quinn. He settled back into a plush seat, the town of Bunyan already out of sight.

The scent of pine needles drifted in, that and a raw wind. Quinn reached over and slammed down the window of the railcar; then, safely isolated from all reminders of Bunyan, he leaned back and shut his eyes. The aroma of cigar smoke enveloped him.

Damnation, but grieving women could be even more trouble than a house full of bored bachelors, and Theodore might botch it.

If he were smart, he'd confront this widow himself—after the funeral, of course.

2

"*EARTH TO EARTH*. Ashes to ashes. Dust to dust."

Morna reached for Conor's hand and held on tight.

Eyes downcast, Morna stood at the grave site in shock. God's timing was getting worse by the day. Or perhaps she ought to look on the good side and thank Him for putting wee Conor in her care. Without her, where would the lad be? Oh, yes, God knew best. And that was the only comfort.

On the clergyman droned, but Morna was too busy rehearsing her speech to the owner to listen. Oh, the nerve of them saying it might be wisest to move on. *Widows with children have no place in a company town.*

And then someone entered the graveyard late. Briefly, she glanced at him, then the fineness of his appearance caused her to take a second, longer look. Without a doubt, this stranger was not just another mill worker like those gathered at the grave site. Although he was definitely tall and big enough to do the backbreaking work, the refined elegance of his appearance scorned that possibility. He was immaculately dressed in clothing of a cut and richness that set him apart. If he felt any grief for Mick O'Brien, or empathy for the weeping lad at her side, it and all other emotion was concealed. His mouth was set in a firm line while his eyes scanned the assembled mourners and finally settled on Morna.

As their gazes locked, a tiny spark radiated from him to Morna and back. It was he who looked away first. Morna gazed upon his face another minute or so. She had never met him before, of that she was certain, and yet it seemed she had looked into his eyes somewhere in the past. But where? In a parlor in Ireland? In a remote village from her childhood? No, impossible. She would have recognized his face. And this face was new. Whatever she'd seen in his eyes now she could not recall. They were blue, nothing more. Again, he glanced at her, eyes worldly. Heavens. Mercy. A blush stole across her face. The other mourners would see her staring like a hussy. So she forced herself to look at the coffin and the preacher, and she clutched firmly to Conor's shoulder.

All the while the preacher talked, she felt the heat of the stranger's stare. Finally, her curiosity unbearable, she lifted her eyes and stared back across the pinewood coffin, unable to take her eyes off him.

Conor, sandy hair tousled from the wind, pressed close to her skirt, clutching the black bombazine fabric in one first while in his other he held tight to his precious blue button. Perhaps she shouldn't have brought him to the grave site, for the lad had endured too much grief in too short a time.

But they had only the town largesse on which to fall back. And this was the place where the people who could decide Conor's future were assembled.

Aye, Morna might be ambitious, but not bereft of compassion. Her own dreams could wait. She had to do right by Conor, who had nobody to care for him but her. Judging by what she'd seen of this town so far, nobody would step forward and take him. Well, she would make sure of Conor's future before even thinking of her own.

She was in shock—shock at the crude behavior of America, shock at the callous rules of this town, and yes, shock at her immediate attraction to the man opposite her. The clergyman looked up to turn a page in his Bible, glanced from her to him, and cleared his throat.

Again, Morna discreetly lowered her eyes. But staring at the dirt didn't erase the picture of the stranger's face. He looked angry, as if calculating how much this funeral was costing his company in time and money.

The sun shone brightly, but it held scant warmth. A bitter cold enveloped them, and the trees were yet to bud. Pine bows were strewn upon the coffin. The air was filled with pungent scents—pine and turned-over dirt and newly sawed wood.

Theodore Montgomery, who up until now she had assumed to be the most powerful man in town, glanced nervously at the stranger. And with that nervous glance, all his authority dissolved. She'd been under the impression Theodore Montgomery managed the town, just as a landlord managed land back in Ireland. Only one man could make a landlord quake, and that was the owner of the land. Morna had a strong suspicion this stranger might be the owner of the town.

At last, it ended. Morna urged Conor forward to lay a pine twig on his father's casket, then drew him by the hand and led him toward the gate. By now the stranger was outside on the road, and she hurried by, hoping to avoid his eyes at all costs.

Theodore blocked her path. "Please, ma'am, allow me to introduce you to the owner. Mr. Quinn Montgomery . . ."

She stopped and turned. So she'd been right. She forced her voice to remain cool and collected. "I have been waiting for the pleasure of his acquaintance," she said. "But we shall have our discussion away from here. I find discussing business in a graveyard to be lacking in sensitivity." She walked away, toward the business buildings of town. She didn't stop until she came to the veranda of the company store, where the skinny balding owner, Otis, was already sweeping the porch, as calmly as if funerals for mill hands were everyday occurrences in this town.

"Otis," Theodore said. "Go inside and fetch an ale for Quinn."

Otis glanced over Theodore's shoulder and paled. He set the broom by the stoop and vanished. A cat jumped off the rocker on the wooden veranda and left it swaying back and forth as if a ghost had fled as well.

Morna had nowhere to hide, nor could she have moved a step. Once again, she was caught in the spell of those deep blue eyes.

Mr. Quinn Montgomery was coming toward her, watching her, as if sizing her up. She was suddenly self-conscious, and her hand went up to her hair, to tuck a wisp back under her shawl. The other women all wore hats, and she felt underdressed, out of place. There were so many new customs and manners to learn, even for a well-bred Irish lady like herself. Conor, meanwhile, clung to the folds of her skirt again. She reached for his hand and clutched it tightly.

Quinn Montgomery came stalking after her, like a wild boar in need of a meal. Beside him, Theodore hurried.

Who was this Theodore to tell her, Morna Patterson, what to do? But that was just it. They didn't know who she was, and she felt no need to tell.

"Mrs. O'Brien, please, we need to talk," Theodore insisted.

She whirled on him. "I'm not Mrs. O'Brien."

"What?" Both men's gazes narrowed on her.

By now a crowd of townspeople had walked back up Main Street, but she was beyond caring who heard what. This was the town where she would start over, and they had best all know it, including the owner.

"Who *are* you, then?" Theodore asked.

A woman pushed forward before Morna could answer. "Dear, I'm Edith Hargrove, and my husband's the company store manager. Perhaps I can be of help. Does she not speak English?" Edith asked. "Otis, come out here."

"Sure and I speak fine English."

"She's not Mick's wife," Theodore blurted out.

"Not Mick's wife? But she just mourned at his funeral."

"For the boy's sake. The boy's an orphan." Calmly, she sketched out the tale. Quinn Montgomery listened in silence.

Edith Hargrove clucked. "Orphans can't stay. Nor can single women. It's a matter of financial support."

"What if I told you I had money?"

Mrs. Edith Hargrove laughed.

Quinn Montgomery pushed forward, filling up both the street and the sky, and Morna became aware of only him. "Nonsense," he said. "Irishwomen don't have money of their own, and if they did, they wouldn't come here."

"I came."

"And the child?" Quinn looked at poor Conor as if he were the underside of a rotten log.

Morna laid a protective arm about the boy's shoulders. "Mr. O'Brien's son." Once again, she sketched out Conor's plight. "So you see, I'm all he has." And she would spit on Mr. Montgomery's shiny new boots before she'd pay a widow's tax.

Mrs. Hargrove sniffed. "Well, I was telling Otis the child surely didn't look like either of you." As if on cue, the screen door banged and Otis reappeared, bottle of ale in hand, his tie done up right and proper.

He handed the ale to Quinn Montgomery, who shook his head and declined. "Give it to Theodore, and make sure it comes out of his wages."

There was an awkward lull. Even Edith had the good grace to hold her tongue while the owner pulled the town manager off to the side for some business talk. Theodore kept casting nervous glances back at Morna, so it didn't take a fortune-teller to know it was her fate under discussion here.

Edith was more blunt about it. "You'll fare best if you leave."

Morna counted ten leprechauns in her imagination, took a deep breath, and prayed for a patient tongue. Ignoring this last pronouncement, Morna addressed Edith's earlier comment.

"The child resembles his mother, may God have mercy on her soul." Way more mercy than what this town was doling out. The bachelors though looked decent enough, and her heart went out to them much as it would to an unwanted child.

Edith Hargrove raised her brows and smiled. "Any sort of woman other than a wife or family member is against the rules, except for once a year when the town manager organizes a trainload of women, special ones for the bachelors, and we virtuous women look the other way. . . . No rules for single women—not even respectable single women. The ones who visit know family or . . . well, they don't come. We have a hotel, of course, but the company prefers to let the rooms to men."

"Be still, Edith," her husband said. "Let Mr. Montgomery do the talking."

Indeed, it was from Quinn Montgomery that Morna wanted answers. She looked at him and raised her voice. "What kind of rule is that? What kind of town is this?"

He gave her his full attention, while Theodore shrank back. "Ah, but company towns are different from other towns," Quinn said. "The company makes the rules, not the people . . . and as to that, I don't even know who you are. If you had to assume a dead woman's identity, I expect you're hiding something."

"My past is just that—past. I've come to start over."

"This is not a town for starting over. In this town, we have rules to abide by, and no one's past can hide from the rules."

She bristled. Such righteousness. "I'm staying."

"You'll change your mind, Miss Morna Patterson."

Mr. Quinn Montgomery turned, the expression on his chiseled face as hard as granite, his dark blue eyes unfathomable. His elegant clothing left no secret as to where he spent his profits. No miser this man, at least when it came to himself. She doubted even a summer sun would ruffle him.

Yet for all his confidence, he was not perfect in all ways. He was too forbidding for that. Perhaps his face was too chiseled, his brows a touch too heavy. Still, despite her dislike of his town, his wealth, his remoteness, she was drawn to the most basic thing about Quinn Montgomery: his strong masculinity. For the first time in her life, a man was not an object of scorn and competition, but somebody who took her breath away. It had taken all of ten seconds for her to realize his power, and she was still fighting her attraction to him as she answered him.

"I beg leave of you to give this little boy a home. You can't turn him out in the middle of the woods. You can't."

Quinn Montgomery's gaze spent all of five seconds on Conor, and then returned to Morna. His gaze roved up and down her black dress, lingering a second longer than necessary on the row of buttons lining her bodice, counting them the way he probably did his rows of houses.

"Theodore," he said, not bothering to look away from Morna. "Give the young lady and boy a tent."

"Give them something? You mean, just ask Otis to give it out for free?"

"You can take the cost from Mr. O'Brien's last paycheck. Surely, if you can work out a bottle of ale, you and Otis can manage to rent a tent. You're the two I've put my trust in here. Can you handle my affairs and rules or not?"

Theodore flushed a deep red while Otis gulped and ran a shaky hand over his bald head.

"You'd charge rent?" Morna asked, aghast. "For an orphaned child? And a piece of canvas yet?"

Theodore stepped forward. "Everyone pays rent in a company town, miss, even children. How else do you think the mill turns a profit to bring more families out here?"

"I thought sawing down trees perhaps," she said softly. Her family had turned a profit from lacemaking. This— this company-town idea was akin to a wicked English landlord charging tenants rent to work the very land. Perhaps America was not going to be so different for a female after all.

"I'm sorry, Miss Patterson, but it's all business. Nothing gets in the way of the company. That's why bachelors are a last resort as workers, you see," Quinn explained.

"No, I don't see."

"Because . . . well, because in the absence of . . . well, man's nature . . ." Mr. Quinn Montgomery seemed at a loss for words. He scowled at Theodore. "You explain it, Theodore." He cleared his throat, subject closed. "Get one of the bachelors to help put it up . . . and watch over her. I don't want any more brawling by men with nothing but time on their hands."

He turned and climbed into a dust-free wagon drawn by a sweat-free horse. There were no footprints where he'd walked. He was that impeccable, that above the rules. Not even the dirt dared get in his way.

In moments he was gone, with no trace he'd been there except Morna's memory of his eyes, blue and remote, gazing on her bodice. That and her quickened heartbeat—

Otis dumped a pile of warm white canvas in her arms. "Your tent."

She stared, her heart falling to her knees, and her dismay must have showed on her face.

"Well, don't look so shocked, Miss Patterson from Kilkenny. Surely, a tent at a fair rent is superior to the third class of an immigrant ship. You don't want to be back there again? If you'd rather we arrange passage back to Ireland—"

"No—I mean, thank you."

Edith Hargrove moved up beside him. "Oh, have a *little* mercy, Otis. For the child's sake. It'll only be a few days, I wager." Then she turned to Morna. "You'll need food, dear, from the company store—and an extra rug to wrap the boy in at night."

Otis stepped up. "Be certain our darling daughter, Nellie, waits on you. She'll be fair."

Edith took the tent from Morna and dumped it on the road. "That is enough, Otis. Send for Arne to help," she ordered. "The rest of you people go about your business."

As soon as the crowd dispersed, she pulled Morna aside and whispered in her ear. "Pay no attention. These men think every last dime must be accounted for or they'll be failures. When the tent is pitched, I'll provide the loan of bedding and a bowl and pitcher. A woman needs the basics of civilization. And you will dine with us tonight. The boy needs something warm. It won't be so bad. I didn't mean to shock you earlier, you know, but it's better if a young lady understands the realities here, don't you agree?"

Morna was grateful that someone in this town put compassion ahead of rules. "You didn't shock me, Mrs. Hargrove. I've come from worse than anything this town can give me."

Edith Hargrove drew herself up tall. "Oh, but you misunderstand. There's nothing bad here. Bunyan is practically perfect. We work hard to keep it clean and free from . . . well, unsavory influences. If there seem to be a lot of rules, that's why. It's well intentioned. A model town, really. We're quite proud, but you have to understand, it's a town for families."

"I do understand, and all the families will be perfectly safe from me. I don't steal, pickpocket, or consort with other women's husbands, so you see you've nothing to fear."

Two crimson spots appeared on Edith's face, and she added quickly, "Because of the boy and all, Quinn Montgomery bent the rules and has allowed you to linger a few days . . . perhaps without rent. He never bends the rules. This is a first. He is a good man, just not one for mingling with the town. In fact, it's been months since he's come here in person."

For a minute all was quiet, except for the distant whine of saws slicing up logs in the mill. The sound was ever present, Morna realized, like the pulsing heartbeat of the town.

Edith allowed her words to sink in, then cleared her throat and brushed a speck of sawdust off her somber black dress. "But beyond that, well, my dear, your prospects here are bleak indeed. We've simply no place to put up single women, so don't be expecting a tea-party welcome. Just soup."

"Soup would be more practical."

Edith would not let the subject drop. She apparently felt the need to justify the rules. "Bachelors are one thing because at least they work, but women have no recourse. Why, with your pretty looks—that reddish hair and trim figure—well, you could do much better in, say, Chicago, where there's at least maid's work to be had. You could pick and choose. Hold out for a fine house, which you'll never have here."

Did this town have no mercy?

"You're too helpful, but I want to want to stay here awhile. The boy needs me."

Morna wished she'd never dreamed of taking on the world. But . . . well, Morna had a good head on her. It was a blessing she'd not waste. No company town and its rules could outwit her for long.

A muscular young towhead, round of face and polite of manner, appeared out of nowhere and retrieved the mound of canvas. Arne to the rescue. He was the first smiling face she'd seen. "Vich place is it I should set the tent, miss?"

Rage bubbled over. Not at Arne, who was trying to

help. But at the cool calculating Theodore. And Quinn Montgomery as well.

"Tell me, Arne, the company doesn't own all the land around here, does it?"

Edith, her husband and daughter eavesdropped shamelessly.

"No, miss, the company is big, but Michigan is bigger, bigger maybe than all of my home in Sverige."

"Fine, then, put it outside company property."

Arne's eyes grew wide, and Edith gasped. Nellie hid a giggle behind her hand. Her father glowered at her.

"Is there some rule against that?"

"No, miss. But it's a big vide, vild voods out there. The company property, it has no boundaries in the voods."

The woods did not consume the entire world . . . nor did the woods completely encircle this town. There was water and, well, every town had a border of some kind. Surely, Quinn Montgomery's company had borders.

"Tell me," she asked Arne. "Where does the company property end on this side, away from the big woods and all those company trees?"

Arne's face relaxed. "Oh, ja, simple. It ends just a few paces beside the bachelor boardinghouse. The bachelors, ve have to live at the edge of the property line."

Morna's head for business did not fail her. She could always find the fly in the ointment, so to speak. Theodore Hargrove and his boss had not thought of everything. Nor had Edith Hargrove and her sanctimonious advice.

"Set the thing up one foot on the other side of the company property. . . . Conor needs some mothering, but he also needs male influence. I believe if you bachelors have a small boy to play with, you might not have time to get into brawls . . . and such."

"Ja, perhaps."

"Then meet me at this company store. Conor and I have to furnish the thing." Bedding from Edith was just the start.

Smiling, Edith rejoined her and walked as far as the door of the Bunyan Store. "Be sure to have Nellie take care of you now. . . ."

Once again, the prim Edith looked Morna up and down, pausing at her lace shawl. "Such decisiveness for a little thing. I realize you're not a lumberjack's wife nor a poor Irishman's wife, but still, for an immigrant, you know, Morna, you're not at all what I would have expected."

Morna smiled wearily. "Nor, Mrs. Hargrove, is this town at all what I imagined."

And certainly not its owner either.

Morna watched in satisfaction as Arne pitched her tent. He laid down the canvas and then moved around it, pounding in one stake after another. Her tent was right next to the boardinghouse, and in that Morna found great satisfaction. The town might not like it, but since Arne was pitching the tent on public land, no one, not even that scowling Quinn Montgomery, could chase her away.

As she stood watching her tent go up, a group of scruffy bachelors came trooping out to watch also. They were dressed in the same clothing they'd worn at the funeral—plaid shirts and cut-off pants. Their red underwear and unshaven faces were pathetic, but at least they smiled.

She smiled back. "Hello. I'm sure Conor wants to thank you for attending his father's funeral. Perhaps later you would be so kind as to tell him a bit about his father. They never met, you know."

They stared back shyly.

"I'm Morna Patterson," she hastened to add, "and I've taken care of Conor since his ma died on the ship. Poor lad."

At last one of the men stepped forward and took the lead in speaking. "I'm Widowmaker, the cook for these fellows. Arne there, who's helping with your tent, he's on the Greenchain and sometimes stacks. Nice and strong."

"Are you in charge, then?"

"Yep. They do what I say else they don't eat. Mick O'Brien was a good man. We'd be right pleased to tell Conor about him . . . but first, we brung the boy his father's effects—from the boardinghouse, you know. His favorite pie was blackberry, and I put some berries up last summer. So now I got one fresh-baked—for the boy. As a mark of respect."

He signaled one of the bachelors forward, and someone held out a steaming pie that was leaking purple juice all over its crust. The fellow tiptoed forward, set it at her feet, and then rushed back into line.

"Why, thank you. It looks—delicious, doesn't it, Conor? And look, there's a package from your da."

Conor hid behind her skirts, so it was Morna who reached out for the package. It was an old patched brown quilt. Morna set it down on a stump by Conor. The pie and the package sat side by side.

The bachelors stared at Morna, and she stared back, touched by their humble hospitality, so different from that haughty Quinn Montgomery.

"Go ahead," she said. "Open it. It might have more of them blue buttons in it."

Widowmaker was shaking his head. "Buttons?" He snorted. "Naw. He ran out and couldn't afford none. That's one of the reasons why the fight broke out. Because he showed up to work not buttoned right."

This statement, while baffling, did not alarm her. Conor, meanwhile, unwrapped the blanket and stared down at a carefully folded pile of red underwear, woolen socks, and plaid shirts. A deck of cards and pocketknife sat on top.

"We got another pair of Mick's socks still drying on the woodpile. We'll give him those later . . . figured you wouldn't mind since we'll be neighbors."

Widowmaker held out an ax. "Go ahead, young fellow. Take it. It was your pa's. We thought you'd want it, and even if you don't, every man needs an ax in a mill town. We'll show you how to use it later. After you're settled."

"Conor's too young to use an ax," Morna said.

"Not at all. I was four when my own pa put an ax in my hands. Better to learn young. Less dangerous to know how something works than to not know. You got control over it that way. Sort of like fire. The sooner you learn to control it the better."

He waved them on. "Well, I'll keep it until you have time to teach him."

With a resigned smile, Widowmaker sat down on the nearest stump, the wood completely hidden by his girth. The other bachelors pressed close behind him as if waiting for his cue.

"Well, don't stand there. Tell the pretty lady your names so she'll know you're human. And tell her your job, in case she needs some wood. . . . You start, Cookee."

A slender young man whisked off his knit cap. "I'm Cookee."

"She knows that," bellowed Widowmaker. "Tell her something new."

"I'm Widowmaker's helper . . . 'cuz . . . 'cuz I got seasick riding on the saw and I'm too puny to lift the boards, and my eyes are too bad to—"

"Shuddup, Cookee, or you'll give my cooking a bad reputation. Next."

Cookee plopped down on a stump and the next man in line doffed his hat and plucked his suspenders and stammered out an introduction. "I'm Cleatface, and I sharpen the saws."

He plopped down on another stump, and Cookee slunk back to the kitchen.

A handsome man with a black mustache and snapping black eyes stepped forward. Unlike the rest, his red underwear didn't show, and he was smiling with confidence. "Pierre, miss, and I'm pleased to meet you. I'm the sawyer, and I'm saving up a stake to go to the Northwest someday."

"Pierre, how nice," she managed. One well-groomed man in the lot wasn't bad.

Pierre stood with one foot on a stump in a casual pose. A most eligible bachelor.

Then the rest blurted out their names. Dogger, who rode the saw. Finn, a trimmerman, also known for his home brew. And finally Bruno, who said he worked with Arne on the Greenchain and stacking. "We are the strongest of the lot."

"Yeah, but not the smartest," Widowmaker snapped. "Hurry up, Arne. If you're so strong you should have that tent up by now."

The land all around was covered in stumps and the bachelors sat on them, as fascinated by Morna as by the tent pitched so close to their boardinghouse. "You need hot water, we got some. And outdoor facilities, too. You can share them."

Morna blushed.

"You're very kind, Mr. Widow—"

"Aw, don't bother with the fancy part. No one calls us mister, not even the town ladies."

"You mean they just call you by last names?" In her world it seemed impossibly familiar. Not only that, she could not help wondering at such strange names. "Forgive me if I seem rude," she said, "but your names are so unusual."

The men snickered and smiled, and to a man their eyes were twinkling.

"Not in a lumber town, they ain't," the cook said. "And my name is just plain Widowmaker, and it's a name you'll get used to." He smiled kindly. "Fact is, you're a lot stranger. You know, a young woman come here from Ireland, I mean."

They all gawked at her as if she'd turned into a leprechaun.

"So," Widowmaker went on, "why'd you want to come here? There ain't no men but us, and we ain't exactly what the town calls the eligible sort. We're the dregs."

Well, Morna would never say something *that* uncharitable. True, these men needed lessons in grooming and proper speech patterns and doubtless table manners, too. Yes, certainly rougher than the sorts she had met in the salons of Dublin. But kinder in manner, too. More open. Gentler than, say, Horace.

They looked like men with secret pasts. But then, she, too, had her secrets. She intended to start over here, and in America she knew her social standing counted for naught. Nor did she want it to. Moreover, these kindly men might turn out to be her only friends, and in the world she'd known, humble men such as these were too easily intimidated by women of class. So she'd keep her background to herself.

"Actually, I—I came because this was supposed to be the little boy's home." There. That was, after all, the truth. "And I hope you'll be so kind as to befriend him."

"Mick's lad. 'Course we will. Anything you or him needs, you just say the word."

"Water perhaps. For washing." She felt sticky and cold both. And so utterly tired she didn't care about the familiarity of her request.

There was a lot of throat clearing. Perhaps they needed time to get used to her. Who knew what the proprieties were? Especially with men named Cleatface and Digger.

She pulled her shawl close and turned to go, but Widowmaker stepped forward. "Not so fast. The little lady needs hospitality," he said to the men. "You don't see anyone else offering it. It's up to us."

He bawled at Arne again. "My stew is drying up, and the pretty lady and lad are growing cold."

"Maybe we should invite her in the boardinghouse for supper tomorrow."

"Thank you," Morna said, charmed by these men. Edith Hargrove would hate it, probably tell her there were rules against eating with the bachelors, but these men had known Conor's father. And they were the friendliest people she'd met so far. Moreover this town did not own her.

She stood then, at a loss for words. An awkward silence filled the air as the bachelors stared back.

"You moving on soon?" Pierre asked. "That Quinn Montgomery doesn't take to women alone. A lonely sort.

If you ask me, he's afraid of women. Tall tales around here say some woman left him high and dry."

"Yeah," Cleatface added. "Took off with another man."

Morna didn't feel the least bit sorry for him.

"Shut your mouth, Cleatface, else the lady'll think your brain got poked along with your face." This was Widowmaker, and now he stood up. "Time to go."

At once, the bachelors stood at attention. Widowmaker turned, and Morna glanced over at their log house. It looked homey, grand in a rustic way.

A wagon came 'round the bend from town then.

Someone whistled low. "Well, speak of the devil," Cleatface said. "It's Quinn Montgomery himself. And that darn cousin of his. He ain't gonna fire us, is he, Widow, all 'cuz of that fight?"

"Naw," Pierre said. "Accidents happen, and he needs us to work the mill."

Quinn climbed down and waited by his wagon. Widowmaker held up a hand to signal the rest to stay back, and went over to see what the owner of the company town wanted.

Briefly, Quinn's gaze rested on Morna, and she felt her pulse speed up, her cheeks grow warm. It was disloyal to these nice millworkers to feel so attracted to the man. She couldn't explain it. Quinn Montgomery was so stiff and rule-bound, he almost made her smile. Yet he stirred something elemental in her. Moreover, curiosity swept through her. Was he really afraid of women? Was there any truth to the men's tales?

She realized she'd been staring. He looked away, and with a blush, she bent to pick up Widowmaker's pie. Gingerly, she carried it to the tent, in front of which Arne was standing, like a butler. Inside was her trunk and some blankets. She sat the pie on the trunk and hurried out for a last look at Quinn.

He was already in his wagon and flicking the reins on the horse. Widowmaker returned, face long.

In the background came pounding, and there was Theodore Montgomery up on the veranda of the log house banging up a sign. Morna squinted to read it.

Widowmaker told them what it said. "For Sale. He's selling the boardinghouse."

"And when it's sold," Cleatface said, "then we'll have nowhere to live, so we'll have to quit. See? I told you it'd be hopeless to keep our jobs."

Already, Morna's mind was turning over the possibilities. "How much is he selling it for?" she asked casually.

They all shrugged. "What does it matter? We can't none of us buy it—even if he sells it cheap, which he will. These woods are purty near all chopped down, and he's looking to sell it all sooner or later. . . . Looks like we won't be neighbors for long, then."

"That depends," Morna said, "on how long it takes to sell."

"Yeah," they all mumbled, and with a last wave shuffled back to their boardinghouse.

That evening, Morna and Conor ate with the Hargroves, and what with both Edith and Nellie staring at her suspiciously, it was the longest hour of her life. As soon as it was socially acceptable, she pleaded tiredness, grabbed Conor by the hand, and departed. Together she and the little boy dined on blackberry pie in their tent, and later when Conor was asleep on a pile of blankets, Morna counted out all her gold pieces, her dowry.

In her mind's eye, she kept seeing that "For Sale" sign. She'd searched Theodore out before dinner and he had told her the price.

"No one will want to buy it, but Quinn said to try," Theodore had remarked.

Theodore was wrong. Someone would buy the place. Morna was not going to let a lot of silly rules outwit her. She couldn't wait to see Quinn's face when he found out.

3

THE NEXT DAY Morna snipped the stitching of her corset and retrieved another handful of gold and silver coins to go with the ones she had counted out the night before. British coins, but if Quinn Montgomery was in a hurry to sell, he ought not to be particular about where the money came from. It was legally hers. Her dowry, free and clear now that Horace had been sent packing.

And with it, she bought the Bunyan boardinghouse.

Morna was ushered into an office upstairs in the company store. It was lit by a single lamp, and at the desk, chair turned toward the window, sat a man. Cigar smoke wafted up.

"You come to buy the boardinghouse?" he asked in a smoother voice than she'd expected.

"Yes, I have," she replied.

At the sound of her voice, the man swung round in his chair. "I wasn't expecting a woman."

No, she guessed not. "Does it make a difference?"

"I thought you don't have a husband?"

Again—"Does that make a difference?"

He tilted his mouth in a smile. Something told her this man liked women more than he liked his job as town manager. He was certainly dressed like a dandy.

"I have the money. Do you want to sell or not?"

"What are your plans for it?"

"Why, to run a boardinghouse, of course. That's why I came to America—to make my own way."

"Ambitious sort, huh?"

She didn't reply. She was not here to discuss herself; she was here to do business.

"Well, I'm not sure, you being a woman and all, but I guess if you got the money, Quinn won't care."

"I'll deal with Mr. Montgomery if you prefer."

"You deal with me, not him. Maybe after we conduct the transaction, we can celebrate your new purchase over dinner?"

"I don't think so. I have a child with me who needs looking after. Here's my money. Cash gold." She picked up her valise and began scooping handfuls out onto the desk.

Mr. Theodore Montgomery's eyes grew wide. "I thought you just came from Ireland."

"We're not all poor. Is it a sale?"

He bit into one of the coins, then grinned. "Yeah, why not? The boardinghouse is all yours."

"I'd like the deed, please."

He cocked one eyebrow. "Clever about business, then, aren't you?"

"I know a thing or two."

He smiled at that. "Well, that's more than the owner knows, so I wish you luck here."

Within a half hour, the news spread, faster than logs floating down a river full of spring runoff. Shutters and doors, usually closed up tight, were flung open and the women of Bunyan met in clusters to spread the news.

Their whispers carried loudly from house to house and shop to shop. The town ladies did not even bother to lower their voices when Morna and Conor passed by on the way back to their tent.

Edith Hargrove's voice was loudest. "Well, I declare, now there's no inviting her to tea, no matter how curious we are about her fancy shawl. A woman who'd own that place is surely no lady."

"Why won't they have you to tea, Morna?" Conor asked the third time after hearing this remark. "Don't they like you?"

"They don't know me." There was no telling Conor the truth, of course. Ladies did not become landladies of bachelor boardinghouses. But Morna didn't care. She wanted a business, and this was her chance. She had not left Ireland because of a shortage of tea parties. And so for now, what the town ladies thought of her was of scant consequence.

Truth be told, she was more anxious to know what the bachelors thought, and so, with Conor in her wake, she marched straight to the two-story boardinghouse. *Her* boardinghouse.

She knocked, the door opened, and she stepped inside. The bachelors were lined up at rough-hewn tables, finishing pie and tea. At her news, there was a momentary silence, as if no one could believe their ears.

Widowmaker stood and cupped his ear. "A lot of us suffer from half deafness, miss. From all the years spent around mills. Would you mind repeating that news?"

She did.

A cheer went up, a noise loud enough to deafen Morna. The men slapped each other on the back and whistled and clapped so loudly that for a few minutes the sound of the mill was blocked out.

Widowmaker called for another place to be set at the head of one of the tables, and it was Pierre, handsome

Pierre, who offered Morna his arm and escorted her over. Cookee set pie and tea in front of her.

"I know it's not as fine as what the town ladies could offer, but—"

"That's not so, Widowmaker," she said, interrupting. She swallowed a forkful of blueberries and crust and savored her new status as a property owner in America. "Most delicious," she said, "and far finer than having tea with the town ladies."

"You gonna make us change our ways?" Cleatface asked. "You gonna move in with us? You gonna make us clean the place? You gonna make us say grace?"

Widowmaker produced a rolling pin from under his apron and bopped the saw sharpener on the head. "She can do whatever she wants, Cleatface. If she hadn't bought this place, you'd be out of work, so count your blessings. If she wants she can make you scrub the floor."

Cleatface hunched down. "Aw, I was only curious."

Morna stood. "Gentlemen, I have only one rule and that's no fighting. Beyond that, I hope we can be friends." She lifted her mug of tea. "A toast to a good friendship from your new landlady."

"Here, here!" There was a lot of banging of mugs on the table and Finn broke out his Kalijja drink for seconds. Morna gamely tasted the Finnish brew shuddered, and swallowed. "Wonderful!" she proclaimed.

"What does Quinn Montgomery think of you buying up his building?" Pierre asked good-naturedly after the celebrating died down.

Morna wasn't sure, but she put on a brave front. "I expect he'll be quite happy to sell so quickly."

When the telegram reached Quinn, he was unbuttoning the gown of his latest paramour, the lovely Louise, of Chicago and Emerald Island.

He allowed the telegram to sit untouched on the silver tray while he finished with her buttons. Then while she slipped her gown down over her hips, he casually reached for the telegram, ripped it open, and read.

The bachelor boardinghouse had been sold for five hundred dollars gold coin. Cash. At first, Quinn felt quite proud of his foresight and good luck. Other companies would call him crazy, but Quinn Montgomery could always see beyond the booming times of Bunyan. A boom only lasted as long as the trees did, he reminded himself. One day the trees would be gone, and the company would move on and leave the little town behind. If a man didn't start selling early, he could get caught with a lot of useless houses. So there was a method to this madness.

It seemed too good to be true, however.

"Quinn," Louise said softly.

He looked up. She was standing there in nothing but lace and muslin.

After a second's debate, he handed her a robe of silk and made his apologies. "I need to contact my town manager."

The lovely Louise threw it at his head. "You only wanted to know if you could have me."

"It's business, Louise. Urgent business."

"Don't think I'll give you another chance like this— not without . . . not without legal license."

So it was marriage or nothing. Too bad. Quinn had hoped she might have wanted him for himself, not the money that came with marriage.

"I'm sorry, Louise."

"I'm not. I hate you, Quinn. Don't think you'll find another lady who'll want you. You'll not, you know. The only thing you have to recommend you is your fortune."

Quinn gave her an ironic smile. "In that case, it's all

the more urgent I see about protecting my fortune. Excuse me while I answer this message."

The dressing gown hit him on the back. He peeled it off and deposited it on the walnut table by the door before walking out.

Five minutes later he had Theodore on the telephone— the only one in all of Bunyan, installed only a few days previously just so Quinn and his hapless cousin could communicate. Quinn demanded more details about the sale.

Theodore talked all around the essential facts. "The bachelors say they're not moving out yet."

Quinn smelled a rat. Again, images of finely manicured hands, the fine fabric of Miss Morna Patterson's black dress, and her elegant lace shawl teased him.

"Who bought the place?" he asked.

On the other end of the receiver, Theodore gulped. It was amazing how a man could gulp in Bunyan and it would carry right through these newfangled telephone lines.

"Who gave you five hundred dollars in gold?" he demanded.

"The Irish lady. Miss Morna Patterson . . . Actually, some of it was silver."

Quinn went frigid. "You sold her the bachelor boardinghouse?"

"Y-you said to sell," Theodore stammered defensively.

"I didn't mean to *her*!"

"You never said that."

"Dammit, Theodore, you have no imagination when it comes to bending rules. Find me a house. I'll have to come up there and stay awhile."

"Of course, Quinn . . . except there are no vacant houses."

"Then a hotel room."

The place was full of millworkers.

"Then rent me a room in the boardinghouse."

Unwisely, Theodore laughed.

"What's so funny? I'm a bachelor, aren't I? Never mind, I'll take care of it when I get there . . . And Theodore?" He paused. "You're fired," he told him. "From now on I'll manage the town."

And before Theodore could argue, Quinn slammed down the phone.

He sank against a pine rocker, the better to absorb the blow. The Irish chit—Miss Morna Patterson, whoever she was—was turning into a nuisance. Fast.

No woman was going to buy him out. He'd go live there and manage the place himself before he'd let that happen.

Morna stared in horror from the blue knit boy's cap to the laddie's woolen cape. Both she and Conor needed a few articles of warm clothing to last them through the chilly spring days. She was still trying to decide if she and Conor could move up to the second floor of the boardinghouse and not create undue scandal in town.

To do so would not win her any invitations to tea, but then again, the tent was cold, and there was nowhere else to live. Was not a landlady entitled to live in her own building? The fact that it contained nothing but single men was but a detail. The bachelors told her an attic room existed, a room long boarded up, but none of them was inclined to tear the boards out and expose the staircase. Superstitious lot, and so the matter remained unsettled.

And until it was settled, warm clothes were a necessity. But she balked at the prices.

She had to budget her money now that she'd spent so much on the boardinghouse. For though the price of the boardinghouse had been reasonable, her resources were now more limited.

Nellie sighed impatiently. "I told you—two dollars for one. Three for five dollars."

"Do you know how much more expensive that is than in this catalog book? They're only twenty-five cents each."

"Well, deal with the catalog book, then," Nellie said airily, "but I'm warning you, the mail from Montgomery Ward to this post office is mighty slow at times."

So slow, the hapless citizens of Bunyan gave up and spent their money at the company store instead. Nellie's father must have highway robbers in his ancestry, Morna decided. And Nellie took after him. Her black hair was the only reminder of her mother, Edith.

Nellie will treat you fair. Edith and her daughter needed to have a mother-daughter talk about the definition of fair. Clearly, Otis was in charge of his daughter, just as back in Ireland, Liam Patterson had been in charge of Morna.

"How much are you charging for a woolen skirt?" Morna asked. Sure and Ireland was cheaper to live in than this place.

Nellie did not waver as she repeated the price.

It was outright robbery, more than a year's worth of potatoes cost back in Ireland. If her grandfather possessed coins for this one skirt, he'd have been a rich man. Her father was rich enough, but would have rejected it as a waste of hard-earned money.

"I believe I shall try at another shop, thank you, Nellie," she said. Morna liked to visit shops, and it was no trouble to her to compare blanket prices.

Nellie swallowed back a giggle, then regained her

composure, face once again smug. "We haven't got but one store in all of Bunyan, and this is it. Bunyan's a little town, you see. There aren't any other towns for miles around. Just woods. The people what live out in the woods and all, well, they all ride in here to make their purchases." The girl tilted her head. "Green as new-cut timber, aren't you?"

"Maybe, but I take root fast." Morna fingered a knit cap for Conor, weighing cost versus the cold.

"I'm awful sorry about the little boy's father," Nellie said.

Morna looked up.

"Poor lad," Nellie added. "'Course, without the mother here, he still can't move up a rung here in Bunyan. Bachelors are low men on the totem pole and get all the dirty jobs. That way if one of 'em dies, there's not as many folks to grieve."

"Well, now, that's not very smart," Morna said just to be polite. "How's a nice girl like you ever going to get married?"

"My papa's the store manager. He'll pick me out a nice bachelor when the time comes."

The snooty little lass. She could have held her own in a Dublin parlor.

"Do you want to buy the cloak or the lad's cap then, miss?" she asked.

"I'll take one boy's cap, this knit one. To keep Conor's ears warm." Compared with this cap, the boardinghouse had been a bargain. Quinn Montgomery must have been desperate to sell. He was not, on the other hand, desperate to move the goods out of this store. Unless, as Nellie said, people had nowhere else to shop.

Mr. Quinn Montgomery would not understand, though.

His fancy tailored clothes did not come from here. Only the money with which to buy at expensive shops.

But there she was daydreaming about the man again. She bought Conor a peppermint stick and was waiting for the rest to be wrapped in brown paper and string. No extra charge—praise be. That's when handsome Pierre and Arne came bursting in.

They slipped off their slouch hats as soon as they saw her. Polite as could be.

Nellie stopped tying the knot on Morna's package and stared. "I've never seen the man with the mustache before," she whispered. "Is he a bachelor?"

"You mean, you don't know them all?"

"Oh, no, miss. They come and go. He's a new one. Leastways, he's never come in here since he arrived in town."

Morna nodded. "He probably can't afford to shop here."

Nellie's expression had lost all trace of smugness and instead wore an expression of awe. She was clearly smitten at first sight.

Morna smiled at Pierre and Arne.

Otis came out from the back room and glared at them. "Why aren't you two at work?"

Arne gulped and looked down at his feet. "I forgot my shirt button. I need a new shirt."

"Take care of it, Nellie, and don't dawdle. You know what to sell them."

Arne sighed and reached into his pocket for a leather pouch. "There goes my stake."

Morna studied his shirt—light blue and open at the neck. It looked perfectly fine to her. Again, curiosity about town rules got to her. "A new shirt? Why?"

He glanced at Nellie.

Miss Nellie spared him a smile. A small smile for Arne. A shy, smitten smile for Pierre, her gaze lingering on the handsome sawyer, taking in his dark good looks.

"Do you both want blue buttons?"

Arne nodded. "Ja, Pierre's a bachelor, too."

Morna was openmouthed as the light dawned. "Do you mean you have to wear blue buttons to work?"

"Buttoned up to the neck," Arne said. "I—I have to follow the rules."

Nellie handed Morna's package over the counter. Arne made a move for it, but Morna kept it. "Buy what you need. I won't go anywhere until you're ready." Nellie moved automatically toward the display cabinet. Curious, Morna took Conor's hand to eavesdrop on this transaction.

Nellie, smile in place, waited. In the case were rows and rows of buttons—all blue and white ones.

Morna looked at the buttons more closely, attention caught. Young Conor had saved a blue button from his papa's envelope. Sent by his father. Why were blue buttons so important around this place? Even little Conor pressed his nose against the glass, staring at the blue buttons, just like his father's. His peppermint mouth made an imprint on the glass, and Nellie scowled. Morna pulled him back and wiped at the glass with her hand. That didn't work, so she spit in her hand and then wiped off the smudge with her dress hem. Heaven help them, there might be a rule against leaving marks on the glass in this place.

Quietly she moved up behind big Arne to listen in.

"They're two dollars apiece," Nellie said. Her gaze never left Pierre, who was smiling back, as if equally smitten.

Morna gasped. "Why, that's outright robbery." Mr.

Quinn Montgomery and Theodore were no different than
the greedy landlords of Ireland. Getting rich off the poor.
She was going to hate the man if it killed her.

Arne sighed and gave a shrug. "I guess I'd better buy
one, even though my stake's not very big yet."

"That will be two dollars," Nellie said, and turned to
Pierre with a blush. "Too bad you can't buy white ones.
They're only one dollar."

Pierre returned her gaze. "I wish I could, miss, but
rules are rules. White ones for married men, isn't that
so?" Pierre returned Nellie's smile.

"Well, you don't have to wear blue buttons outside
the mill, do you?" Nellie asked. "I mean, like at the
lumberman-day social . . . are you going?"

Arne gave his friend a smile. "Go on, tell her, Pierre.
Tell her we lured you to work here so us bachelors could
win the log-chopping contest."

"Then you'll be at the social—you know, the dancing?"

Pierre shrugged. Arne knew the answer. "You know
we can't, Nellie. It's company rules. Bachelors can
compete with logs, but then we go home."

Rules. Rules. Rules. Morna pushed forward and stood
by the glass showcase. Who did Mr. Quinn Montgomery
think he was? Blue buttons and no dancing. "Excuse
me," she said sweetly, "but I'm so new here. It seems I
haven't grasped the American concept of dressing. What
does it matter what color buttons are?"

"Bachelors have to vear blue buttons at their collar,"
Arne explained, face coloring with embarrassment.

Instinct told her what was going on. Still, the question
begged to be asked. "Why ever for?"

Pierre stared into Nellie's eyes, as if he liked what he
saw. "I've got the rule memorized," he said teasingly.

"To tell us apart at the mill and around town. Company policy. Bachelors are marked men. Last hired. First fired, and if there are any accidents, it's always us blamed. Have I explained it quite right, Miss Nellie?"

"Precisely." Nellie Hargrove sighed. "And a dollar extra to sew them on."

"I sew my own on," Pierre said.

"I'll bet I could sew them better."

He smiled at Nellie. "I bet you could, too, Miss Nellie, but I'll settle for my poor sewing. Otherwise, I'll never save up a stake. Unless you lower the price."

Nellie bit her lip, obviously torn. "I can't," she said. "Papa would get angry. He keeps the books and watches every penny."

Arne leaned close to Morna. "Her papa also cuts off the buttons that are sewn on sloppily. Says it's a matter of neatness. But everyone knows he's drumming up sewing for Nellie."

Morna had known many a village widower who could mend his shirts and sew on the odd button. This was beyond the pale. "I'll teach them how to sew on a button."

"Sorry, only wives are allowed to buy needles and thread." Nellie's tone was slightly exasperated, as if these rules should be obvious. Or she feared giving away town secrets. "You're not a wife, or even a proper widow."

Quinn Montgomery was heartless, charging double for bachelors . . . and exempting himself from the rules. She remembered how fine he'd been dressed, right to the pristine white button at his neck. Double standards. Outlandish prices. No wonder the poor bachelors lost their temper and got in fights. Having no social life was only a part of it.

Sure and God must be frowning on this place. And if He wasn't, He ought to be.

Inspiration struck, and she handed her package back to Arne. "I'll buy some needles and thread, please," she said.

Nellie hesitated.

"I'm a woman," she pointed out.

"I said wives buy needles and thread."

"You didn't say anything about landladies, and I'm a landlady now. I'll buy thread, needles, and buttons." She smiled and pushed a silver dollar across the counter. "Blue ones."

Thankfully, no rule restricted her. Yet. "I still don't understand this."

"This is a family town, miss," Nellie explained as if to a child. "Management does all it can to encourage families to come and stay."

Morna waited till she was out on the boardwalk, where the clattering of horse hooves on the board street kept her words from eavesdroppers. "Run along and play, Conor. It's all right. It's me the town doesn't want, but they'll let you play."

As soon as little Conor was out of earshot, Morna turned to Arne, his shirt still missing its top button.

"No wonder it took Mr. O'Brien five years to send passage money for Conor. How ever do you manage here, Arne?"

Arne looked around nervously as if to make sure no one was eavesdropping. "Oh, you're right about that. A lot of bachelors get stuck in all the rules. And they're even stricter at the mill. Theodore says we can't show up at the mill with missing buttons."

"What happens?"

"A fine. A dollar a missing button, and a man's got a hard enough time saving a stake vithout the company taking it back in fines."

Mr. Quinn Montgomery ought to be the one fined for greed, but she held her tongue. He might turn out to be a worthy business adversary. And besting a man at his own business tickled Morna's fancy far more than playing childish word games with him.

It was like a bad nursery rhyme gone awry. "Let's see—men can't work at the mill unless they come buttoned up. But bachelors have to wear blue buttons. And even if they can afford blue buttons, they can't buy thread and needle if they haven't got a wife. . . ."

Arne nodded and finished for her. "And so some of us have to keep buying brand-new shirts, and that takes pretty near all of our pay, so if ve vanted to move on and find a vife, ve can't ever save the money . . . it's hard cuz ve never get out of debt to the store."

Oh, balderdash. "Arne, go back to the boardinghouse and strip off that shirt. I'm going to sew your button on for you. First one free, and then you decide if you like my sewing." He would, of course, for Morna could tat lace, a task far more complicated than pulling a needle and thread through buttonholes.

Later as Arne stood bare-chested, she snipped a thread, shook out his blue shirt, and handed it back. "There you go. Try that button for size."

Already he was shrugging into it; his fingers flew rapidly up the front, buttoning it, and at the top, by the collar, he fastened a blue button. The bachelor's button.

"Well?" Morna prompted.

"It's just fine, Miss Patterson. *Takk*—I mean, thank you."

"Call me Morna." While Arne proudly strutted about, showing off her sewing job, Morna stared off at the company store way up Main Street and thought. "Tell me, Arne," she asked, when he stopped to take a breather, "about how many shirts would you say are piled up in the boardinghouse waiting for buttons?"

Arne's brows drew together in puzzlement as he deliberated. "Oh, dozens at least."

Morna smiled. Visions of beautiful blue buttons danced before her. The same color as Mr. Quinn Montgomery's eyes, if she recalled correctly. She'd love to see the look in them when he found out what she was going to propose to Arne.

"Well, now I have unlimited access to thread and blue buttons. You have far too many shirts needing mending. Let's make a deal about those shirts, Arne. I could use a table and bench. Are you allowed to nail some boards together in your spare time?"

"Oh, ja, I am good vorking the wood into furniture."

"Very good, I shall pay you to make me some simple furniture . . . and while you're doing that, I have a proposition for the bachelors."

Arne blushed. Quickly, Morna got to the point. "It's quite innocent and I think the bachelors will benefit financially. . . ."

An hour later Morna sat by a small mountain of shirts, a pile of blue buttons on the table. A callus was rubbing her middle finger raw from pulling the needle in and out of tiny buttonholes. But that didn't matter. For the prettiest sight of all in this greedy town so far was the jar filling up with silver dollars for her work. And she never even stopped when the mill whistle blew. There was money to be made.

Morna had found her second business.

Quinn was not surprised to see Theodore waiting for him on the railroad platform. He'd been right to come here as quickly as he could. The news was worse than he'd known. Halfway through Theodore's account, Quinn erupted.

"Dammit, I don't want bachelors hanging around that Irish female with naked chests exposed for all the town and her to see while they get their buttons sewed on. I want them all evicted and her, too. This is a family town, Theodore. Have you forgotten that? Single women and fatherless children have no place here! Accidents happen because a bachelor starts daydreaming about felling a woman instead of a tree."

Quinn stopped, aware he'd yelled at Theodore within hearing of Otis Hargrove, and that was a first. A businessman first and foremost, Quinn prided himself on remaining in control at all times. That Patterson woman still bothered him, and he was just beginning to figure out why.

"But I can't stop her," Theodore was sputtering.

"You have to," Quinn said between gritted teeth. "This town is in the business of creating lumber, not match-making."

Silence. Sullen silence. Theodore had sulked from the time he was a child.

"Never mind, I told you you're fired."

Theodore, in a casual gesture, ran a hand over his immaculate sleeve and then gave a wry smile. He was the handsomest of all the Montgomerys, and also the most deceitful. Quinn never had liked him. At one time he had loathed the man, then decided having him around to keep an eye on him might be the best way to keep the family name from being ruined. If anyone could ruin the Montgomery name, Theodore could.

Now he shrugged. "I thought we had an agreement, Quinn. I work here in exchange for my family. You know, keep your scandals in the family, so to speak."

Quinn balled his hands into fists, then forced himself to relax. Once upon a time he'd have fought Theodore, but not anymore. Lately he'd controlled his habits with this job. Now he didn't want him around, period, no matter the personal cost. "You've abused the arrangement. Your silence isn't worth it." Or maybe hiding the past wasn't worth it.

"The scandals in your past could be worth a lot to the right newspapers."

Quinn tensed. Theodore always had his mind working, which is why he'd functioned so long as town manager. No more. "Go ahead, then. Tell all you want about Sarah. You're the one whose name is on the line. I was a damn fool to think I could hide things this long."

Theodore shrank back, obviously surprised.

"Get out, I say. Pack up and leave."

"May I wait for the next train?" Theodore sneered.

"You can ride out on a logjam as far as I care."

Laughing softly, Theodore sauntered away. "You take life too seriously, Quinn," he said over his shoulder. His voice rose as distance spread between them. "That's what drove Sarah to do what she did, you know—you take this puny little town too seriously, too. Good riddance to it."

Quinn couldn't resist that. "And you, cousin, you don't have a respectable bone in your body. Your morals smell like an alley cat's. If I had my way you'd be banned from the Montgomery family."

Theodore paused and turned. "You always were jealous of me, weren't you?"

"Disgusted is the word."

"You should have told me, then. I'd never have come visiting so long ago—when Sarah invited me for supper—"

"Get out."

Quinn could have said more, but the good people of Bunyan were starting to pause on the boardwalk and listen. He could imagine their thoughts. The owner of Bunyan, the man who made the rules, practically brawling in public. Quinn had to set the example.

He looked from side to side. "Well, don't stare. This is private family business. Go on about your business and pass the word that I'm the new town manager."

They scattered like squirrels chasing after a safe hole in a storm.

For once, Quinn couldn't isolate himself from his town. But it wasn't the monotonous row houses and pine trees he was seeing. It was a pretty lass with whiskey-colored hair and snapping green eyes . . . and a trim figure. . . . And something more.

She didn't talk or walk like an Irish peasant. Her hands were not the hands of a woman who'd toiled in the soil. Her clothing was too well stitched and of a finer fabric than homespun. She was of a finer class than immigrants—and more intrigued him: her money.

And her gall. Her utter gall. How dare she start sewing on buttons for bachelors?

Quinn tugged at his shirt collar, trying to recall who did *his* buttons. He certainly didn't stand around half-naked while a seamstress or tailor fitted him. And he'd be damned if the bachelors of Bunyan would do so.

Oh, that Irish woman was worse than the forest brush. She was like sap, gumming up the smooth-running, well-oiled machinery of his perfectly controlled little town . . . and though he hated admitting it, she was gumming up his thoughts as well. The reddish hair. The wide green eyes. The alabaster skin. No woman within a thousand miles of Lake Huron quite looked the same now, and he cursed his fate. Did the woman have to resemble Sarah quite so closely? It was bad luck, and Quinn liked his life more in control so that luck was not a factor. Especially when it came to women.

But he did not allow himself to worry over his attraction, for he intended to get Miss Patterson out of here at once, and he had the perfect plan.

4

THE TOWN OF Bunyan, Morna decided, resembled its owner in many ways. As she and Conor walked up Sixth Street past the mill, she gazed around, incredulous. What struck her about the little town was identical to the thing that struck her about Quinn Montgomery.

Perfection. Controlled perfection. An emotionless facade.

Every house was freshly painted.

Not a shingle was out of place, that she could see.

With few exceptions, the yards were as well-groomed as Quinn.

On the houses, the shutters were all opened to let in exactly the same quantity of light. On the stoops, dogs sat quietly, as if they, too, knew the rules.

Only a few things marred the order: chickens running loose in one yard, one house painted gray instead of regulation tan.

And only one that she could see allowed its garbage to collect out on the back stoop.

This sense of order involved more than the upkeep of the identical houses. It was evident in the planning of the place.

Every door faced east or west; the town streets were perfectly lined up.

Even the names were orderly, if uninspired. First Street. Second Street. Third Street.

And going north and south, the names were equally predictable though more interesting to Conor. Fir Street. Pine Street. Birch Street. Maple Street.

One by one, Morna read the names for Conor so he'd not be lost. But again, it was not a town in which to get lost. It was too well laid out. Regimental. Precise.

A woman stood on her porch sweeping, and Morna raised her hand to wave, as she would have done back home. The woman hurried inside and shut the door. The shades on most houses were down. No flowers softened the square houses. On Main Street—also known as Sixth—there was one of every business needed for families, a company school, a company church, and farther up, past Montgomery Mills, a company infirmary.

It was so quiet, their footsteps echoed on the boardwalk. No dogs barked. No cats chased other cats. The few wagons that passed had such well-oiled wheels, nothing squeaked. There was no laughter from playing children. The few children she saw were sitting quietly, and as she and Conor approached, they dispersed and ran home.

"What do all those signs say?" Conor, who was anxious to learn to read, was dragging a twig along the row of wooden signs, rattling the quiet.

One by one, Morna read them aloud.

"No spitting.

No drinking.

No cussing.

No loitering.

No eating.

No hopscotch lines on boardwalk.

No public displays of affection."

"What's a public display of affection?" Conor asked.

Morna looked down at the boy, sandy curls blowing in the breeze. "Well, now, nothing you need to worry about, Conor. And from the looks of this place, I doubt much of it ever happens, so I'd not fret. Your da and your ma would not want that."

Snatching up his hand in hers, she hurried him along to the cemetery.

A few wild violets plucked from the edge of the woods were laid on the grave of Conor's father. A prayer was said. A kind thought of his mother, too. Morna did not believe it would help Conor to ignore his loss, but rather to talk about it.

"Who was that big man with the beard at Da's funeral?"

"The owner of the town."

"He came for Pa?"

Morna was more cynical than young Conor. A man like Quinn Montgomery never came to the funerals of his employees without an ulterior motive. What it was she had yet to discover.

"He came because . . . well, to be kind."

"Why do they call him Moose?"

Morna was taken aback. "Who does that?"

"Some of the boys. They won't say it to his face, but they dared me to."

"I expect it's because he's so big a man."

Morna would never forget her first look at Quinn Montgomery. The impeccable grooming. The shock of dark hair, his beard half grown out. His neck was large, his forehead broad, his nose strong. The rest was hidden by the beard, well trimmed, but a bit forbidding when coupled with his other features. His hands were like bear paws. Of course his suits would have to be custom-tailored.

"Big as a tree. Did you know he owns the woods . . . most all of them?"

"Yes, I'd heard." It was time to change the subject. "I'm glad to hear you're making friends."

Conor was quiet. "They're not my friends. They say I'm a no-good Irish like my da . . . and there are rules for new boys."

"What rules?"

"Before I can play, I have to go into the woods alone to prove I'm brave enough and—"

"Conor, they're only teasing you." Some things never changed, no matter the country or town.

"They tease me about my suit, too."

Morna sighed in frustration. In her social class, children had dressed up, so naturally she'd selected the best reefer suit in the company store and ignored the expense. She realized now she'd erred. To fit in, Conor needed coarser playclothes—something in scruffy corduroy and with patched elbows like the other boys.

"I'll make something over so you only have to wear this suit for best. How's that?"

Conor's face relaxed. "Yes. Then I can play in the woods and not worry about tearing my trousers."

"Oh, no, you can't."

"Why? The big boys sneak off into the woods."

"They say it's dangerous. But maybe we can explore the trees nearby."

"All we have is stumps near us."

True. But from a distance there was a nice view of white pines. "You can draw pictures of the trees. Make a book of them."

"A book? I can't read, Morna." He turned big green eyes at her, frustration in the welling tears.

"Ah, now, that's not difficult. You like to draw

pictures, don't you?" All children did. At his nod, she smiled. "You can make a picture book. I have writing paper in my satchel, and then you can sit and show the bachelors the pictures, and in turn they'll tell you about your da. And in time, the other boys will envy you all the tales you hear. How does that sound?"

"I'll draw a picture of Ma . . . and . . . and the blue button Da sent me."

A tremulous smile flitted across his face, and Morna wanted to encourage it, so she didn't argue about the blue button to which he still clung.

"Yes, a picture book of trees," Morna said, pleased with her idea and Conor's enthusiasm. "Why, I've never seen such trees, not in all Ireland." It was the only good thing about this town so far. Trees to gaze at, and even though the boardinghouse boasted only stumps, the view of white pines was magnificent.

It was time to leave the cemetery.

Conor hesitated and then crept around the grave. "I'm here, Papa. I've come to Bunyan." That was all, then he laid a hand on the mound of fresh dirt.

"Should I draw a picture for Quinn Montgomery, too?"

A fleeting image of the handsome owner crossed Morna's mind. He was too perfect to be captured on paper. If Morna were doing the drawing, she'd sketch a bank overflowing with money, and then she'd label it MR. MONTGOMERY.

"Whatever would make you happy, Conor. It's for you to decide." She gathered her shawl over her shoulders and led Conor back to the boardwalk.

The few people on the boardwalk parted for them or else stood in clusters whispering. The name "Mr. Montgomery" floated out of every conversation, and people cast anxious eyes toward the hotel or else the sky. She didn't want to know the gossip, for the owner was like Zeus, capable of hurling thunderbolts into people, and now that she had her own little business and her own boardinghouse, Mr. Montgomery was of little concern to her.

She looked up. The sky was gray, with a threat of spring rain.

"I don't like this place," Conor said.

Neither did Morna, but it's where she'd found her new start. And she was going to make some changes—and maybe even make Mr. Quinn Montgomery change some of his rules.

If she had to live here, she had a say in what went on. That was the first rule of business her papa had taught her when she was no more than knee-high to a leprechaun. In business, the owner has to know the people. And she told Conor so, but Conor was more intent on his blue button than on Morna's words.

Once again, he was rolling the little blue button, stopping on the boardwalk to catch it and spin it like a wee top.

Morna was anxious to divert him with talk of paper and crayons. "I expect a pine tree might be a more interesting subject than Bunyan. The bark is rough and the branches are uneven. And a tree is full of wee things hiding out—bugs and caterpillars and the like. They all call it home."

"I'll draw them, too."

"I'll give you some money to go buy crayons at the company store."

They arrived back at the tent just in time to greet Arne, who was hauling over a table of newly sawed planks to Morna.

Arne grinned cheerfully at them. "Ve vant you to come for midday meal—Dogger and Pierre and Finn and, well, all of them. Even Cleatface. Vill you? The cook is gut."

"Is Widowmaker cooking?"

Arne beamed and snapped the suspenders that seemed part of the lumbermen's uniform. "Ja."

"Arne, I don't want to be rude, but I find many of the men's names very curious."

Arne let his suspenders fall flat and stared down at his boots. They were cleated, and his pants were cut high at the ankle. "Don't be alarmed, miss. Ve got nothing else much to do, so ve have nicknames. Ven Vidowmaker came, his cooking vas perty bad. Ja. His flapjacks so tough ve used to yoke at him it vould take a hacksaw instead of a knife to cut them, but he's learned some."

"I'm glad to hear that, Arne. So what did he do to get his name?"

"Oh, he's a lumberyack, vorks in the voods felling trees, and he's outlived two vomen. It's not really how the vord is used. Vidowmakers, you see, are branches that fall from on high and kill a man. And that makes vidows. Ve vas running out of animal names and ve couldn't call everyone skunk. Besides, the company doctor started a rule ve had to have baths every veek because ve smelled like sweatin' pigs who'd vallowed in sheet, he said, and so . . . vell, I better be careful of my tongue. Your ears better not be delicate, miss. The men aren't too refined. I expect you'll be vanting a rule banning cussing inside the boardinghouse."

"There's a difference, Arne, between a rule for rule's sake and common courtesy around ladies. Let's go greet the men. We've a lot to talk about."

"Yah, like vat vill Mr. Montgomery do next?"

"Forget Mr. Montgomery—except when you're at work or in town."

Arne shook his head. "No one can do that, Miss Morna. Haven't you heard the talk?"

She shook her head.

"Vhen Mr. Montgomery found out Theodore sold you our boardinghouse, he said he's coming back here to manage the town himself. Everyone is purty nervous, you bet."

"Well, they needn't be. Maybe he'll learn what running a business is all about." She sailed ahead and into the common dining room of the boardinghouse. So Quinn Montgomery was scared of her—or mad at her. Well, good. She'd show him she wasn't afraid of him.

That evening, Morna and little Conor went over to the boardinghouse dining room for dinner, and the bachelors and she sat around the stove and at the tables sharing their stories. Morna skimped on her life in Ireland, instead telling tales of fairies and leprechauns. And after that, naturally, the bachelors started in on tall tales. One by one, they tried to outdo each other with tales of the darkest woods, the heaviest ax, the sharpest saw, the biggest log, the strongest man.

Widowmaker went last. "All right, now. I've heard all those tales over and over. I've got a new one, and it's about Bunyan."

"This town ain't got no tall tales," Digger said, cupping his ear, the better to hear.

"Does, too. I just ain't told it. Remember, I been here longer than any of you here. I was here when Quinn Montgomery started this town, and I heard it then."

"Well, get on with it, then," Cleatface muttered, yawning and scratching an armpit. "Everyone knows the place was named after Paul Bunyan 'cuz Mr. Montgomery had no imagination. So I don't expect this tall tale will be any good either."

"Maybe. Maybe not," Widowmaker said. "But you listen up, or I'll see you don't get any apple pie for dessert."

Cleatface shifted and sat at attention.

All eyes were on Widowmaker, even little Conor's, who sat in Morna's lap, rapt with attention.

"Anyway, some folks say Paul Bunyan came through here with his bride and was thinking these woods would be the perfect place to settle down and raise a family. But his wife didn't like it here. And they had a falling-out. And before big Paul could sweet-talk her back, well, a lumberjack bigger 'n Paul came down from the northland—from Pierre's land—"

"Canada," Pierre supplied.

"Yeah," Widowmaker said with a grateful nod, "and she fell in love with him and vanished into the dark woods, and the last anybody guessed, she went back to a big city. Well, now, Paul, he was strong and had stamina and could walk farther and go without sleep and food longer than anyone. So he searched and searched, hoping to win her back."

"Did he find her?" asked Conor.

"Nope. The only thing he ever found was a trail of tiny blue buttons from her gown. And Paul watered those buttons with his tears, and little blue flowers sprung up where the buttons had been. No one's ever seen the buttons since, of course, or the flowers—"

"What about in that secluded woods?" Morna asked. "There has to be a reason they're not touched by the loggers." She was intrigued by one patch of trees that appeared untouched by logging.

"Naw, that's some sentimental thing of Quinn Montgomery's. Anyways, Paul vowed to be a bachelor forever more and that's how us bachelors ended up wearing blue buttons."

Cleatface groaned and tore open the button at his neck. "You're an old woman, Widowmaker," he said. "Been spending too much time in the kitchen."

"You complaining about the food?"

Cleatface held up his hands in apology. "No, no. It's the best."

Cooks, Morna deduced, were a rare commodity in towns like this. Especially prized among bachelors.

"Well," Widowmaker said, standing and stretching, "it's the closest thing I can figure out to why us bachelors have to wear these danged blue buttons. Part of the town legend."

"I liked your tall tale," Morna said, then hastily added, "I liked everyone's tall tale." Secretly, though, it was Widowmaker's that intrigued her, and as she headed off to put Conor to bed, she wondered how much of it was tall and how much might be really true. . . .

Quinn paused outside the company store and stared up at the second-floor window that was the town office. Theodore's former office.

Ten years ago Quinn had sworn he'd never set foot in this place again, and except for occasional visits to the depot, he'd managed to keep his vow.

When Quinn arrived at the store, he was aware of all the stares, and without acknowledging anyone, he followed Otis up the stairs to the office.

"The best room in the store." Otis moved to lift the window shade.

The view was to the east and north. Directly below

was the boardwalk and the street. Beyond, the woods stretched out everywhere, a sea of dark green. At once, his shoulders slumped as the old pain whipsawed through him. Looking at those trees was all it took. It used to be like an ax to a tree trunk—raw and bleeding. Now it was dull, the way he imagined a rotting tree must die. Day by day. Season by season. Someday when all the trees were cut—all but one bower—maybe then he could move on and forget. He snapped the shade down.

"Mr. Montgomery—"

"I like it dark. Light the lamp. I like it shady in here, and I want Nellie and Edith to stay downstairs until I'm out for the day, understood? Give them orders never to lift that blind, is that clear?"

"Mr. Montgomery, may I inquire how long you're planning to stay?"

"Until Miss Patterson moves on."

"You'll be wanting a room, then? I mean, you're staying awhile."

"Yes, unfortunately."

"Sir, in my humble opinion, I thought the town wasn't running quite smoothly. We have so many rules, sir, that frankly, they start to bump into each other."

"Rules are functional. I make them so I won't have to be bothered with this ugly place, but now it seems I've been given no choice."

Otis's face flushed a dull red, and he was silent.

Technically, it wasn't Otis's fault. The town had been humming like a well-oiled machine, the people all orderly and hidden away in their houses like ants under a fallen log. And then Miss Morna Patterson had come with her uppity notions . . . claiming to bring a child to his father. Hah! An excuse to get her hooks into his town. His.

Every square foot of it. Even the wretched log dwelling where he housed the bachelors.

And while he might detest it, that didn't mean he was ready to sell it to a woman. The instant Theodore had told him of the sale, he'd known that. Vision be damned. He had memories here. A history. Heartbreaking, yes. But that made it all the harder to part with any piece of it.

Quinn paced the utilitarian room, touched the rolltop desk of rich pine wood, the silver inkwell and letter opener. He paced about, pausing at the sideboard where he briefly touched the whiskey decanter, glanced with disdain at the velvet chair behind the desk and the bookcase full of law books. Theodore spared himself no luxury.

The walls, on the other hand, were painted drab green with only a company calendar to adorn the walls. A small braid rug no bigger than the girth of a tree was all that separated his feet from spartan wood floors. Theodore had tried to turn a sow's ear into a silk purse.

"How did my cousin stand this place?"

"I thought you'd be proud of it, sir. It's the finest room in town, other than the hotel lobby. Since it's all paid off, and all. I expect you'll not want to stay long——"

"As long as it takes," he snapped.

Quinn shrugged off his coat and glared at Otis. The little man shrank back.

"I'm afraid I don't understand your anger."

Quinn stopped in his tracks. Nor did he. The woman was pretty and desirable. He'd been unable to keep his eyes off her from the first moment he saw her.

"I don't want single women around here."

Especially not women with tangled red-gold hair and

dewy eyes and skin like alabaster. He had desired her on sight and hated her all at the same time. He'd assumed she would deposit the boy with a family and leave, so he'd never have to deal with her. Buying the bachelor boardinghouse left him speechless, and feeling unaccountably betrayed.

Quinn Montgomery trusted no woman and never would. He took them on his terms. That's why Miss Patterson had to go.

And he had a plan to checkmate her. Two days here and she'd be running with her pretty mane of hair behind her . . . running. A vision in white. White nightdress so thin he could see the outline of long limbs through it. And in the rain it would be soaked and clinging to her curves. She would taste of rain.

Desire was a deep dark forest within Quinn, and there were only certain paths he allowed himself to walk along. Those that led to women of easy virtue. Those that led to women who understood that he wanted one night, not a lifetime. Brunette women. Blond women. Faded women. Older women. Married women. But never beautiful young ones with tangled reddish hair.

The noon whistle cut through the room like a banshee, shrill in its wail.

He looked. Otis was staring at him strangely. No one ever saw Quinn deep in reverie.

He sank into the chair and leaned his elbows on the desk and raked his hands through his hair. "Get my bags to the hotel," he said.

Otis departed for the hallway without a word and clanged back in a few minutes later.

"Otis, where is she now? Not in the woods. I don't want anyone in the woods but the lumbermen, the men from the sawmill." There were places, just as in his dreams, that no one went but him.

"Where is she?"

"I—I don't know, sir. Was I supposed to follow her? I believe I saw her walking with the boy away from the cemetery. Likely she's at the boardinghouse. All of the bachelors lined up for baths this morning—"

"Enough! Give me my hotel key." He needed a bath himself.

"Uh, it's not ready," Otis replied, a bit uncertainly.

"When then?"

Otis ran a hand over his bald spot, always a sign that he was hiding some vital information. He flushed a dull shade of red, a dead giveaway. "Spit it out, man. What's the matter?"

"I'm afraid, sir, the hotel is all booked up. Your room won't be ready for a week . . . unless we throw someone out. That's against the rules, of course."

"Nonsense. Theodore has a perfectly good room."

"He sublet it to a newlywed couple—at a handy profit, I believe."

Quinn might have known.

"I could make up a pallet for you here."

"I'd sooner sleep in the hotel lobby. Never mind, Otis. I'll wait for a room to open up."

"Wait where?"

Quinn waved a hand wearily. Damnation. He'd have to solve the problem of the Irish landlady more quickly now, or he'd be sitting up trying to sleep in chairs for a month.

Which wasn't at all the problem. She was the problem.

How could he maintain a perfect family town when a beautiful woman was practically living with a bunch of roughneck bachelors? Not in his town. It was just asking for trouble.

She was trouble. But if he had his way, she wouldn't be in business as a landlady to bachelors for long.

And he'd do anything to get his way.

5

$\mathcal{M}$ORNA SAT IN the rocker by the boardinghouse
fireplace and tackled another button. Heartache and
disappointment were far away in Ireland. Now she had a
town and a piece of property. She was content—except
for two things: the tent and Conor's reluctance to let her
out of his sight.

Right now he was sprawled on the floor in front of the
fireplace playing dominoes with Arne.

"Maybe we should move into the attic," she said as
much to herself as anyone. Canvas did not keep out the
cool spring air of night.

Arne looked up. "I would wait for a house to rent,
miss. The attic has ghosts."

This was ridiculous. Ghosties lived in Ireland. "I can't
imagine a ghost putting up with Quinn Montgomery's
company-town rules for a minute."

"Yeah, well, it is a tall tale," Arne said.

"And nothing more," she sad, and snapped off a length
of blue thread. Over and over they debated the merits of
living in the attic. Would the town brand her wanton or
not? They had not pursued the matter because half the
attic was boarded off; that made Morna nervous not
knowing why. Tall tales about ghosts would not help wee
Conor to sleep.

And then the knock unexpectedly shook the door.

Conor jumped up and a row of dominoes fell to the floor.

Morna pulled the boy onto her lap. "It's nothing, Conor," she said softly. "Probably someone from the mill." They worked around the clock, three shifts, and Morna still wasn't used to them coming and going.

Cleatface flung open the door. "Yeah?" he growled.

"Good afternoon, gentlemen."

At the formal greeting—and the too familiar voice, Morna tensed. She held Conor more tightly in her arms to control her own shaking.

It was Quinn Montgomery himself.

He stepped inside the door and stopped, looking around with a funny expression—almost one of nostalgia. Then, as if aware everyone was staring at him, waiting for the sky to fall, he cleared his throat.

Why, he was nervous, Morna realized, and her heart almost went out to him. A big giant of a man like that and he was actually shy. That gruff manner, all the grouchy talk about rules, it hid a mild-mannered man. Curious. How very different from her first impression at the cemetery.

He rammed his hands down into the pockets of his greatcoat, for outside the wind was blowing fierce. It swirled inside, rattling dishes and lifting the skirt of the tablecloths.

Cleatface pushed the door shut. "Would you like to stay for supper?"

Quinn Montgomery looked at the plank tables set with cracked and mismatched bowls. He shook his head. "Thank you, no, and I won't waste your time with fancy words." Briefly his gaze lit on Morna and then he deliberately turned away from her and spoke to the men alone. "I'll tell you how it is, men. Straight and honest. You're terminated."

"We're what?" Dogger, who was nearly deaf, cupped his hand about one ear. "Did he say we got termites?"

Cleatface shook his head, expression shocked, obviously at a loss for words.

Around the room, the sawmill workers sagged against the walls and benches. Only Dogger remained baffled. He cupped both ears. "What'd he say? Speak up, someone. What is it?"

"You're fired." The two stark syllables crashed about the room like a pair of felled trees.

It was Morna who found her voice first. She unwrapped Conor from her arms, set him down, and stood, angry.

"What do you mean, they're fired?" Just because he was bigger than everyone didn't mean he could do something so unjust.

Slowly, he turned and looked at her. A stab of something electric shot through her, weakening her knees. He had the bluest eyes. And to her chagrin she couldn't tear her gaze away.

"Fire?" said Dogger in some alarm. "Is there a fire?"

"No, Dogger," Cleatface shouted back. "We've lost our jobs."

"Lost what?"

"Jobs . . . fired." Cleatface pulled a finger across his throat in a slashing motion.

The light dawned in Dogger's eyes, and he sank down onto a bench. "Sometimes it is better to be deaf. This news I do not need. Where will a deaf man go?"

It was Quinn Montgomery who turned away first, who broke the intense look between him and Morna. Without a reply, Quinn headed out the door of the boardinghouse.

She was ashamed, staring so when these men had just lost their jobs. Her face was flushed, and she busied herself pushing needles and thread into her sewing basket. Maybe no one noticed how long she'd stared at Quinn. She had to pull herself together.

The bachelors, to a man, stood there, still in shock. Not Morna. She broke past them and, picking up her skirts, hurried after Quinn. How dare he? Who did he think he was? By now, she was out the door.

"What grounds do you have for firing them?" she called, dodging one stump and then another. "Stop."

"I own the town. I don't need grounds or reasons."

"But you don't have a heart or a bit of compassion—"

He turned and looked at her, something like pity in his eyes. "I'm sorry you wasted your money, Miss Patterson, but this is better for the town and for you. You'll see."

"What rule did they break? Tell me that."

He looked down at her, eyes unexpectedly full of humor as if he found something about her amusing. It wasn't funny, especially not the way her insides turned little flip-flops. He stroked his beard. She stared, trying to imagine his face clean-shaven. It wasn't handsome, but rugged, yes. And those blue eyes . . .

"Why are you staring?" he asked, and turned away, as if self-conscious.

"I—I didn't mean to."

"Like you didn't mean to buy my boardinghouse?"

"You wanted to sell it." She dashed around so she could look up at him again. "You put it up for sale."

He averted his gaze. "That's not the point."

She planted her hands on her hips. "Why don't you try living by your own rules for a change?"

"Did you have one in mind?"

"Frankly, Mr. Quinn Montgomery, this town's got too

many rules to count." She looked at his shirt. "Why don't you wear a blue button? You're a bachelor."

He half smiled. "What else do you know about me?"

"Enough. And let me tell you, you'll never own me. But you may engage my sewing services—for a fee."

A wide smile split his beard. "I have no intention of wearing a blue button. I'm the owner."

"And above the rules. I know. You'd never dare eat with the bachelors. I saw you turn up your nose at their table. And you are a bachelor. I suppose you'd never entertain the thought of sharing their bunk room with them either. Never mind that it would let you know them and what they need." .

"They don't need anything but a job."

"Thanks to you. But you're wrong in thinking they cause trouble because they're bachelors. It's because of your rules, because this town shuns them, won't include them. They go to the mill, then they come back to the boardinghouse and sit around with cards and harmonicas and tall tales. They're lonely men, and lonely men don't put their hearts into their work. I've been here less than a week, and even I can see what's wrong. They're people, too. But you'd never know that because you're too high-and-mighty to share quarters with them. Bachelor quarters."

"Is that an invitation to your house?"

"You get nothing from me for free. I'm as much a businessman as you."

He pulled a cigar out of his pocket. "Then I'm glad to have a place in town—at the hotel."

He was lying. Everyone knew the hotel was filled up. Maybe he'd thrown someone out on the street. Well, it was his town. More the pity. She looked down at the ground. His blue eyes were uncommonly disturbing. "I just think you owe them a reason."

"I don't know how to elaborate," he said. "With numbers, I excel. With words, I'm usually at a loss, unless it's a letter."

His expression did not waver, nor did his gaze leave her.

She waited.

He squirmed. "I'm cutting back on employees," he said. "Starting today. There's no more reason than that."

There was a long silence . . . except for the sound of underwear and blankets snapping on the line, the flap of wings from a flock of gulls, and faraway, the ever-present echo of an ax hitting wood.

"It's me, isn't it? You're only doing that so they'll leave and I'll have no one to rent this house to."

"If you're as astute a businesswoman as you say, I have no doubt you'll think of something. But to play landlady to bachelors . . . well, as the town ladies would say, it's shocking."

"You, shocked? I find that hard to believe."

"Nothing shocks me, Morna. But this town has standards. It's a family town, and an unmarried lady in charge of the bachelor sleeping quarters? Won't do. Too scandalous for the good families who rent my houses."

"The town needs to mind its own business, then. Good day."

She walked away and left him there amid the stumps.

He didn't say another word, nor did she hear him walk away. She glanced once over her shoulder. He was standing there, watching her, cigar in hand, dark hair in place. Not even the wind could ruffle him. His beard disguised his expression, except for his eyes, and she could swear there was amusement in them.

She didn't care. He was a big heartless lout, and if she'd felt any stirrings toward him earlier, it must have been pity. Not attraction. Never. Impossible!

Determined to put him out of mind, she turned back and quickened her step. But what she saw at the boarding-house made her stop dead in her tracks.

The bachelors were all lined up, making no secret of eavesdropping on her and Quinn.

Widowmaker strolled down from the veranda, walked to the covered hole that was his outdoor oven, and lifted out the pot of steaming beans as if that was his sole purpose in being outside.

Cleatface stepped down from the veranda, and he was holding a butcher knife. "It's your turn, Widowmaker."

Widowmaker tasted the beans, nodded, and turning, stood and lifted his chin. Cleatface advanced and raised the knife.

"No!" Morna shouted. All her hard work sewing.

Cleatface didn't turn. "Sorry to waste such nice sewing, Miss Morna, but if we're fired, we ain't gonna be marked men no more." Then he grabbed a handful of shirt material and proceeded to saw away at the blue button.

Cleatface sawed the button off and it fell to the ground. "As long as we're unemployed, we're not wearing these blasted blue buttons no more. Dumbest rule in the world."

Conor was scurrying along, collecting blue buttons in a jar. Already, the jar jangled with buttons. Blue buttons with thread trailing off them.

Morna rallied then. "Take heart now," she said as bracingly as possible. "In Ireland, I declare, high-and-mighty Quinn Montgomery would have been tarred and feathered for what he just did."

"This ain't Ireland," Widowmaker growled. "Meaning no disrespect, miss, but tar and feather's all good and well, but they don't help us earn a stake."

Conor picked up the last button from beside Widow-maker's boot and then brought the jar over to Morna. "Cleatface said they're yours."

"You're a good lad, Conor," Cleatface said. "Your da would have been proud of you. Be glad he didn't live to see this day."

Conor looked at the bachelors, his friends. They were lined up, all dressed alike in red underwear poking out from the rolled-up sleeves of their plaid flannel shirts. They reminded him of himself—boys without mothers.

"Don't worry," he said. "Morna will take care of you."

They laughed, and Conor felt a blush rise up his face.

"Aw, leave the boy alone," Pierre said. "He's one of us."

Conor glowed, proud to be included. One of them. Just like his da.

They stood in a crooked line, and one by one he met their defeated faces. Widowmaker. Cookee. Pierre. Dogger. Finn. Cleatface. Arne and Bruno. They might be scruffy and rough talking and yes, even smelly. But they were strong.

"Someday when I grow up, I'll be as strong as you. Da wrote that he was strongest . . . after Pierre."

"Ain't true," said one of the others. "I'm the strongest one. Pierre might be handsome and have all the ladies eyeing him, but he can't compete with me at lifting lumber."

Morna clapped her hands for order. "Gentlemen, no teasing Conor, and absolutely no fighting. You know that's my only stipulation as your landlady."

They laughed uneasily and bent their heads to scuff

their boots in the ground or else kick a stump in frustration. "We can't stay without jobs, Morna."

Landlady rules were the furthest things from their minds. "I'm sorry. . . . Don't worry," she said more gently. "I'll think of something. I will."

Their faces were bleak, their eyes shiny, as if they were fighting tears. Widowmaker turned and lifted the lid on the beans again. He tasted and wiped his hand across his mouth. "No use fussing over us. We always knew we were the first to go. That's how it is in a company town."

"Well, don't pack yet. And no one owes me rent till May first. You've all got time to hunt out the best place to go and pack and . . ." Now it was her own composure failing.

Pierre smiled at her. "You'll never make a profit giving us charity."

"Oh, it's not charity. I'll make you all scrub down the bunkroom and dining room."

A moan went up, but they smiled, albeit wanly.

"Let's eat," Widowmaker said, and they all trooped in. Hunger did not wait for problems to be solved.

As one, they dug into the same fare as last night. Beans and bread and fried potatoes and pork. They drank tea and no one spoke a word.

Morna stirred her beans and broke off a piece of bread.

Everything in this little town seemed to say bachelors were not welcome, and it made no sense. Over and over in her mind she chewed on the last thing Widowmaker had said before carrying in the beans.

We never know when we bachelors are gonna be turned away from work. It's hard to make a stake because everyone lives for today. Spends at the company store, and so when the job ends, no one will have a stake to move on.

The men slumped down around the plank table, faces

long. Widowmaker unknotted his apron and joined them. "Guess there's no hurry to eat, seeing no one's got anyplace to go—until we pack, leastways."

Cleatface pushed back his plate and slung himself up from the bench. With a long face, he shuffled off toward the bunk room. He came back moments later and tossed a duffelbag by the door.

"What are you doing?" Morna asked.

"Might as well scrub my share and move on west," he said. "They say there's lots of trees waiting to be cut there and not enough men."

"I said there's no rush. Another week."

"I can't pay rent here come May Day, let alone get together a stake."

"He only did this because of me." Guilt weighed down on Morna.

Widowmaker gulped and washed his food down with a loud slurp of tea. "Ain't so," he said. "Quinn Montgomery didn't want bachelors here. Our days were numbered when he put this house up for sale. Cleatface is right. Like we kept trying to tell ya, when you're single, you know the job can end anytime. Any payday can be the last."

She moved to the head of the table where the men, expressions dejected, sat staring at their plates. "I think it galls him to have a woman buy his property up."

"Now, you don't know that. Lookee, like we said, one day soon, he's going to sell this entire town. He don't care about the people."

"How do you know?"

"We all know. When the trees go, we go. And it don't take a genius to see how few trees are left. Trouble is, some people can't afford to move just because he says, but I guess that's our problem."

"If he thinks all I can do is sew on buttons, he's got a think coming." She stood. "What if I were to hire you?"

They looked at her with puzzled expressions.

"I need a house to live in. I could hire you to build one for me."

"Oh, miss, I'd not press our case. It'll only put your reputation at risk."

"My reputation?" She laughed shortly. "This town already thinks I'm a fallen woman, so what will it hurt if I go and try to get him to change his mind?"

Cleatface shuffled his feet; the cleats on his boots made big pockmarks in the dirt. "Aw, let her. If we go, she loses the rent on this big house. Give her a shot with Quinn."

She looked up at the ring of sad-faced bachelors who'd gathered round. "Thanks, Cleatface. I'll be back for Conor as soon as I change. I intend to meet Mr. Montgomery in style."

She marched toward the tent, half a dozen clucking lumbermen on her heels.

"He won't take kindly to a single lady calling on a single man in his town. And the town, well, the ladies, they'll gossip, label you loose. Now, we know you ain't, but the town ladies get mighty fussy about guarding the rules."

"Fie on the rules. This is a free country. If I give him a piece of my mind, what can he do? Send me back to Ireland? And as for the town ladies, they ought to tend more to their baking and less to gossip."

Widowmaker broke into a slow smile. "You know, for a woman, you got a lot of spirit. Wish I could see you tell him off. It'd make us all feel a bit better."

"Where do I find him?"

"Heck, miss, he don't socialize with the likes of us.

Fact is, he never comes to Bunyan, so your guess is as good as ours. He'll be hiding out somewhere, but only someone like Otis will know where."

Very well. She'd visit the company store on some pretext and do some prying of her own. "Wash up, Conor. I'll buy you a treat."

Conor grinned. He liked Morna. She could take care of anything. She was brave like a man, not all delicate and weepy. But just in case she couldn't fix things for the bachelors, Conor had his da's treasure map; the map mailed in Da's letter. A map leading from Ireland to Michigan. If he searched hard, he might find the treasure and he'd help the bachelors. They were his friends, and he liked them. But he had to keep it a secret because Morna would never let him go out in those woods. And where else would his da hide a treasure but there?

He sat out on the veranda waiting for her to return from the tent. It didn't take long.

"Ready?"

"Conor, are you coming with me?" Morna asked. "To town. To mail a letter to Ireland. To find Mr. Montgomery. Maybe to buy a peppermint stick."

He stuffed the blue button down his pocket and hurried after her. A trip to town always meant a peppermint stick. No maybes about it. The treasure hunt would have to wait a bit.

6

$\mathcal{A}$T THE BUNYAN Company Store, Nellie Hargrove expected another day of boredom. But, truth be told, this ugly little town of Bunyan had ceased to be boring the day Miss Morna arrived with her silk shawls and that orphan child in tow. She'd set tongues to wagging, brought none other than the owner, the richest man in the state, to live here, and then, to cap it all off, had done the daring deed—bought a house full of bachelors to manage as landlady.

Oh, yes, Nellie thanked her lucky stars. For she'd been within a week or so of running away to Chicago to join her elder sister, who had all the excitement of marriage and a tall brownstone on a bustling city street. Now it was Nellie whose letters to Chicago carried the more exciting news. And Cora begged her younger sister for more frequent letters with "more delicious news."

The door to the store squeaked on its hinges. Nellie looked up. In walked none other than the Irish landlady herself. Nellie warmed to the task of prying juicy tidbits out of her. Oh, yes, the town might be bearable for another year yet.

Nellie quickly moved to the post office counter, determined to talk to Morna. Her mother glided up behind her and hissed in her ear, "Don't you go getting friendly. She's an improper woman."

Nellie crossed her fingers behind her back. "Yes, Mama."

She turned back to the little barred window that served as Bunyan's post office.

Nellie looked at the fine lace of Morna's shawl. All the ladies in town were gossiping about it. Company women did not dress so. She was dressed far too fine for the rest of them, which was suspicious. Poor Irish did not buy up log boardinghouses, either. Unless, of course, she earned her money by less than savory means. Nellie wondered what really went on in that boardinghouse.

"May I help you?" she asked.

"Postage to Ireland, please. You can mail letters that far?"

Hoity-toity, too. "Of course I can," Nellie said in an injured voice. "We send letters across the Atlantic all the time. I used to send 'em for Conor's own pa."

"Of course, that was foolish of me."

Nellie didn't think Morna Patterson was foolish at all. She thought she was lucky to have all those eligible men to herself.

"Will that be all? No furniture or anything?"

"Why?"

"Well, you see, everyone's wondering when you'll move into the boardinghouse to look out for all those bachelors."

Morna stared mutely. She bet they were busier than hens laying eggs. "I'm not sure, Nellie."

"You mean you might?"

"Well, I do own the house. Usually it's common for landladies to live in a room of their own. The only trouble is this house has its extra room boarded up."

"You mean the attic room?" Nellie had heard about a locked-up room. Some said it was a tall tale but not her pa. He had it on good authority—from Theodore.

"Tell me, Nellie, do you believe the tall tales about my boardinghouse? The ones the bachelors tell?"

Nellie shrugged, not sure she wanted to confide in this bold Irish woman. "I'm not allowed to talk to the bachelors, but if I did, I'd not put any stock in them."

"But you've heard some?"

On second thought, maybe it wouldn't hurt to tell Morna a little bit. That way Morna might tell her about the bachelors. "Some people—the older folks—say there was a time before the town was here when that house was all alone in the woods."

"Who built it? Mr. Montgomery?"

Nellie shrugged. "Montgomerys and their kin built everything here. All I know is the log boardinghouse came first, before the town." She began polishing the counter. "Ma says you're invited to tea this afternoon."

"Thank you, Nellie. You're most kind," Morna said. "Could you tell me one more thing?"

Nellie looked up. "What's that?"

"Where can I find Quinn Montgomery?"

Oh, yes, she was a bold one. Nellie knew he wasn't upstairs in the office. "Sleeping at the hotel."

"Good. He'll be easy to find."

"You mean you'd call on him in the hotel?" Nellie's sister's life began to look positively dull.

"Why shouldn't I?"

"I should warn you—the town women, well, they're talking."

Morna gazed back calmly. "You mean that I'm some wicked madam because of that boardinghouse? A lady's got to earn a living, and I never heard of other ladies with boardinghouses losing their reputations for talking. Or is there a rule against that, too?"

Once again the door to the store squeaked open and the little boy—Conor—came bouncing in, followed by a man, a man Nellie had been hoping to see again.

She craned her neck to see around Conor, who was jumping up and down at the candy counter. Behind him stood Pierre, the handsomest man Nellie had ever seen. The blue button on his shirt gave him away as a bachelor, and she could scarcely take her eyes off him.

The bachelors always sent the same old crotchety fellow to buy their staples, and so she'd assumed they were all alike. Ugly. Dirty. Uncouth. How wrong she was.

Well, now, that was shortsighted of her ma and pa to keep the bachelors away from town socials when handsome men like this were available for dancing.

Morna walked over to him. "Pierre, maybe you'd better wait here while I find Mr. Montgomery."

"Pierre can wait here," Nellie offered, sweet as pie.

Her mother swooped around the corner from the cracker barrel. "No loitering, I fear. You know that, Nellie. Especially by bachelors."

And so Pierre, taking the hint, retreated outside to the veranda.

"The town should start letting the bachelors come to the picnic dance, Ma. Maybe it's time that rule was abolished."

Edith Hargrove swept the floor where Pierre had trod, as if to sweep out vermin that came with bachelors. "Nellie Hargrove, you take your eyes off that young man. He's a common sawyer or cook or heaven knows what. You're going to marry fine, or not at all."

"Shush, Ma," Nellie said, aware Morna was standing there, smiling.

"Tell me, does Quinn Montgomery have a lady?" Morna asked.

"Him?" It was her ma who spoke up. "Maybe on his fine island out on the lake. But he thinks he's too fine for the likes of anyone in this town—even my Nellie. Looks don't mean everything, I tell her, but she'll not believe me. Surely you understand, being landlady to a house full of unkempt men."

"I don't know," Morna admitted truthfully. Horace had been uncommonly pleasant on the eyes. But inside he'd been rotten to the core. She rather wanted to see a man's soul before she decided these things. "I think how a man looks inside matters, too," she said. "The bachelors tell me trees are all different inside. Some with wide rings of growth. Some all rotting inside. And no matter how handsome or tall the tree, you can't know these things till you cut it down."

Morna Patterson strolled out, lace shawl loose about her shoulders.

Edith Hargrove drew in a scandalized breath. "I've seen some Irish in my day, and let me tell you, none as brazen as that one. Oh, but she's a bold one. Quinn Montgomery will appreciate a nice young lady like you when he's done dealing with her. You're a lily compared to that wild piece of clover."

Nellie wouldn't go that far, but she was not about to allow a woman of Morna Patterson's reputation to have all the men. She would figure out a way to meet Pierre, even if it meant first agreeing to flirt with Quinn Montgomery. He was too big and frightening to ever think of in the romantic sense. It didn't matter how much her mother admired his fortune. But she could stand to flirt with him a little bit if it helped to catch the eye of handsome Pierre.

Morna took a sip of tea and wished everyone would quit staring at her. She would rather be in town tracking down Quinn Montgomery in some chicken coop. But then, when she'd accepted an invitation to tea at the Hargroves' house, she'd known she was on the menu along with all the egg sandwiches and apricot tarts.

It was simple fare; she'd known much more elegance in her father's home. But she wasn't about to tell these ladies so. That was her secret, her past. It was bad enough that she'd worn her best lace shawl, for it was attracting too much curiosity.

"That's a very fine shawl you've brought from Ireland," Edith noted. "I confess I thought you were a poor immigrant lass."

"I brought my dowry, and this shawl . . . well, it belongs in the family." Which was not exactly the truth, but not a lie either.

Teacups clattered, and Nellie dropped her napkin to the floor.

"Well," Edith went on, "we are pleased you could join us. As you might have guessed, we like to get to know the new . . . ladies . . . who move to Bunyan, though I must admit you're the first unattached one to come in a long while."

"So I gathered." Morna wondered where all this was leading. She had a hunch, but one never knew with strangers, and Americans to boot.

"Forgive my boldness, but is it true you've bought the bachelor boardinghouse?"

"Quite."

"I thought it might be better off sold to a gentleman."

"And why do you think that?" Morna set down her cup.

"For the obvious reason. How can I say it discreetly?"

Morna said it for her. "You fear I'm compromising my reputation by owning a house full of men."

Raised eyebrows went up all over the room. Faces swiveled from Edith to Morna, as if hanging on every syllable.

"I was under the impression running a boardinghouse was a perfectly respectable occupation in America."

"For married women, widows. Yes. But I must warn you, my dear, that some ladies—there are ladies who declined to come for tea today because they're having doubts about the wisdom of your choice of business."

To Morna they were all a bunch of old cats with nothing better to do with their time than meow. "Perhaps they weren't thirsty."

Edith Hargrove was silent a moment, as if gathering her wits. "Miss Patterson, you're taking offense. I'm only trying to help. Might I suggest you sell the boardinghouse and look for more suitable work? Perhaps the hotel needs a maid."

"I'm not a maid. I came here to own a business."

"The only person who owns anything in this town is Quinn Montgomery."

"And he's paid not a whit of attention to it. Oh, it looks neat and all, but I think he's more interested in counting his profits than knowing the families."

"I've heard he's come back to run the town in place of his cousin. Nellie's quite sweet on him." It was a cautionary remark.

"Mama, please . . ." Nellie pleaded, and turned away in her chair to stare out the window. "There's Pierre," she said suddenly.

Edith stood. "Nellie, stop staring at that wretched bachelor. It's unbecoming of your station in town."

"They're quite nice men, actually," Morna said, trying to keep her voice even. She hated the way this town dismissed her bachelors as some inferior species.

Edith touched her napkin to the corner of her mouth. "Well, you know what I meant, surely. They're hard workers, of course, but a bit rough about the edges. Not refined."

"They're bachelors without benefit of training in social graces," Morna pointed out. "As a matter of fact, I intend to instruct the men in table manners and even teach them to write a bit, if they wish. Letters to family for starters. They're very eager to fit in. Anyone can see that by their anxiety over the blue buttons. Perhaps if they were included more in the town activities, they would lose their rough edges. They say they have to keep separate, except at work."

Edith shook her head. "It's against the rules for them to mingle—except for logging days. And then, of course, we need them to show off their skills."

"They want to be more than needed for their work skills. Everyone does." She looked around the room. "How did the blue-button rule get started anyway? Does anyone know?"

The ladies either shrugged or gazed into their teacups. Such a docile bunch. Clearly, if Edith didn't answer, no one would. And Edith did.

"It was Quinn Montgomery, of course. Him and his cousin Theodore. One or the other sets all the rules. There's nothing special about it. Blue buttons come cheap, and I imagine they thought it would be a handy way to sort out the workers. Why do you ask?"

Morna, accustomed as she was to the fairy stories of

her native Ireland, would not have been surprised at anything.

"Conor had a blue button his father mailed to him. It seems special. I thought perhaps a tall tale—is that the American term?"

"This town already has too many tall tales. No, I'm afraid it's a practicality. Mr. Hargrove buys blue buttons—and white ones, too—by the barrel. They're good for business and identification, but nothing romantic."

"They're also good for keeping the men from ever earning a stake. Now that I'm sewing them on, they'll not be buying so many at the company store. If you'll pardon my boldness, the prices are rather steep. Especially for my boarders. I intend to give them a fair deal, for they're fair and kind men."

Edith gave her a bemused look. "My, my, such a passionate defense of them. But then they are your boarders. A word of caution, though. We ladies hope you will be circumspect. It's already bad enough having Mr. Montgomery sleeping in the hotel lobby. This is, after all, a family town, and we're already having a bit of difficulty explaining to our youngsters why a young woman is spending so much time in the same boardinghouse with the bachelors."

Morna's temper rarely flared. But a lady of her breeding could only have her dignity questioned so many times.

"Because I bought it. I own it. And I am the landlady. And I run a respectable establishment." The subject was closed. She would rather deal with Quinn.

"Really, Miss Patterson—"

Morna stood abruptly and gathered up her shawl.

"Mrs. Hargrove, I must be—what is the American term?—running along? I have a business meeting in town."

With Quinn Montgomery.

7

QUINN MONTGOMERY WAS thoroughly annoyed. He'd fired the bachelors, but now he was stranded in this town.

Sitting in the maroon velvet chair by the potted fern in the lobby of the Bunyan Hotel, he stared at the newspaper. No rooms in the hotel. And it was against company rules to evict anyone. Even he as owner could not argue with that rule.

A woman and bunch of bachelor lumbermen had reduced him to renting a chair. And of course, Theodore. His bungling cousin who knew even less about managing towns than about the practice of law.

Well, he could endure a night sitting up a chair, for no woman was going to best him. He'd no sooner allowed a picture of Miss Morna Patterson's reddish-gold hair to flit through his mind than her voice drifted across the lobby. He slid his newspaper down to nose level so he could peer over the edge of it and stare. There she was, the landlady to a bunch of rough-talking, loose-living bachelors. Unobserved, he gazed at her.

She was Sarah all over again. Like a lovely elf returned from the woods to haunt his days.

As if haunting his nights weren't enough.

It was a punch to the gut. He looked at her, part by part, searching for differences. First, the hair. It was the same reddish color. The face. In profile, the high cheekbones, the full mouth, the impertinent nose and impatient chin.

It was Sarah all over again, and yet it wasn't.

With relief, the differences began to hit home. This woman was taller. Spoke with an Irish accent. She was bossier, less flighty. In fact, now that he looked at her hair again, it was curlier. Wisps blew about her hat.

And her clothing. Far more elegant than anything Sarah ever wore. Than anything she'd ever find in his company store. She didn't belong in a lumber town. Certainly not in Bunyan, and he was going to make certain her stay was short.

A single woman with a stash of money traveling alone—a beautiful woman allegedly with no past . . . well, he was too cynical to have any illusions. A woman who looked like her could have only one motive for connecting herself with a boardinghouse full of bachelors, and he wasn't ready to see his town taken over by a woman of ill repute.

It didn't make him ache to touch her anymore. But that was only because of the similarities to Sarah, and well, he did have a past. Too much past. He had only to look in the mirror every day to see the scars of the past in his eyes, in the beard he'd grown to hide his homely face; a face Sarah had jeered at.

Morna glanced over.

He pulled the newspaper back up so it hid his face.

After a minute he slid it down and waited for her to lash into him.

But she smiled. Annoyed at himself for getting caught staring, he raised it again and forced himself to study the curlicues on the letter *C* in an advertisement for corsets from some Detroit emporium. It was one of those Gothic letters with trailing tendrils. . . .

A gloved hand pushed the paper down, and he was staring at the elegant lace shawl of Miss Morna Patterson. He let the paper slide to the floor and looked up into her face.

"Are you aware, Mr. Montgomery," she said slowly, as if addressing a child, "that not even the English Parliament has imposed on Ireland as many rules as you've given this town full of gray boxes?"

Impertinent chit.

A muscle twitched in his mouth, and he bent his head. He usually avoided eye contact with women, with anyone. It was easier not to see their dislike. And Miss Patterson disliked him. She was only more skilled at hiding it than Sarah had been.

"Each of my rules has a reason," he said to the newspaper. "This is a family town, Miss Patterson. Are you aware that in Bunyan there are rules against unattached females calling on single gentlemen at hotels?"

She arched one brow. "Really, Mr. Montgomery. Whatever will people think? That I came to seduce you?"

Her words cut to the quick. Women never seduced him, except for his money. . . .

He stood so he could tower over her. "They'll think, Miss Patterson, that you're a loose woman—all the more so since you've purchased a house full of bachelors."

"There was no law against it."

"You must realize that when a young woman steals into America using another woman's identity, not to mention her child, and then produces a vast amount of cash in order to purchase a house full of single men, people don't need much imagination to draw unseemly conclusions."

"About what? The house? There are tall tales about its past."

He averted his face. "I don't discuss the past."

Morna stared at his profile. He had straight features, strong cheekbones and jaw. Turned as he was this way, she could never say he was—well, Nellie was unkind in saying he was ugly. Mysterious was more like it. His face was mostly hidden by the full growth of his beard—dark and thick, it hid him from temple to jaw. She did not find it handsome, yet it oddly suited him, and she sensed that he was a gentle man underneath. The mild manners, the reluctance to socialize, would be explained by his face.

"Will you tell me about it?"

"About what?"

She shrank back a bit at his abrupt tone. "The house. The tall tales. Unless the stories are connected."

"My past is nobody's business. It's your future that you should mind. The entire town is whispering, and as a result yards are in disarray and men are late for work. Their gossip about you indirectly affects the number of logs that get sawed and thus my productivity—"

"Perhaps you should give your employees something more to occupy themselves with than trivial gossip."

"You are not a trivial event, Miss Patterson. Why did you come here? Are you escaping some scandal in Ireland? You're not the first to come to America for that reason, but if it *is* the reason, I want you to know this town is not a haven for you. Perhaps farther west—"

"I have as much right to stay here as you do. As to why I came, your citizens would never guess—not in a million years. . . . We all have our secrets, Mr. Montgomery. You may hide yours with a beard, but that doesn't mean mine are less painful."

Quinn didn't flinch. "Do you find my face somehow painful to look upon?" he asked.

"Of course not. You mistake my meaning. It's what people are inside, how they treat a lady, that I count. Our looks are not important, though I find it interesting that you choose to hide yours."

"Many men wear beards."

"Many men have something to hide . . . but as I said, it's what inside that counts."

"And what do you think I am inside?"

"Someone kind, who won't let that kindness out because you think wrongly you're being judged by appearances only."

"As you are judged."

"Because nature favored me with what some call a pretty face is no guarantee that I'm kind inside. Like you, I have to prove myself, prove I have nothing but business on my mind."

He found himself swimming in extraordinary green eyes.

"Mr. Montgomery, you needn't worry. In my previous life I was an honest woman, and I have no designs on a bunch of lumbermen. But I do need their rent. And they need their jobs. That wasn't nice of you to fire them."

He laughed. "No one's ever accused me of being nice." He turned his gaze full on her then, and couldn't stop the tug of attraction he felt. That hair was so much like Sarah's it made him ache. "You'd have an easier go of it in a different sort of town. A bigger city would be easier for you."

"I'm not leaving, Mr. Montgomery, and you can't make me. Unlike the rest of this town, you don't own me.

Unlike you, I'm not afraid of the tall tales inside that house. Furthermore, I'm going to hire the bachelors myself—to build a house for me."

"The deuce you will."

"I don't appreciate profanity." She waited a moment. He pretended to read the newspaper. "You can't stop me."

Suddenly his blue eyes met hers. "There's a rule here that says you need a permit for a new house."

"Which you give out, I suppose?"

"When I want new houses, and I do not want any new houses. Nice try, Morna, but I'm afraid you'll have to forget the idea of hiring the bachelors as carpenters."

He turned away again, his expression stony.

"Why are you so desperate to be rid of me?" she asked. "You're practically twisting the rules to have me gone, and all I've really done is bring an orphaned lad here and hire out to do sewing. Why?"

Quinn wasn't about to tell her why. Instead, he stared at the rich reddish-gold hair that framed her face. It was the hair that disturbed him. Tempted him. She was the ghost, a ghost from his past. That's how much she reminded him of Sarah. Only he'd never tell her so.

"Will you change your mind?" she asked gently.

Her skirt rustled lightly against his leg. His nerves were poised on edge. She was beautiful, and he liked her. But he didn't trust any woman that reminded him of Sarah.

"Is that a no?" she asked.

Her voice was soft. He pictured himself alone with her, unpinning the lovely hair, kissing the nape of her neck. He shifted uncomfortably in his chair.

"Will you rent me a room in the boardinghouse?"

Her mouth dropped open. "What for?"

"I'm a bachelor and I need a place to stay."

"You're staying here in the hotel."

"In a chair," he corrected her. "It appears there is no room at this particular inn. And now that I think on it, I'd prefer to stay in the boardinghouse, where I might rent a bed—and board."

"With the bachelors?"

"In the attic. I like a bit of privacy."

"How do you know it's habitable? Most of it is boarded up."

"Because I know that house, Miss Patterson, and I know the tall tales, and I know not one bachelor would dare to sleep up there. They've warned you off it, haven't they? With what? Tales about it being haunted? Did they say the same about the room in back?"

She looked suddenly paler. "A room in back . . . I hadn't explored up there yet. The attic is boarded up, but no one knows why. . . ."

His intuition was uncanny. This was precisely why she'd delayed her decision to move in.

"Part of the attic is boarded. Part is open."

"I see."

"The boarded-up room could be yours. There's no need to tear down boards. I have the key to the door."

"Now you're bribing me. Why would you want to live there?"

"Because I'm a bachelor . . . Are you sure you're not afraid of me . . . ?"

His presence could create all kinds of trouble for her bachelors. "Of course not. But I'm not sure you'd be happy in the boardinghouse. It lacks many of the amenities to which you've become accustomed."

"How do you know what I'm used to? How do you know anything about that boardinghouse?"

His voice was rough, and she blinked. Something about the way he spoke of the house gave her pause. He knew something of the place that he was not sharing with her.

For from the moment she'd first laid eyes on him, she'd known one thing: Quinn Montgomery made her dizzy with his mysterious aura. She liked his straight profile, his dark, immaculately groomed hair, the directness of his gaze. But most of all she liked the thick dark beard, wild and unkempt as the underbrush in a neatly ordered forest. The one thing about him that he allowed to be unruly. That, she realized, was the mystery about the man. The unexpected combination of order and unruliness. He was hiding something behind all those rules, and that lent him the air of mystery.

"Miss Patterson?"

He was waiting, staring at her.

Quickly, she debated her choices. Let him in her boardinghouse, and she'd live on the edge of a precipice. He invited sympathy, and from there it was but a short step to intimacy.

"Well, you want your bachelors to have jobs, don't you?" he asked, voice cool.

"You know I do. Is this blackmail?"

He smiled. She was quick and intelligent. Far different from Sarah, whose conversation was girlish. "I wouldn't call it that. All business deals involve compromise. Surely a woman who professes to be a . . . uh . . . businesswoman realizes that."

"Of course. So what are we trading?"

He looked at her, and a sudden idea took shape. "We trade nothing yet. I propose instead a wager."

"A what?"

"You are a businesswoman, are you not? Don't sound so shocked."

"I'm listening. Go on."

"Prove your virtue and the bachelors stay on at the mill forever. But if I seduce you, not only do the bachelors leave but I win back my boardinghouse."

Morna caught her breath audibly. "That's ridiculous. You'll never win."

"Then what's so hard about agreeing to it?" He smiled at her.

For a moment she was silent, then to Quinn's satisfaction she nodded. "You play dangerous games, Quinn, and yet something about it intrigues me."

The die was cast.

Quinn knew she'd be unable to resist. She was a gambler, this one, or she'd not have turned up here in Bunyan like she did with nothing to her name but an orphaned child and a trunk. True, the town would be shocked at this gamble, but then they would never know. The bachelors would never know.

No one would know. Only pretty Morna and Quinn Montgomery. However it turned out, he'd at least have some amusement, some diversion.

"I said I agree," Morna repeated thoughtfully. "But I have one condition of my own. The bachelors go back to work until the wager is settled."

Why not? His mill would produce more lumber. So after a quick shrug, he nodded. He was enjoying watching Morna Patterson stand in front of him, breasts heaving. She crossed her arms.

"And I warn you I doubt you'll like living with them."

"I'll be the judge of that."

"How do you know so much about that place? My place?"

He rose from the chair and circled her, like a predator. "I used to own the place, remember? I own this town, Morna. I know more about it than anyone. I owned this town when it was nothing but woods. I made it, and I'll decide who lives here and when to burn and destroy it if I want."

"Why?"

Quinn was taken aback. No one had ever asked him why. He hid the reason in a recess of his heart, the way nocturnal creatures might hide inside a hollow log. Because my heart is a hollow thing, he might have said, but he couldn't say it out loud. Words, someone once wrote, were invented to hide thoughts.

"One more thing," he added. "I want the attic."

"It's shut up. Boarded over." She tilted her chin up a notch, and a beam of light coming in the door caught that remarkable hair.

Quinn wanted her.

"We'll unboard it. There are two rooms up there. You can have the one that's decorated."

"How handy for your wager."

He smiled at the rosy flush on her face. "A door separates the attic rooms. You could even push an armoire in front of it if you really want to win the wager."

Arms folded, eyes blazing, she glared at him.

"I don't care if you say no and leave," he heard himself say. He was never going to want another woman as long as he lived. Not in that way. Not with his soul.

"No," she said. "I want to move into the house. . . . But I have my own rules inside."

"As landlady, you're entitled."

"You won't be exempt."

He raised one eyebrow, bemused. "Won't I? Tell me why."

"The men are learning to behave like gentlemen, and you'll be no different. Just because you own the town gives you no special privileges. You'll hang your socks up like everyone. We'll all do our share. You might even have to chop kindling."

"Would it surprise you to know I can handle an ax?"

"Yes."

"Likewise, Morna I will be surprised if *you* can handle an ax . . . perhaps I shall have to give you lessons."

"I'll learn from the millworkers, thank you. Don't ask for any special favors. I won't tolerate favoritism. You're no more, no less, than my other boarders."

"Except I live upstairs."

"Mind you, Quinn, I'm only agreeing to that *request* because I think the bachelors would be unhappy having the owner of the town bunking with them. Now don't ask for another thing."

"I wouldn't dream of asking for more. But you can't expect to run a bachelor boardinghouse and not be watched—by the entire town. I have a duty to the town."

"You presume too much."

"We'll see."

Anger flickered across her face, but she was too clever to give vent to it. He watched her battle with self-control. "When do the bachelors start work at the mill?"

"Tomorrow."

"And when do I get the key to the locked room—a key I should have received upon buying the house."

"Theodore didn't have it."

Blunt and to the point.

He dug into his pocket and dangled a key in front of her. "I suggest you take the upstairs room for a practical reason—so the bachelors can't watch you disrobe by kerosene lantern."

"They don't."

Even more to the point. A stab of heat shot through his groin. He swallowed hard, looked away from her. "You may rent the empty attic after I leave." He smiled. "I don't expect you'll like this town for long. Not after I close the mill, then there'll be nothing to bargain with."

"I'll worry about that when the time comes. I've learned, Quinn Montgomery, to live in today."

As had he. Today. No past. And the future—he looked no further than the day when the trees would be gone.

"You're a woman of wisdom, then, Miss Morna Patterson, and a pleasure doing business with you."

"It's a deal, then?" she asked.

He nodded. He was making a mistake striking deals with a woman who looked like her. A bigger mistake opening up that attic, especially the back room, and allowing her to access to it. No good would come of the deed. No good came of anything Quinn did these days.

He looked at her, while inside the hollow cavern of his soul a voice cried out, *Say no. Back out.*

She took a step toward him. The sweet scent of her rustled from the folds of her gown. Her shawl slipped and the lace grazed his knee.

"We have a deal. With one last understanding—the bachelors work."

"Yes." He smiled at her, and she stammered some more words.

"I'm not what you think, you know. This is perfectly innocent. You've judged me wrong, you'll see."

"No one ever is what they seem, Morna. Nothing is what it seems." And before she could start asking difficult questions, he walked away and went to collect his bags.

She'd struck a deal with the devil, but there was no use

telling her that. Or she would not be so eager to turn her attic over to him. Everywhere he went was hell on earth. For a fleeting minute he'd glimpsed heaven—just a piece of it—in her eyes, and he wanted to have it again.

In that fleeting second, he'd said the word *yes*.

And he wasn't sorry.

An hour later Arne was hauling Quinn Montgomery's luggage to the boardinghouse.

An hour and five minutes later the word had spread up and down Main Street. Quinn Montgomery had gone to live in the bachelor boardinghouse.

Well, said the butcher's wife, that's an appropriate place.

Ah, said the milliner's wife, but he's never wanted to live there before—until that woman, that Irishwoman, moved here and bought the place.

Edith cleared her throat and held up a blue button. "Ladies, please, you know idle gossip is a waste of time. He's gone, of course, to keep an eye on her."

8

"*B*REAK OUT THE brew, men. We need a toast."
Cleatface came running into the dining room. "We got
our jobs back. Mr. Quinn Montgomery changed his
mind!"

Everyone's face lit up, and the men crowded around
Cleatface asking for details.

Morna put aside her sewing. Their happiness filled her
heart, but now came the part she'd been putting off. She
stood. If she didn't tell them shortly, they'd open the
front door and find out anyway.

"Gentlemen, there's more to it than that. . . ."

Pierre turned to her. "See, I told you it was too good to
be true."

"Aw, don't pour cold water on things, Pierre. I expect
he wants us decked out in blue buttons like before—so's
the town knows who the bachelors are."

Morna had already begun sewing on buttons. "It's
something more, I fear."

Their smiles faded a bit.

She took a deep breath for courage. "I've rented him a
bed here."

"Holy sawdust!"

Widowmaker dropped the pot of baked beans he was

holding on to the floor. The bachelors' supper spread in a widening pool upon the pine floor. The mongrel Queenie promptly bounded over and lapped it up.

Like hounds scenting disaster, the other bachelors came running from their bunks, clad only in socks and sawed-off pants and snapping suspenders over their shoulders as they came. As the news spread, they sank down one by one.

Arne buried his face in his hands a minute then looked up hopefully. "Is he taking the bed out of here?"

"No."

More moans. As usual, Dogger arrived late. At the sight of the dog licking the last of the baked beans, he knelt, teary-eyed. "I been smelling those beans all day, just a-waiting for supper."

"Dogger, get up." Pierre and Arne pulled him to his feet and each held an elbow to steady him. "You got your job back," Arne said right into his ear.

"Blackmail," Cleatface muttered.

"I had no choice." Morna wished they'd be happier about the news. "It was the condition for giving you your jobs back."

"Well, I'd rather move on than sleep under the same roof as him." Pierre's handsome face was flushed with anger.

"Shuddup, all of you," Widowmaker yelled. "You all need jobs and you know it. Heck, you ain't even got supper now, let alone a stake to start over somewhere else."

"I rented him the attic," Morna said. "So it's not like he'll be with you, really."

"He's coming to spy on us."

"On me, I fear," Morna said. "But if I can stand it, so can you."

"She's right, men," Pierre said. "What kind of cowards are you all? We're the ones who run the saws and all. It might be fun to have a rich greenhorn in here watching us."

"He'll be watching Morna."

"All the better. We'll watch him watch Morna. . . . Now, let's say a benediction for our supper." They formed a circle around Queenie, who was lapping up the last of the beans.

Morna no sooner relaxed than movement at the door caught her eye.

Quinn Montgomery stood in the doorway. And he was staring in bewilderment at the last rites for the spilled supper. He was also dressed up in suit, white shirt, and tie, and looked so hopelessly out of place among the rough-and-tumble millworkers that she almost smiled.

Or it might have been because she was ridiculously glad to see him. She smiled tentatively.

Last rites for the beans were over. One by one the bachelors followed her gaze.

"Blast my buttons," Cleatface said. "I hoped you was joshing us."

Quinn stepped in and dropped his valise onto the floor. "Good evening." His gaze was only for Morna.

Her heart pounded crazily. "Now, why would I do— do that?" she said. "Mr. Montgomery fully intends to send you back to work—and with a raise."

Quinn froze in place, eyebrows raised quizzically. "That wasn't in the bargain," he whispered.

She tilted her head at him. "But it's such a good idea." She turned away from those blue eyes and addressed the bachelors. "The exact amount hasn't been worked out yet, but it's a sign of how much Mr. Montgomery values your work. As much as he values the married men."

Pierre leaned back against the wall and crossed his arms. The mouths of the other bachelors dropped open, the expressions on their faces ranging from disbelief to skepticism.

"What changed his mind?" Pierre asked. "You?"

Quinn took a step toward Pierre.

"I assure you, your landlady is a most persuasive woman. But perhaps you already know that. She's kindly consented to let me have the attic room for no charge."

"I didn't."

"But how else do you expect me to accept a drafty room with a reputation for harboring ghosts?"

"That's a tall tale."

"Living rent-free will allow me to offer the men that raise you spoke of."

She drew in a breath. Whatever she did, she must not allow this man to make her lose her temper. Oh, he was ruthless, and no matter how cleverly she tried to outwit him, he always managed to outwit her.

One thing she'd learned from her father, though, was the art of doing business: when to hold the line, give in . . . or compromise. The men had their jobs back. Victory in the war was hers, so she figured she could give in on a battle over rent.

"All right, then. As soon as you're settled in, I expect the key to the other room we discussed."

The men all swung from Quinn to Morna. "Criminy, he's not going to open up the back room?"

"Why not? Don't tell me it's haunted, too?"

"No, it's just that—well, no one's ever seen it. Who knows what's in there?"

"I'll be in there," Morna said, and sat down in the rocker by the fire, like the queen of her domain. "And I'll have no more silly stories. Please step aside and allow

Mr. Montgomery to settle in. Everyone will wash and comb their hair before supper. Maybe with more attention to our grooming, there'll be less time for telling tales."

She picked up her sewing and glanced up only long enough to watch Quinn, key in hand, carry his valise up the rickety wooden stairs to the attic door. The men watched him, too.

"Criminy," Cleatface moaned. "He's really gonna live with us."

"It'll be dusty up there," Cookee said reassuringly. "And there'll be spiderwebs. You think he's afraid of spiders?"

"No." It was a unanimous chorus of voices.

"Well," offered Arne in a consoling tone, "it's not like he's in the bunkroom vith us . . . I mean, it could be vorse."

"Ain't a good idea having the boss under the same roof with our landlady," Cleatface muttered.

"Shuddup, Cleatface," said Widowmaker. "Could be he don't like us under the same roof with her."

"Heck, we're gonna look out for her. I don't trust him one bit. Any man what would have the poor sense to fire us can't be trusted around our landlady."

"We'll see," Pierre said thoughtfully. "For now, I'd count my blessings."

Morna looked up at Pierre and gave him a grateful smile. Pierre smiled back.

They were still smiling at each other when Quinn descended the stairs, and Widowmaker bustled back to his little kitchen, calling, "Time to eat. Everyone sit."

It was a silent dinner, with only Morna and Pierre making an attempt at conversation. Something about Pierre's French-trapper ancestors. She couldn't quite concentrate. Quinn Montgomery's blue eyes were fixed on her the entire time. Her appetite failed. The fried potatoes and bread and salt pork didn't appeal. She burned her tongue on her tea and spilled the sugar.

When Widowmaker brought in a big apple pie, she stood. "I think I'll skip dessert."

Quinn stood, too. "Save mine till later. I assume Morna wants the key to her room now, so you can get out of that tent."

She gulped. "Yes, it'll be good for Conor to sleep under a roof again."

"Where does the boy sleep now?"

"With me."

"He belongs with the men."

"He's terrified of the dark. He's so newly orphaned, and—and he's been having bad dreams."

"I think he should bunk with the men."

"I—I'll suggest it. As long as I'm close by . . . is this room close by?"

"Close enough to hear the men snore through the walls."

"Hey, we don't snore."

Morna put a finger to her lips. "Quiet, please." She swung back to Quinn. "Will you give me the key or do I have to chop down the door?"

"I don't know. It's been a long time since I tried to open the room."

"Dessert?" Widowmaker asked.

Suddenly everyone decided they were too full. And since they were too full, they might as well stand by in case Quinn Montgomery needed someone with brawn to help out.

"I think he can do it himself," Morna said, hoping

they'd take the hint and return to their bunk room. "Don't you men have socks to wash or cards to play?"

Later. "Mr. Montgomery," whispered Cleatface, "is going to have his work cut out running this town. And watching him saw open that shut-up room is going to be the start of some fun."

"Hush up," Morna said. "He's got a key."

"Won't work. Mark my words."

"You be polite to him or you'll be thrown out." Too late, Morna realized what she'd started—a rivalry between the millworkers and the boss. With her as the landlady, though, she'd be the peacekeeper, too. And above all, peace would reign in her house.

No matter what she had to do to keep it.

She only wished her heart would listen as well. Quinn Montgomery looked at her so intently. Her pulse reacted so fiercely. She'd never felt she was in danger of losing her way until she met his gaze.

Conor came running up to her and clutched her skirts. "You won't leave me, Morna, will you? You won't make me stay alone in the tent?"

She patted his curls. "Of course not, Conor. We're only going to move inside."

Quinn watched them, and she raised her brows a fraction and shrugged. I told you so, she said silently.

"Conor has been through a lot of change and grief. I think I'll let him decide where he wants to sleep."

Quinn nodded. He felt for the boy, but it was the landlady, Morna, whose sleeping arrangements bothered him. Wherever she slept in this house, he'd be uneasy. Oh, he wasn't worried about winning their wager. It was the way she made his pulse slam heavier against his ribs.

"Widowmaker, I'm going to disrupt your kitchen."

"What for?"

"Because the entrance to the spare room is behind your cupboards. I could let your landlady go in and out of her new room through the connecting door up in my attic, but somehow I think everyone would be happier if she had her own entrance—these backstairs."

This time Widowmaker dropped his wooden spoon, which Queenie sniffed and abandoned. "There can't be a stairway behind the kitchen. There's nothing back there but a wall."

"Didn't you ever notice how outside it juts out from the kitchen farther than it does inside?"

"Not enough to make it a staircase. A closet maybe."

Quinn gave an enigmatic smile. Morna, more and more curious, drew closer.

"Push that cupboard out of the way," Quinn ordered, "and someone bring me an ax."

Arne handed one over.

To Morna, it appeared to be nothing but a wall of logs. Maybe this was Quinn's way of trying to scare her out.

"You said it had a door with a key," she said.

"It does. But first we have to uncover the door."

"Holy cow," said Cleatface. "This place really does have a secret staircase."

"Stand back," said Quinn. As he raised the ax, the bachelors scattered. He brought it down with a mighty whack and a crack, and the wall in the kitchen split. Over and over Quinn took the ax to the wood. Finally, when he leaned on the ax to catch his breath, the bachelors rushed forward, crowding each other in their eagerness to tackle the boards bare-handed. In a few minutes more, the space was cleared, and Quinn gestured for Morna to come and see.

This was crazy. Maybe the tent wasn't so bad after all.

But Quinn Montgomery was a compelling man. She could not resist him.

Inside, the scent of pinewood was overpowering, and it was dark. Widowmaker handed her a kerosene lantern, which cast big shadows all about her. Gradually her eyes focused.

Quinn was sitting on a rickety set of stairs. In his outstretched hand was a key. "Go ahead," he said. "Take it."

"Where's the door?"

He jerked a thumb over his shoulder to indicate up above.

"You mean there are two sets of stairs leading up?"

"When the house was built this was intended as the servants' staircase. Only servants never came to work here. Instead the room upstairs was closed up and locked. Go ahead. You own it now. You might as well look at it, or do you believe all those tall tales about ghosts and whatnot?"

"You tell me," she said. "Are they true?"

"Take the key," he said, standing and holding out his hand.

A golden key lay in his palm. "You do it, please."

Quinn walked up the stairs, twisted the key into a lock of gold, jerked it away, and gave the door a push. With a squeak of rusty hinges, it gave way, and Morna stepped inside, holding up the lantern for her first look.

It was splendid. The things she could see anyway. Much of the furniture was covered, ghostlike, in white sheets.

Behind her, the bachelors stood whispering in the doorway and on the stairway like gossips. Only Quinn followed her in.

"It might need dusting."

She was speechless.

"You want a better light," Widowmaker said from the doorway. "In case of bats and mice."

Quinn turned. "We've waited a long time to walk in here again, and I don't want company."

"Maybe Morna wants to be chaperoned."

Quinn glowered at Widowmaker.

Morna cringed. If cooks weren't so hard to find, he'd send Widowmaker packing. "I'm fine, Widowmaker. Tell the men to bring all their shirts into the dining room."

"We already sewed our own buttons on. Least we could do, after all you done."

She smiled at him. "I'll be fine. Now let me look."

While Quinn waited in the doorway, a spiderweb just above his shoulder, Morna held up the lantern and slowly walked about the room, exploring.

It wasn't large—about half the attic—but it was more elegant than anything she'd expected to see in this town. Like an Irish castle plucked up and set down here in humble Bunyan. So utterly different from the rest of this regulation sawmill town.

Slowly, the ghostly shapes of furniture were coming into focus. She pulled the sheets off to reveal one treasure after another. A velvet chair, a settee, a mahogany table. Dust filled the air. A piano. A whatnot, still loaded with fine china pieces.

She sneezed. Heavens, she'd have to buy cleaning supplies at the company store and pay exorbitant prices. Oh, but for this room, it'd be worth it. The tattered lace at the window would have to go, too.

Clearly, the place had been a grand room, but it was at the wrong end of town, the opposite end from all the fancy homes of the managers. It looked as if the occupant had just walked out and left it. The previous owner, though, was Quinn. . . .

She spun around, shining the lantern now on this corner, now that wall, then at last came to the doorway where Quinn Montgomery still lounged. The lantern light caught at his face, highlighting the dark beard, the somber blue eyes. His arms were folded, his gaze on her.

"Sure and it's a beautiful room you've been hiding away in this town. Were you going to let me buy the house and never tell me about it?"

"You'd have found it eventually. Through the door on the attic side."

"Connecting with your quarters?" Suddenly the implications of that connection took shape. She'd sleep one thin door away from Quinn.

"Locked . . . unless you open the door." He indicated with a nod the shadowed doorway connecting the two parts of the upper story. "You can sleep in peace, I assure you."

"I intend to."

"Do you like it, then?" Quinn asked.

"It's beautiful."

"Beauty is in the eye of the beholder. I don't care for it. That's why I didn't mention it. But I hate the thought of the boy out in the cold in a tent."

"Yes."

"You can dust off one corner for tonight."

"Yes, it's perfect. . . ." Right down to the elegant brass headboard. "Did you live here?" she asked.

"For a while."

"Why did you leave?"

"I didn't want to live here anymore."

This room had the touch of a woman. "Did you live here alone?"

"No. I built this house for a woman, and she decorated this room."

"What happened to her?" Morna barely breathed the words.

"She wasn't fond of living in the woods. Nor, for that matter, was I. So after she left, I built the rest of the town and the sawmill and proceeded to cut down the woods."

"Will she come back? When all the trees are cut down. I mean?"

He gazed at her a long moment. "I don't know."

Whoever she was, this must be the ghost everyone talked about. Not a real ghost, but a memory from the past.

"I'll send some men out to gather your things."

Which was a polite way of saying the subject was closed.

He went downstairs, but she stood there at the doorway, stunned. . . .

This beautiful room and everything in it was all hers.

Except for one thing.

The past that it held.

Quinn Montgomery's past. The key, she suspected, to his heart. Which was a ridiculous thing to worry about in any case because she despised the man.

9

CONOR LAY IN the dark, a button caught tight in his hand. He missed his mama. He wished they'd never left their home in Ireland. Now he had no mama, and no papa either. And the button was all he had left. All the men wore blue buttons. His papa was not as special as Conor had thought. He had been a man like all those red-underweared men downstairs.

He thought awhile longer. In one of his letters, Papa had written about a treasure. Now, why would a father write his boy about treasure unless he meant for him to find it and help his ma? Only now Conor had no ma. He bit his lip, tears welling.

His papa had written about the treasure. He'd used some of the treasure to buy their boat tickets to America. So the treasure had to be real. Even the bachelors said so. Well, not exactly, but in one of their tall tales, they went on and on about the lumberjack and the lady who stole away into the woods and got lost. It was not Conor's favorite tall tale, mainly because he did not like any stories involving lasses. Conor much preferred tales of daring and fun. He liked Paul Bunyan tales. But he'd perked up and listened to the tale about treasure—despite the bothersome part about some female.

Treasure. Hidden treasure. For the first time since Mama and Papa died, he felt a rush of boyish thrill. For the first time this funny town with all its company rules held some excitement for him.

Of course he had no idea exactly what the treasure was—a pot of gold perhaps? But maybe something else. Jewels? Fairy dust? American money? Maybe in this town the people thought wood chips were treasure. Whatever it was, Papa had used it to buy boat tickets, so it must be something wonderful.

Maybe if he could find it, he could use it to take Morna away from that grouchy Mr. Montgomery. He suspected she'd rather be back in Ireland. He twirled the button between his index finger and thumb, watching the way the moonlight twinkled off it as he did so. Then he rolled over.

The button slipped out of his grasp. In the next second, it dropped to the floor. He leaned over the edge of the bed to pick it up—but it never landed. He could see clearly by the moonlight. It was rolling. It was rolling right toward the door that separated this room from the attic room next door. And as far as Conor was concerned, that next-door attic room contained one very scary man. It was, the bachelors teased him, the room where the ghost walked. Conor had no reason to doubt them.

Sitting up, covers clutched in his hands, he frantically searched for Morna, fast asleep in her bed.

"Morna!"

Morna awoke with a start and sat up, pushing hair out of her eyes. It took a minute to blink away sleep. She missed the smell of canvas, the hard ground. Then she remembered where she was—in a bed in the upstairs room of the boardinghouse.

"Morna!" Another cry was followed by sobs.

Conor.

In another second, she threw back the quilt and got out of bed. The floor beneath her bare feet was freezing cold as she hurried to the source of the cries without stopping to throw on a shawl.

The little boy was sleeping on a mattress on the floor across the room from her. He was, in fact, practically blocking the door to the attic, Quinn's lair. "I'm coming," she whispered urgently, desperate not to awaken the sleeping lion next door.

Inch by inch, she felt her way along to the window, threw up the shade to let in moonlight, and then crossed directly to Conor.

She wasted no time in embracing him. "Hush now. It's only a dream."

"No! No! The button's gone."

"A bad dream. Conor, it'll be there in the morning."

But Conor would not be consoled. "I lost Da's button. Find it, Morna." He flung his arms about her neck. "It went through the door and the ghost is going to get it."

Somehow, Morna feared Quinn far more than any imaginary ghost. Still she couldn't help but smile at the predicament. "Here now, it probably dropped on the floor." Over and over she tired to reassure him. Really, the bachelors were going to have to stop telling these tall tales when Conor was around. The child had gone through too much pain lately to hear such nonsense. "Hush, Conor, we'll find it at daylight."

"No!"

"Then I'll feel around for it now. Where did you drop it?"

With a sniffle and a rub of his nose, Conor pointed at the door.

Morna followed where he pointed.

"Down there," Conor said, voice wobbling. "Da's treasure map said I could never lose the button."

Treasure map? This was the first Morna had heard of maps. More tall tales growing larger with darkness.

She leaned across the mattress. "I expect it fell on the floor, and if I reach down, I shall touch it."

"No, you won't," Conor said in a small and shaky voice.

"How do you know?" she said while leaning across the bed.

"Because the button went through the door."

Impossible. And it was on the very tip of her tongue to say so when her hand touched the bottom of the door. It did not meet the floor. She encountered a gap high enough for a button to roll on through to the attic.

Quinn's part of the attic.

"Did it go into the other room?" she asked.

Conor nodded. "Yes. Get it, please. You're not afraid of him, are you?"

Morna gulped and prayed her voice would not betray the fib.

"Of course not. Quinn Montgomery is an old grouch. I'll find it and he'll never know I was there." She reached for the doorknob.

She wished she felt as confident as her words.

Quinn woke up to a creak. Two creaks. Footsteps.

Slowly, so the mattress would not squeak and give him away, he turned his head and opened his eyes.

A ghost stood directly in front of the window. He'd not bothered with the shutters, and the moonlight streamed in behind the figure. Half-asleep, he allowed himself to believe it was Sarah. The ghost of Sarah. All right, so he did believe in ghosts.

She was dressed as he remembered, in a white flowing gown, and her hair was long and flowing and unmistakably reddish.

He shifted and half sat up. "Sarah?"

Like an apparition of the past, the figure moved toward him.

He forgot to breathe.

Halfway between the window and his bed, the figure stopped, bent down, and picked up something from the floor. "Sarah," he whispered.

"It's me, Morna."

He was fully awake by now, and the past day came back to him. The place. The month. The reason. All of it pressed down on him as if a tree suddenly fell and pinned him. His head spun. He'd drunk some of Finn's concoction and was drunk.

But when he heard her voice again, he knew he was stark sober.

"I'm sorry. . . . Conor had a nightmare. He refuses to be comforted until I bring him his button. He's clutched it ever since we met on the ship and—"

"I thought—"

"That I was a ghost?"

"I thought you were someone else . . ."

"Oh."

Lucid now, Quinn allowed himself to stare. Morna was more beautiful than ever. And he wanted comfort, too.

When she walked over to his bed, desire stirred in his loins, but disappointment cut through him. He'd almost begun to believe she was as pure and innocent as she declared. He'd almost decided to call off the bet and behave like a gentleman.

But apparently, his first impression had been correct. She was a loose woman, with a houseful of bachelors from which to choose.

Not at all appropriate for a family town. He'd best deal with her straightaway. Throwing back the covers, he got up.

Her eyes grew wide.

He looked down at his long underwear.

"Surely, you're not embarrassed by my attire, Miss Patterson."

"Don't you have a robe?"

"Yes, but the bachelors all run around in long underwear—"

"Not in front of me, they don't."

He shrugged on a robe that was hanging over a nearby chair.

"Did you find it?"

"What?"

"The blue button of Conor's."

As answer, she held out her hand and showed him. The tiny button shone in the pale light of the moon.

He nodded. "Conor will be happy, then."

"Yes."

She looked so innocent, so sweet and guileless, with the moonlight behind her. He still wondered about her, though. Was she really an innocent? Or someone more experienced? She seemed in no hurry to leave.

"Did you lose anything else?"

She shook her head. Embarrassed, she turned to leave.

With one quick step, he blocked her exit and touched her shoulder, right where a lock of her hair waved.

Neither of them moved. For Quinn, breathing came hard.

"I'm sorry." Her words were a whisper. "About waking you."

"I'm not," he said, and allowed his thumb and forefinger to smooth that lock of her hair to its very end.

Maybe now was as good a time as any to find out if his suspicions about the landlady were correct. . . .

She seemed to have forgotten all about the bet.

With an ease that came from experience, he moved closer and stared down into her face, shadowed in the darkness. The moonlight highlighted her hair. Its color was muted, but it flowed long down her back, just as Sarah's had.

"You are so like her," he murmured.

"Who?" she whispered.

"Someone I once knew," he said, and with each word his mouth moved closer to hers, inexorably drawn to the past. Her mouth was entirely different from Sarah's. It tasted sweeter, softer, and then he was kissing her, and was glad it was not Sarah.

His hands tangled in the hair at the nape of her neck, pressing her closer. A single pulse beat between them, and she swayed against his body.

"Morna!"

It was Conor's voice.

She broke off the kiss, looked up at him with disturbed eyes and a stricken face. "I—I don't kiss men I've barely met. I know you have a bet against such a notion, but you'll not win that easily. You're going to lose, Quinn Montgomery, as I live and breathe. I don't know who you thought you were kissing, but Morna Patterson you'll never kiss again, and you will lose, as God is my witness."

She broke away and hurried back toward the door that separated them, her white gown flowing, glowing in the moonlight.

He liked the taste of her, the feel of her in his arms. And she was wrong. When he'd kissed her, he had not been thinking about the past.

He wanted to win the bet, and he would.

But not for the original stakes.

It was as simple as that.

And to Quinn, women were never more complicated.

There was no rush. He had much to do around this godforsaken town. Oh, yes, in this case, time was on his side.

In the morning, Morna arose early, while dark still streaked the sky. Below, Widowmaker was rattling pots on the stove, and she washed and dressed quickly. She wanted to be occupied about the house before Quinn Montgomery appeared. Halfway down the stairs, she stopped. Quinn's voice, its deep timbre unmistakable, drifted up from the dining room, where he spoke to Widowmaker.

Trembling, she hugged her arms about herself. The memory of his lips on hers weakened her and frightened her.

She stood there a few moments composing her facial expression. Her gown was gray, her hair was pinned up in a tidy knot. She looked properly chaste and could not possibly give away her inner turmoil.

Reaching out, she found the rail and slid her hand along its surface the rest of the way to the door. She paused in the doorway. Quinn stood with his back to her, tall and straight.

She stood absolutely silent, taking in the breadth of his back and the absurdity of his dark suit in this sawmill boardinghouse. In her imagination she ran her hand up the fabric of his sleeve.

Widowmaker and he were talking about the virtues of coffee versus tea. "Everyone likes their tea in this place. Same in the lumber camps. Coffee's a highfalutin' drink, and while that may sound strange to you, it ain't to us. Half of us came down over the border from Canada, you know, and tea it is. If you're wanting coffee, you'll have to make your own."

Quinn turned a hundred and eighty degrees in one motion, as if he'd known all along she was standing there, and with his words he did not miss a beat.

"Is that the kind of fare you serve at your boarding-house, Miss Morna Patterson?"

"Excuse me?"

"Tea? I want coffee."

"I've only just acquired the place, if you'll recall, and furthermore, this is not a restaurant. It's a boardinghouse. My boardinghouse."

"For a while, Morna Patterson."

With long and graceful strides for a man so big, he came toward her. She stood rooted to the spot, her pulse in her throat. She wanted to holler to Widowmaker to stay in the room with her, but another part of her wanted to be alone and close to Quinn in the darkness, as she had been last night.

But Widowmaker shook his head as if annoyed at another mouth to feed and vanished into his kitchen.

Morna stood looking up at Quinn, at his mouth, his smile. She was ashamed to remember how she'd nearly lost her head last night.

Quinn seemed to have eyes in the back of his head, for Widowmaker had no sooner left the room than he reached out and grazed her lips with his thumb.

She batted his hand away and backed up a step, right into the wall. "You take brazen liberties."

"It is my town."

"And once again, my house."

He smiled fleetingly. "What," he asked softly, "were you doing traipsing about up in the attic dressed like a ghost?"

"What were you doing kissing a ghost?"

"My mistake, and my loss."

"You will never win back this boardinghouse. If you wanted it so badly, you should have thought before you allowed Theodore to tack a 'For Sale' sign upon it."

"I have lived too much of my life in the past, Morna, and so I don't talk about it or relive it."

"Nor do I."

"Then you aren't going to tell me why you came here."

"I already did. It was because of Conor."

"Ah, yes, and it is because of Conor you were tiptoeing around in the attic chasing after a blue button." The scoffing in his voice was gentle.

"It was true. He had a nightmare and would not be comforted unless I found the button. His da's blue button. His sole comfort. That and a treasure map."

Quinn's eyes narrowed. "What treasure? This town is full of lumberjacks, not pirates."

She gave a little shrug and used the chance to move around Quinn and head to her place at the end of the table.

From the grumbling noises and cranky talk coming from the bunk room, the bachelors were stirring and would soon be filing in for breakfast.

Outside, the whistle on the mill blew shrilly, the wake-up alarm for the town. From the kitchen came Widowmaker's whistling.

"Sit down, Quinn, and wait for your tea. As soon as the men are all here, I intend to give them a talking to about their tall tales. I believe Conor could do with fewer stories in this place. His imagination is overwrought from losing both parents. He doesn't need any more stimulation."

"Small boys like stories."

"Did you lose your parents?"

"No, but I liked the tall tales. You coddle him."

"You have no feelings."

"Feelings don't keep this town running."

"What does?"

"A manager."

"You fired Theodore."

"Then I shall run it, and without pity or mercy on womanly sympathy."

"I hope you fail."

Quinn eyed first Morna and then the cup of tea Widowmaker plunked down in front of him. He hated tea. He desperately wanted coffee. Almost as desperately as he wanted to shove back his chair and span the length of this plank table and yank pretty Morna Patterson back into his arms. Last night had not been enough, and this verbal sparring was getting them nowhere.

He lifted his mug and gulped. Hot tea burned his tongue. He swore under his breath.

"I owe you a new set of underwear," came a voice from the bunk room. "You was right, Cleatface, the owner's not only still here, but he's having breakfast with the pretty lady."

Scowling, Quinn reached for a milk pitcher and sloshed some into his tea. He should have fired the surly lot of them while he had the chance. Grumpily, he watched them file in, unshaven and with red underwear showing beneath their plaid shirts. Disgusting garb. Come to think of it, he had fired them and then rehired them. He must have been crazy, or seen a ghost.

Once again he glanced down toward Morna. She was smiling at the other men. Jealousy coursed through Quinn, and he hated himself for it. He was supposed to be immune to jealousy. Once it had destroyed his life; he'd vowed it would never master him again, and so he clenched his fist and banged on the table as if to chase it away.

The table shook. His tea sloshed over, and so did everyone else's. Morna, white-faced, rose and threw down her napkin.

"Mr. Montgomery! I thought you of all people would display manners, be an example through whom I might instruct these other men in the niceties of table manners."

Quinn was instantly ashamed at his weakness. He could only stare back at her in silence, for if he spoke, his voice would betray his shakiness.

Morna remained standing. "I see then that everyone here is in need of table manners, so I may as well set down the rules of this table."

Quinn glanced around at the men. To a man, they sat, mouths open, spoons clenched in fists, oatmeal and hotcakes untouched in front of them.

"Manners," croaked Cleatface. "You didn't say nothing about manners. We never had to use manners. We're lumbermen."

Quinn leaned back in his chair, breakfast forgotten, thinking, Let's see how the spunky little miss from Ireland talked her way around a bunch of roughneck mill hands.

"You are lumbermen and gentlemen both."

"Hmmph. That won't set good with the foreman."

"Here in my boardinghouse you're gentlemen. That means using your napkins, eating with utensils rather than fingers, not licking your plates, saying please when you want something passed across the table."

"Aw, Miss Morna, we ain't high-society types."

"You're my boarders . . . and furthermore, there's no vulgar language at the table. Is that much clear?"

They nodded. One by one, she called their names, and they nodded in turn again.

"Very good."

Everyone, even Quinn, relaxed, and either spooned up the oatmeal, or poured syrup over their flapjacks.

They were still chewing when she spoke again. "I'll talk while you eat—because I can't have you be late for work now that you're newly hired back . . ." She paused to spare Quinn a look, and it was not as kind as the one she gave the other men.

He looked down at his flapjacks, strangely dejected.

She walked up one side of the table and down the other. As she talked, she touched each man's shoulder. Each man, except Quinn.

"Before Conor wakes up, I want to talk about the tall tales in this house. I fear they're too frightening for a lad of his tender years."

The men looked up with interest, but kept on chewing. Syrup dribbled down a few chins.

"Napkins," Morna reminded Dogger, and handed him his. He dapped at his unshaven face, smearing syrup into his stubble.

How, Quinn wondered, could such a refined woman give such uncouth men her undivided attention and ignore him? He was using his napkin, eating with a knife and fork, and . . . still feeling unreasonably jealous. This woman was nothing to him. It was this house. That was it. Old memories were haunting him.

He swallowed his jealousy and plastered a look of amusement on his face.

Morna stood beside him now, still explaining about Conor.

"Perhaps if he could play outside more. I'll encourage that. He's never seen so many trees, and I'm sure things like birds and small animals would amuse him. And then there's a treasure—"

Quinn scraped back his chair and rose to confront Morna. "The boy stays out of the woods."

"But why?"

"The woods are dangerous. Ask any of these men."

"Not the woods right here by the boardinghouse. One little patch of woods." Morna walked to the door, opened it, and pointed outside at a pristine triangle of woods. "No one works in there. Those trees are nothing but a patch of shade."

"Have you gone there?"

"Just to the edge. I thought Conor would enjoy a nature walk with me—"

"Don't. It's a town rule never to go near there. If you want to take him for a walk, stroll by the elms in town."

"That's not the same. They're not big enough to hide things."

"Such as this treasure the boy speaks of."

"That's just a boyish fancy. No, I mean things like squirrels and moss and beetles and wildflowers."

"Boys don't care about such things."

Which was a lie. He had once loved the woods very much; he had once been a boy just like young Conor. A boy needed the woods for playing. In the woods, a boy could pretend to be anything from Robin Hood to a fur trapper. But not in those particular woods. And that was the part he did not want to explain.

"It's my town. I don't need to explain my rules."

Even in anger, her face was beautiful. She shut the door and strode back to her place. "You have too many rules in this town."

Now he had her. "Are your rules of the table forgotten, then?"

"That's entirely different."

"How?" Quinn pushed back his plate of flapjacks. All the bachelors had quit eating. Their glances swiveled from Quinn to Morna to Quinn. They were more fascinated with the debate than eating. It took a lot to make lumbermen forget about food.

"The difference," he said more softly, "is that the rule about the woods is for safety. Your rules do nothing but drive a man crazy. The bachelors don't want to have manners. They only want a paycheck."

"And what for? So they can work for you forever and give it all to the company store? Oh, no, Quinn Montgomery. They want a stake. I know what that means. They want to have a life of their own, a family, a home, and so I'm helping them learn the manners they'll need."

Suddenly the door leading from upstairs swung open and Conor stood framed in the doorway. "Why's everybody yelling?" he asked, rubbing sleep from his eyes.

Morna rushed to the boy's side and embraced him. The bachelors slurped down their tea and wolfed down their flapjacks.

Quinn was left standing alone, watching all of them. The bet was a mistake. He should never have allowed himself to be drawn in. If only she didn't look so much like Sarah, then he might have left well enough alone. She didn't kiss like Sarah, though. Her lips were moister, softer, more fragile.

"Mr. Montgomery, sir?"

Quinn swung around, interrupted from his thoughts.

Pierre, handsome Pierre, stood there holding out a bundle of clothing.

"What's this?"

"I might be taking liberties, sir, but I was thinking you'd want to dress more comfortable as you see to the town. You and I are about the same size," he added, as if to explain why Pierre instead of someone else was giving him clothes.

Quinn glanced askance at the bundle. Red underwear and a plaid shirt. Heavy woolen socks. Crude and ugly and unrefined.

"I doubt I'll need them. Theodore never dressed down."

"Begging you pardon, sir, but you fired Theodore for not doing his job."

For the first time, Quinn acknowledged to himself that he did not fully understand his job. But he wasn't about to let on to these mill hands.

Nor to Morna. She'd already made a fool of him, letting him kiss her and then paying more attention to these rough-hewn men than to him. He didn't like that kind of treatment from women one bit. Now she was mollycoddling the boy, and he was ignored. Most women would abandon their children for a night with him.

All right, he'd play the game for her. He'd dress more like them. He'd show her he could fit in and rule this place both.

Then let's see how easily she pulled away from his kiss.

And for the first time in years, he found himself looking forward instead of back.

10

$\mathcal{I}$N ALL HIS born days, Quinn never thought he'd stoop to this level—dressed in red flannel and plaid. Worst of all, the garments itched. Maybe the mill hands had a good reason for being grumpy and picking fights.

"Good afternoon, Mr. Montgomery." Otis stared as Quinn pushed open the screen door of the company store. A pair of town matrons stared, then turned away and tittered. Quinn banged the door on his thumb.

"Damn!"

He shook his hand and then accidentally backed into a display of buckets. The metal pyramid fell in a clatter. The cat shot past him and hid behind the cracker barrel.

"Can I help you, sir?"

"No! I mean, yes. Do you have any idea what Theodore did as town manager?"

"Mostly smoked upstairs in his office."

"It was a wonder the town didn't burn down."

"Sir, I'm only the store manager, but he and I talked now and then—off company time, of course."

"Stop apologizing and dithering and give me some idea of what he should have been doing. And if you tell anyone I asked for your help, you're fired."

An idle threat and Otis had to know it, for if Quinn

fired Otis, too, then this town would have only him to run it. He didn't relish the idea.

"Perhaps if we walked about town, I can show you. Theodore hired some of it done; he tried his best. But some things have been waiting a long while."

As they strolled about inspecting the paint jobs on company houses and the lack of chicken coops or abundance of dogs in one yard, Quinn tried not to feel the fool. His footsteps echoed on the boardwalk. No one was about. The streets cleared quickly once he'd rounded the bend from the boardinghouse. Most of the buildings were shuttered, but here and there he saw a face peering out in curiosity. He didn't blame them. He was just as surprised that he was here, managing a one-horse sawmill town. Sawdust floated in the air, and the spring air carried a chill.

"I'm surprised the place is in this good of order, considering. It looks like it took care of itself."

Otis jammed tobacco into a pipe and tamped it down. He reached inside his shirt pocket, pulled out a coffee-stained piece of linen manila and thrust it at Quinn.

"What's this?"

"A list. Helps me remember what needs fixing or tending. You can do things in whatever order you want. It ain't got no particular order. Just the things Theodore never got around to."

Quinn read the thing and silently cursed his incompetent cousin. Next, Otis would be asking for a raise or pushing his plump daughter in his direction.

"Where do you suggest I start?" he asked Otis. His tone of humility shocked even himself.

Otis tapped his pipe against his heel. "At the company store, I reckon. For supplies. Everyone starts there."

*   *   *

Nellie Hargrove was bored standing at the counter polishing the glass over and over. When her papa went inside his office with that Mr. Montgomery, she relaxed and propped her elbows on the glass display case and peered in. Inside were the fanciest items in the Bunyan Company Store. The gilt hair combs. The fans. The shawls. The bottles of violet scent and lavender soap.

Nellie could see her face reflected in the mirror polish of the glass. She was young, pretty, and bored. There was absolutely nothing for a girl of eighteen to do in a town like this except sweep sawdust and count the trees. And her father insisted on staying here indefinitely. Nellie knew why, of course—because of this store and the profits it made for the Hargrove family.

Her mother liked the fine things her papa brought home. But someday this town would be dead. Nellie was only a year out of school, and even she knew that. She guessed the older folks knew it, too—anyone could see the forests dwindling, but no one wanted to pull up stakes and start over.

Actually, truth be told—Nellie didn't want to either. Not yet. Oh, she dreamed of cities like Chicago and St. Paul and Detroit, and she might have been tempted to leave on the train and go find work in one of the fancy department stores there—Bloomingdale's, say.

But one thing kept Nellie here.

She was hopelessly smitten with Pierre. Oh, but Pierre was so handsome, even in woolen shirts and suspenders. He had black hair and a black mustache and no one could sharpen the blades on the saws faster than he. If only she hadn't made the mistake of sighing too deeply when her papa was nearby.

He was French-Canadian, her papa snapped, and no

daughter of his was going to go courting with a mill hand, never mind a foreigner. At least, that was her papa's excuse. She knew he had designs for her to marry up, to marry the likes of Mr. Montgomery.

Quinn Montgomery was a frightening man, too severe in both appearance and manner. He was rich, though. She'd give him that, and he could be useful to make Pierre jealous.

Pierre always had a tall tale for her when he came in to buy buttons. And lately, after her papa had warned him not to linger by Nellie too long, Pierre had taken to using sign language, the same way the men talked in the noisy sawmill. One word at a time, he was teaching Nellie to use her hands to talk, so they could be across the room of the big company store and still say hello with his hands. Nellie thought Pierre was oh, so daring. She adored his tales and always made it her business to wait on him when Papa was out of sight.

Papa, of course, had forbidden her to ever look his way unless it was to collect his money. But how could she help but sneak a peek when she handed him his purchase, whether it be buttons or shirts or red underwear?

What made her out of sorts lately was the same thing that had Mr. Montgomery so grouchy—the arrival of that Irish lady. Now that she was living inside the boardinghouse, Pierre wasn't dropping by the company store nearly as much.

And that had Nellie out of sorts as much as bored.

Every day she brushed her hair until it gleamed and pinned it up just so. She'd taken to wearing her best shirtwaist and dark skirt when she worked in the store and sometimes she snuck a bit of her mother's lily-of-the-valley scent. Just in case Pierre came—which was usually the day the men got paid.

Which wasn't for another two days.

The door squeaked open, and she looked up, expecting to see another housewife come to buy overpriced flour or calico at double what it should cost.

Her heart flew to her mouth. Pierre filled the doorway, and he was looking at her.

She smiled and with her hands said hello, thinking to impress him.

He nodded back. That's all. He walked to her. "Morna Patterson sent me on an errand," he said.

At once, Nellie hated Morna Patterson. She'd been here less than a week and not only was she Pierre's landlady, but now he was doing her bidding. With all those bachelors, did that rich Irishwoman have to pick on the same one Nellie liked? It wasn't fair.

"Well, Pierre, I never thought I'd see the day you gave up the best job in the sawmill to do the bidding of a foreigner."

He shrugged, and at his smile she realized her error. Pierre was foreign, too.

"Aw, Nellie, you know your papa doesn't like me hanging around you. He'll fire me if he catches me talking to you, and I haven't got my stake yet to move on."

"What's that got to do with Miss Patterson?"

"She's treating the bachelors real nice. Going to throw us a social."

"You mean a party? There are parties at Papa and Mama's house."

"Yeah, but they never invite us bachelors. You know that."

Nellie's heart was on her sleeve. "Well, that's town custom."

"So we're going to start a new custom."

"You going to invite anyone?" she asked, trying not to sound coy.

"Naw, it's just a card party. Not the sort of thing you refined folks would like."

"Why are you telling me this, Pierre?" She was jealous. Green as a sapling.

"Because I need to buy some things for her, for the bachelor social, I mean, and I need your help."

"If you think I'll sell them cheaper, you're wrong."

"You used to—"

"Hush, Pierre. That was our secret, and Papa is never to know. Those days are gone. If you come buying for the lady who owns the bachelor boardinghouse, I cannot favor her. She must pay the same prices as everyone."

With a sigh, Pierre handed over his list.

As she was wrapping Pierre's package, Mr. Montgomery approached with his own list. Suddenly mischief overcame Nellie. She was young and pretty and bored . . . and miffed at Pierre. What he needed was a good dose of jealousy, and she set about from that moment on to turn her wiles on Quinn Montgomery.

She thrust the brown paper package at Pierre. "There, you're done." She looked over at the owner of this town and batted her eyes the way she used to do at Pierre. "May I help you?"

Pierre stood there a second, flushed, then stalked out.

Papa stood in the background looking on approvingly, so she gave Quinn Montgomery her prettiest smile, merely to please Papa. He was a big imposing man, and he made her nervous, but it was more important to please Papa and teach Pierre a lesson.

Papa came and whispered in her ear.

For Quinn Montgomery, the prices were cut.

She started to protest, for Papa was risking being found out, but that was his problem, and it gave her some satisfaction to know the Irishwoman who had stolen Pierre's affections and time had to pay double.

Pierre had paused in the doorway, looking back at her. He smiled, and she turned her head. She gave him no smile, not as long as he was under the spell of that wicked woman who owned his lodgings. Suddenly she didn't mind being a company-store clerk. For a little while longer. Long enough to make Pierre jealous, and she would or die trying. She bit her lip and kept on smiling. But it was Quinn Montgomery at whom she smiled.

Quinn chose the easiest task on the list—indeed the only task he knew how to do.

If the list had said to charm a finely bred matron, he could have done it.

If the list had said to select a case of fine wine, he'd have done it.

If the list had said to purchase new croquet mallets, he'd gladly comply.

If the list had said to inspect the rooms at the island hotel, he could have done it.

But instead he had to choose between chicken coops and leaky sewers and painting one of these boring little houses and inspecting the sawmill.

He chose to begin with the latter, though he had not a clue what he was supposed to be inspecting it for; the place was noisy. A man could go deaf in here, and it was full of sawdust, and outside in the drying yard, it wasn't dry at all, but damp with a spring rain. The lumber was damp, the men shivering. They all looked alike—dressed in wet plaid wool with heavy caps and big boots.

He nodded to signal his satisfaction and walked out of the sawmill, feeling foolish in his lumberman's clothes. Unfortunately, he would need more than one set of those barbarous garments, so he had stepped inside the store.

Nellie looked at him with doe-eyed naïveté. He supposed if he pretended to court her, it would go easier with Otis, but he wasn't in the mood yet. His thoughts were still on Miss Morna Patterson, who'd gotten him into this embarrassing predicament.

Quickly he purchased more new clothing and blankets and some personal grooming items and then wasted no time in heading back to the boardinghouse.

The list burned a hole in his pocket, but he didn't want to confess to Otis that he had not the slightest idea how to sell chicken coops or how to paint cottages.

Halfway down to the boardinghouse, he paused on his walk. He was too eager to return to that house . . . and the woman who reigned inside.

She was his enemy, his nemesis. So he tried to distract himself, remind himself this place was only a temporary residence. As soon as he wore her down, or else the rambunctious bachelors did, she'd leave, and then he'd sell the entire place.

From the boardwalk just south of the sawmill, he could stare across the expanse of river, where logs were backed up, waiting their turn for the saws. Just a few miles away, at the river's mouth, waited the blue expanse of Lake Huron, and in his mind's eye he could almost see his island sitting like an emerald jewel off the shore.

That was where he belonged—in the luxury of the big white hotel.

Quinn missed his island life, missed the isolation. There, nothing bothered him, no one needed him. The place contained the remnants of an old fort dating from colonial British days. Wealthy women came there on holiday. Oh, they made demands, but of a temporary nature. And afterward, he'd watch them walk about outside on lawns that swept down to the water while deferential waiters served lemonade and vodka, and birds swept from shade trees to the water, circling idly.

He would tour the mill again tomorrow after he thought of a way to improve productivity. He wanted this town gone, cut out of his life.

Then he could move on west like the other big lumbermen were sure to do. Maybe in the Pacific Northwest he could start over in every sense of the word. Maybe he could even beat Weyerhauser to the West. It was his sole joy in the lumber industry, trying to hold his own against the biggest mogul of them all.

Counting his money and women were all that made him forget, and having to return to Bunyan was the worst thing that could have happened to him. It was like stepping back into a past he never wanted to revisit.

Back into betrayal. Betrayal. A heavy word. Still weighing on him like a wooden weight falling out of the sky. Ripping everything in its path, strewing ragged debris everywhere.

That's all Bunyan was to him—the debris left by a woman's betrayal.

Sarah was her name.

She still lay heavy on his mind.

Once, long ago, when this forest had been Quinn's alone, he had pulled a man dead from a tree that had fallen the wrong way. It was the only way he could describe the aftermath of Sarah.

No one in Bunyan knew. They assumed all the tall tales about its origins were true, and he didn't care to enlighten them.

For too soon the town would be no more. It existed for one reason and one reason alone—to aid him in destroying his forest.

Actually, the townspeople were all dumb, for it was clear as the pox on Cleatface's skin that a lumber town existed for one reason only—to demolish a forest . . . and Sarah's memory. When that was done, the town would have served its purpose. What the people did after that was their business.

The mill whistle blew, like a shrill birdcall. And men were stomping out and home.

He'd dawdled too long.

11

*W*HEN THE DOOR to the log house swung open, Morna looked up from her sewing, expecting to see the bachelors. There was a spring chill in the air, and sitting by the fireplace to sew was much cozier than staying upstairs. Conor had more room to play as well. Right now he was in the kitchen with the cook, and it was a good thing or he'd laugh out loud and try to make Morna laugh, too. She didn't feel like laughing.

Quinn Montgomery stared back at her. He looked so out of place, like a little boy dressed up in new clothes he hated. She bit back a smile and had to bend her head over her sewing to keep the smile at bay. Sawdust dusted his shirt and his hair was all windblown.

It was the first time she'd seen him so—so ruffled.

And she suspected that more than the spring breeze had had their hands on him.

He looked vulnerable, slightly defeated, and it was a sight she'd never expected to see, rather like leaves wilting on what she'd assumed was an evergreen.

Yet he was a man who'd never admit he was less than people assumed.

She ignored the sawdust and blown hair and addressed him stiffly. "Good afternoon, Mr. Montgomery. I assume you did everything on your list and are ready to give up and hire a real town manager."

His eyes narrowed on her and he ran a slightly shaky hand through his hair. "You're on my list, Miss Patterson; so as long as you're still here, then, no, my list is not completed, but thank you for asking."

"May I offer you a cup of coffee?" She said it with the formality she'd once used in her family's elegant parlor back in Ireland.

Quinn half smiled at the question and stared at the stove. A coffeepot had now joined the teakettle.

"I managed to obtain some coffee," Morna explained. "And at a fairer price than it's sold for at your company store—"

"Otis sets the prices. They're fair."

"They're outrageous, but then with no competition, Otis can charge what he wants. In any case, I did not buy the coffee from your company store. Pierre gave me some."

"Why?"

"He's a generous man. He gave you your clothes also, didn't he? And don't be expecting anything fancy. Widow-maker brewed it in a big pot, but—"

"It's hot?"

She nodded.

"Yes, then." He reached toward the nearest plank table for a mug.

She moved to the stove and grabbed an apron from the oven door to use as a pot holder. She turned but he was already coming toward her, like a man edging his way out of the safety of the woods and into an open arena. Slightly wary, he never took his eye off of her, not even when he held out his mug for her to pour.

She wished this were another place, another world.

She wished it was her world, not his, and that she was pouring for him in her brother's—no, her own parlor. She would be wearing a gown of silk, not this drab muslin, and pearls rather than blue buttons would decorate her. The scent of candlewax would fill the air—

"You're quiet, Morna."

She had filled the cup and realized she was still staring down at the handle, at the way his hands grasped it. His hands were large, the fingers strong, the skin smooth. She could almost remember how she'd melted inside when he'd caressed her hair.

And now he had said something to her, and she had no idea what it was.

She looked up to find him smiling down at her. "It might be hot."

"It always is, isn't it?" He set the mug on the table and pulled out a chair. "Will you sit down a few minutes and join me? Maybe we can arrange a truce of sorts."

"I don't want one."

"I'd still like you to sit with me."

Now she was the wary one. He waited while she put back the coffeepot. When she turned he was still waiting. She eyed the chair and then moved to it and stiffly sat, hands folded on lap.

"I think, Mr. Montgomery, that we're both going to be in this town together for quite some time—"

"How do you know that?"

"Because I suspect you know little of how to manage this town—"

His gaze shot up. Bold blue eyes bored into her. She rushed on. The room was finally feeling warmer, and she pushed her shawl down.

She rubbed a finger over the blue button she'd been sewing on.

"Because," she said slowly, "I've got a fair idea of what's on your list, and that you've never done any of those things in your life."

"Don't you?"

"Well, the bachelors tell me you'd never been inside the mill till yesterday, so I know you don't know a saw from a log. And as for the town, well, I hardly think you've spent your life until now repairing leaky roofs or ordering cemetery monuments or awarding prizes for the cleanest yard or—"

"I've seen the list."

"Ah, that explains why you're in such a rush to down that coffee."

He looked at her over the rim of his mug and took a long slow sip.

"My nerves have never been steadier. If you must know, I wrote a letter to all the tenants today advising them to tidy their yards."

She gave a scoffing laugh. "Letters are the easy part. I'll believe you know what you're doing when I see you measuring out free lumber for chicken coops."

"You seem, Miss Patterson, to know a lot about running a place for someone so new to America."

She shrugged, stung by his sudden formality. She rather liked the way he said her Christian name. But such feelings were fanciful, and she asked the fairies to guard her from abundance of fancy. He didn't know she came from a wealthy family. He assumed she was a poor immigrant. The bachelors told her he believed she'd used her last penny to buy this boardinghouse. No one knew it was her dowry and that her brother was probably richer than Quinn himself. She'd just as soon he didn't know any different. She was tired of men judging her by her family's wealth. She wondered if Quinn wasn't tired of women admiring him for his wealth as well, but perhaps men were different that way.

In any case, it was none of her business what he did with other women. She wondered if other women called him Mr. Montgomery. As if he were the Prince of Wales or something. So formal.

"What's so amusing, Miss Patterson?"

The smile vanished, chased away by her suddenly rapid pulse. "Nothing . . . well, perhaps a thought about your name. With the others using names like Widowmaker and Cleatface, somehow Mr. Quinn Montgomery and Miss Morna Patterson sound a bit stiff."

"What do you have in mind?"

She smiled and leaned her head back. "I'd rather you use a funny name, the same as the other bachelors."

"I'm not the same as the other bachelors."

"Oh . . . you're a single man, are you not?" She had been taught never to speak with such boldness to a gentleman, but the words just burst out. "I'm sorry," she said, her manners catching up with her. "The bachelors are so open in their speech and opinions that it must be quickly contagious. . . . But it's true, isn't it, that in America, all men are equal, even single ones?"

"That depends what you're referring to—kisses or money or a man's reputation."

"The latter, if you please." But it was his kiss she was thinking of. No man she'd ever known could equal Quinn Montgomery in that regard, and he probably knew it.

He simply looked at her, letting his silence speak volumes.

To hide her blush, she got up and pretended to test the kettle for water. "I came to America hoping to find the equality for which it's so famous. Please help me by calling me Morna, same as everyone else. If you like I'll still humor you and call you Mr. Montgomery, but I warn you it'll sound ridiculous matched with that woolen shirt and red underwear of Pierre's. So I'll call you Quinn. Everyone's equal in my boardinghouse, even you. In the way I threat them."

Outside, whistling and stomping feet signaled the arrival of the bachelors from the mill. Another shift was over.

Quinn pushed aside his mug and stood up.

"Leaving before anyone sees you? You are a private sort, aren't you?"

"You certainly are a bossy one."

"Mmm, not bossy, just taking an interest in my boarders. You'd do well to follow my example with your town. People in your charge respond to personal care and concern."

"Full of advice, I see. Don't waste it on me, Morna. Give it to these worthless bachelors. They're going to need lots of advice on what to do when I get this house back from you, and they're out of work again."

The bachelors stood in the doorway, watching him, then turned as one to her.

"He ain't being mean, is he? It's one thing him owning the mill and all, but he can't sass a woman. You just say the word."

Morna shook her head and held up the shirt to display the newly sewn button. "Quinn Montgomery and I were sharing our housekeeping lists over a cup of coffee. We had a most interesting chat. But enough of him. Tell me about your day."

They didn't need a second invitation. At once, they clustered around the stove, some draped over the log pile, others pulling out benches. They circled her as if she were the hearth, and her smile the warmth of the fire. They warmed to her at once and soon had her laughing as Dogger mimicked Mr. Quinn Montgomery touring the sawmill. All the while, Morna applied salve to their blistered hands, removed splinters, and snipped off any buttons hanging by a thread so she could resew them.

Once, she glanced up. Quinn was standing outside the circle of mill hands, and the expression on his face was unlike any she'd seen yet. Filled with some inexplicable longing. Or pain.

She didn't want to know about his pain. If she took his pain, she might care about him, and after Horace she didn't need to care about any man. She turned back, laughing, to the bachelors. "Who else needs some salve?"

Three men stuck out their hands, all anxious for her ministrations. A few minutes later she glanced up and Quinn had vanished.

"He went upstairs," Pierre said, as if he could read her thoughts.

"Who?" she asked innocently. "Quinn?"

Cleatface chuckled. "Heck, if he'd do some honest work, then he could have you spread salve on his blisters, too. I wager he comes on another mill tour tomorrow. Not just a quick walk like today. No, he'll ask us to let him try everything from the green chain to the loading of lumber."

"He can't do it," Pierre decreed. As sawyer, he had top ranking among the men here.

"If he wants salve rubbed on by Morna bad enough, he'll do it all right. What d'ya bet?"

Morna stood. "Here now, you know my sacred rule in this boardinghouse. No bickering or fighting. Stop it now. Mister—I mean, Quinn, merely needs more time to get used to his new role."

"Heck, Morna, he'll never adjust. Why, today he walked through the mill like he was strolling through the lobby of the Grand Hotel on Mackinac. Not that I been there, but I heard it's full of strollers."

"Do it again, Dogger," someone called out, and Dogger paced across the dining room, hands behind his back, frowning. "And all the time we was using sign language to say naughty jokes and he couldn't understand a single word."

Morna laughed, then a picture of Quinn Montgomery standing vulnerable and proud in the doorway stopped her. Her smile faded.

"I think we ought to give the man a chance to get used to the place. That's only fair."

"Aw, Morna. He don't care about us. We're nothing more'n profits to him."

"Maybe so. Maybe that's what's wrong. He needs to mingle with you." Last night Quinn had taken his supper upstairs. Morna would not accommodate him so today. From now on, everyone ate together or got no food at all.

Quinn gritted his teeth at the announcement. Either he joined the others at the plank tables, or he'd go without supper. This landlady was going to grate on his nerves. Too bad she was so pretty. A waste actually. For while she behaved this way, he could care less about the possibility of moving out and losing the bet.

But she was extremely pretty, and he couldn't look at her enough to satisfy himself. At first he thought of her in comparison to Sarah. Now he thought of her for herself. Not how she resembled Sarah. Rather the reddish-gold hair, the sassy expression in her eyes, the clever way she sparred with him. And yes, her lips. Her kiss. He thought about that most of all.

And then there was her annoying habit of taking charge of things—of him.

Reluctantly, though, he gave in to his hunger pangs and came downstairs. He was still in lumberman clothes, and at the doorway to the dining room, he stopped. To a man, every one of the sawmill bachelors stopped chewing, cutting meat, swallowing, or drinking. Gravy dripped off of forks while everyone stared.

He wasn't here to be stared at. And the devil take the boardinghouse rules. He wasn't here to play by her rules. He was here to win a wager and gain back his boarding-house.

Without a by-your-leave, he heaped up his plate with the standard fare of salt pork and beans and bread and carried it away.

Morna scraped back her chair. "You can't leave this room with that food."

"Watch me." And as easily as if he were strolling out onto the lawn of the Grand Hotel on Mackinac Island, he took his food away. This house had enough bad memories without adding a bunch of crude lumbermen.

He ate on the edge of his bed. Alone.

Within seconds of finishing, someone knocked on the door. Not the door leading up from the dining room, but Morna's door, as he called it. The door separating him from Sarah's room.

Morna slept there now, but he still thought of it as Sarah's room. It had wrenched his gut to look at it again, and yet he had enjoyed watching Morna marvel over its beauty. Maybe it, like his soul, had been locked up too long.

Maybe, too, he was talking to himself like a woman.

Morna banged on the door now. "Quinn, this is my house, and I won't tolerate anyone walking away from my table."

He walked over to the door and stared at it. Only an inch of wood separated them. An inch away from Morna's hair of red, her porcelain skin, her softness.

If he opened the door, she would be close enough to hold.

She would be vulnerable enough for him to keep on holding her, to kiss her, to make love . . . and win the wager.

But not yet. This game of cat and mouse was proving more intriguing to him. . . .

There was a rustling at his feet. He looked down. A slip of white paper was inching through the crack beneath the door.

This could be interesting. Certainly more interesting than making forced conversation with a crew of unshaven, sweaty bachelors. Jealousy still coursed through him, and he fought it back. That had nothing to do with why he came upstairs. It was simply beneath his dignity to consort with that crew downstairs.

He picked up the note, unfolded it, and read.

You are worse than a spoiled child. Do you think you are better than us?

He smiled and examined her handwriting. It was rather fine for an immigrant girl. She must have had access to a convent for her lessons.

He dug a pencil out of the valise in which he'd buried the hapless list of town duties and turned the note over to scribble a reply. *I have work to do.*

He slid it back under the door.

There was silence for a few minutes and then a new note came back. *End the blue-button rule.*

Pause.

Why?

Because it's not fair.

Pause.

Life is not fair. The rule stays.

Pause. Then she banged upon the door.

"Quinn, I know you're listening. I know you're right there on the other side. Hear me now. Your work involves the people in this town, and unless there's a ghost in there, you can't help the people while hiding away."

"I'm not hiding. You're intruding."

"You are stubborn."

"So are you."

Silence. Not a truce, but a stalemate.

He slumped down on the handiest seat—an old leather-bound trunk. Initials were carved on the lid, and he stared down at them. SM. Sarah Montgomery. His long-departed wife. When she'd left, she'd taken nothing, not even this trunk.

Yes, ghosts did dwell in here with him.

Though Sarah's ghost at the moment seemed far away. He wanted to see the ghost of Morna Patterson. Oh, not the ghost, but the white-clad figure in the nightgown. Not slipping out of his grasp, but flesh and blood within his grasp.

He scrawled another note. *Open up the door.*

A long pause. He could almost feel her hold her breath on the other side of the door.

Then a note came back. *Why?*

He scribbled on it: *For a truce.*

Written communication ceased. The attic was so still you could hear a button drop. Only none did.

Instead, the lock turned on Morna's side of the door,

and then the knob gave and the door opened. She stood there, and his pulse hammered heavily all over his body. She was more beautiful than any ghost, and he almost reached out for her.

Then she held up an old photograph in a cracked gold frame. A wedding photo of a beautiful woman and him. Before he'd grown his beard. Morna had been exploring the room. It served him right, he supposed, for locking it up ten years ago without cleaning it out.

He looked into Morna's eyes, at the question in them.

"Her name was Sarah, and you are sleeping in her bed."

"Will she come back?" Morna asked, her voice unusually soft.

"Isn't that what ghosts do—haunt us forever?"

12

$\mathcal{M}$ORNA FELT AS if she'd been felled by a runaway log. For a long minute she stared mute up into Quinn's eyes, searching for more. They gave away nothing, not pain, not grief.

How little she knew about him. This big bearded man who feigned gruffness and lack of caring had a secret.

A wife. A ghost of a wife.

Maybe the tall tales the bachelors told about this place weren't so farfetched.

"This was her room, wasn't it?" She held out her hand to gesture behind her.

"Our room," he corrected.

She didn't need to hear the answer. She knew. Why hadn't it been obvious at once? This was his house. This room would have belonged to a woman he knew.

A woman he loved.

No wonder he regretted selling the place.

No wonder he wanted it back. "She was very beautiful."

"Yes."

The word was rough as a limb torn by a storm.

She was full of questions, but dared not intrude on what was obviously his private grief.

Suddenly he reached for the photo. "I'd like to have that."

She bent her head to hide her confusion. Despite their ridiculous wager, she was drawn to this big man, to his size, his gruffness, his blue eyes, and yes, even to the beard behind which he hid. Even that she liked. He'd once been a fine enough looking man—strong of features, if not handsome. The attraction had nothing to do with how he looked, only with how he made her feel.

"Morna, do you want to know about her?" he asked gently.

She looked up. His eyes were kind, and she couldn't bear kindness. Not from Quinn. She wanted . . . love. She envied the woman in the photo, the ghost in his past.

She wanted him to touch her again. . . .

He set the photo on top of the trunk and, turning back to her, stared down at her. Her eyes locked with the deep blue of his.

"If you don't like the room anymore, I don't blame you."

"You should have told me."

"I don't talk about it."

Morna gathered all her courage. "Why did you call her a ghost?"

"She died."

Morna drew in a breath. "I'm sorry." And here she'd been imagining their wager was something more. If anything, it meant less. He still loved a woman who had died. He loved a ghost.

"I know you can't tell it from the photo, but she had hair almost the exact color as yours. And the same shape face and she was about the same size—"

"Please stop." Morna turned away. "Don't compare me to a dead woman."

"I could never do that."

"But you have." Tears were filling her eyes, humiliating tears. "When you kissed me . . . you said . . ." She swallowed back the sudden lump in her throat. "You asked later why I was walking around like a ghost in the night. Was it her I reminded you of then? Is that why you offered the wager? So you could pretend to win back a woman who's dead? I'm not her, Quinn. I'd rather give you this house than be mistaken for a dead woman."

His eyes were sad, and for a minute all he did was stare at her. He shook his head. "I don't want it that badly." Then he reached out and touched her chin.

She turned her head.

"I want to kiss you again, Morna. You, not someone from the past."

God help her, but she couldn't move, nor could she stop him from bending down. He smelled of pine. The entire room smelled of sweet pine, and she was melting again in this man's arms. His lips touched hers, and she gave an involuntary moan. Trembling, she clung to him and their kiss deepened. His arms gave her shelter, even as his lips drew out desire. He kissed her long and hard and then his kiss grew gentler. A kiss to the corner of her mouth. To the throat, to the hair at her temple.

And then she stood in his arms, her cheek against the very heartbeat of him.

"You see, Sarah is—"

Morna came to her senses and pushed away. "Forgive me, I forgot myself."

"No, Morna, it's not what you think."

"I'm not Sarah. Whoever she is or wherever or whatever she was to you, I'm not her and never will be." He could have seduced her. He would seduce her if she forgot herself like that again. And then she'd have nothing. That's the only reason he was kissing her . . . either that, or because he imagined she was another woman.

"You'll never have me, Quinn. Not that way. Never!"

Blindly, she grabbed for the door frame, felt her way inside her room, and slammed the door on him.

She stood there, back pressed against the wall of her room, gulping back hot tears.

At last she opened her eyes and looked at the room she so adored. The wood, the gilt, the paintings, the dried flowers. All of this had been Sarah's.

Miserable, Morna stared at long last at the bed, at the brass foot and blue velvet coverlet. She might have bought all this, but it would never be hers. Not as long as Quinn Montgomery dwelled here in whatever past haunted him.

And yet she could never throw it out like so much discarded dead wood. She sank down into a straight chair and stared at the bed. She was going to win the wager, but it was going to be much harder to resist the man than she imagined.

The next day was Sunday, and Morna insisted the bachelors attend church. Quinn and Morna sat as far away from each other as possible. Quinn sat up front, as befitted the owner of the town, while Morna sat in back surrounded by bachelors tugging at the necks of their plaid shirts. Dogger's blue button popped off and went rattling onto the floor just as the preacher began his sermon. While matrons stared, Morna stuck out her foot and covered the button with her shoe. As the sermon proceeded, Morna spent more time staring at Quinn from behind than listening.

She was not alone. Every single female in the church cast surreptitious glances his way. Conversation before church had been about the upcoming Lumber Days Social. There was no doubt whom everyone wanted for a dance partner.

"Well, I think it's an injustice that the bachelors in my very own boardinghouse aren't invited," Morna had said outside the church.

Edith Hargrove tried to smooth things over, she and Otis both. "Well, naturally, they're invited to the logging contests. They always win, but to the social? No."

"But don't the eligible ladies want—"

"To dance?" Edith looked over at the motley crew of bachelors and shook her head. "Not with them. Not with any man in a blue-buttoned shirt. It's forbidden. Our daughters do not marry blue buttons."

"Why not?"

"It's the rule," Edith said as if it were obvious. She smiled kindly at Morna. "That's a very lovely shawl you're wearing, dear. If you continue to handle yourself with discretion, perhaps the town ladies will forgive your association with that boardinghouse and invite you to tea again. Be circumspect. It helps to bring the bachelors to church. Most commendable of you." And on that word, Edith turned to her husband, who was nervously running a hand over his bald spot. "Come along, Otis, or we'll lose our pew."

It was a long service, but back at the boardinghouse, Sunday stretched even longer.

Morna and Conor were forbidden to walk in the woods. The town rules meant all businesses were shut, and people had all gone and shut themselves inside their houses again, despite the fine spring weather. Only Nellie and a friend had put on shawls and bonnets and come out to stroll past the boardinghouse, while giggling and casting a curious eye at Pierre, who boldly waved at Nellie.

Morna sat on the porch, wrapped in her warmest shawl, and waved at the young ladies. They saw her, stiffened, and hurried past.

The other bachelors had not noticed. They were engaged in a contest to see who could split the biggest log. Either that or sitting inside around the stove, playing cards or shaving and washing out socks.

"Hey, Morna," Cleatface called over to her. "We've decided it's time for you to have a lesson."

She blinked in bewilderment. Surely they didn't think she was going to participate in their little contest. Her, a slight lady, competing with such brawny men. True, she believed women should be equal when it came to inheriting, but when it came to wielding an ax, well, no—"

They carried the ax to her and explained.

"Aw, we wouldn't put you to a contest, but it's like this—everyone in a lumber town has to know how to work an ax. Even women."

"Why? Won't you chop my kindling?"

"Sure we will. But that's not the point. An ax is a dangerous thing, and in a mill town or lumber camp, there's a superstition that if you know how to handle something dangerous, especially the ax, then you'll never get hurt by it."

She thought that over and stared all the while at the shiny blade of the ax. It was freshly sharpened. The smell of fresh-cut pine lay heavy in the spring air, and the scent made her think of Quinn, of standing close in his arms.

"Come on, you got to know—in case you need to cut stove wood when we're all at work."

"Cook—"

"Cooks come and go."

Conor was jumping up and down. "Can I? Can I?"

"Absolutely not."

"Oh, the boy's got to learn, too."

"With a dull ax."

"Nothing but sharp ones. If you learn right, then there's less chance of getting cut. That goes for the boy, too."

Morna saw no way out. "Very well." One piece of wood couldn't be that hard. If she knicked it, they'd be satisfied. "One swing," she said.

They bargained back. "One log chopped into kindling. With a good swing."

Already they were escorting her to the chopping block. Of all the towns in America, it still amazed her that she'd happened on this scared rabbit of a town, with its silly blue-button rule. Because of a nail, the war was lost. . . . Because of a blue button in a little boy's hand, here she was, Morna Patterson, learning to chop wood. Oh, how her family would laugh to see her now.

The men stiffened and looked back.

She turned, too, ax in hand, ready for her lesson.

Quinn Montgomery had come out on the porch and was watching.

"There's no rule says we can't teach her how to work an ax," they said.

"Go right ahead," Quinn said. "If anything, the rules forbid anyone living here to be ignorant of the ax." His blue eyes were gleaming, and the trace of a smile tilted his mouth.

Cleatface, who never missed an opportunity to boast about his expertise with logs, was giving her instructions. "Now, Miss Morna, you gotta pay no mind to Mr. Quinn

Montgomery. He ain't gonna throw us outta town for swinging an ax. Matter a' fact, we'll give him a lesson, if he asks for it."

"I don't need any lessons, Clarence."

"Cleatface," came the growling reply.

"Cleatface." Quinn pronounced the name carefully, waited for Cleat's satisfied smile, then turned to the others. "I built this town, remember, and I might not have been swinging an ax as long as you, but I wager I can match you log for log."

"You challenging me?"

"Let's see how good a teacher you are, first."

"You wanna teach the landlady yourself, is that it?"

"Shuddup, Cleatface," Widowmaker cautioned. "He's already fired us once."

Morna stepped forward. "Could we get on with the lesson, please?"

Now Quinn stood watching, and she was more self-conscious than ever.

The men were practically jumping up and down like children in anticipation of teaching her the most basic skill of a mill town.

She was appalled that this was their only sport.

She couldn't deny them, but she'd figure out something more for them to do on Sundays than shave and wash out socks and chop wood.

She let her shawl drop and, after unbuttoning her cuffs, rolled up her sleeves. Cookee picked up the shawl and held it for her. She watched Cleatface and then Finn demonstrate the backswing, then she took the ax and imitated them.

Wham. The ax came down on the log with a thud, bounced off the end, and dug into the dirt ground.

Men jumped back a couple feet.

"Keep your eye on the spot you're aiming for."

The words came from Quinn. The men looked at him and nodded. "He's right. Try again."

Once again she swung. This time she hit her mark, and with a whack the log split at the top. Another whack, and it split all the way.

The men let out a cheer that must have carried up the main street, right into the homes where the citizens of Bunyan were doing who knew what on this otherwise quiet Sunday.

She chopped again. It took more muscle power than collecting peat did—for she'd helped the servants back in Ireland once or twice. And it was certainly cleaner than coal.

Once more she chopped.

A button popped on her bodice.

And another.

She left the ax in the log and gathered up her kindling and buttons—plain white ones. A third dangled by its thread. With one hand she clutched her bodice together and with the other handed kindling off to Cleatface.

"Excuse me, gentlemen, modesty requires that I retire and do some button sewing of my own."

She headed for the porch.

"Conor's turn," someone called.

The little boy pedaled his legs across the yard.

"Be careful, now. He's young," she reminded them needlessly.

"All the better to learn while you're young," Quinn said smoothly, reaching out to help her up.

The third button fell on his shoe.

He let go of her and stooped to retrieve it. He dangled it out to her between his thumb and forefinger. "You dropped something."

Color rose, quick and hot, in her face. She'd not spoken with him since yesterday upstairs when they'd kissed. Now she was trying hard to keep her pulse steady, desperately wishing to escape. It was so hard to look at Quinn without trembling, without giving away her longing.

"Hold out your hand," he said. He looked down at her face. His blue eyes studied her as if looking for some signal. "Give me your hand," he repeated.

"I—I can't."

"Why not? After swinging an ax, you can't?"

He knew why not. And he was enjoying having her at a disadvantage.

"I'd pay to see you swing that ax," she said, and moved around him. This was best, to tease each other.

At the door, she stopped, fumbling for the handle with one free finger.

"You won't have to pay, Morna. I wasn't lying. I know my way around an ax. Just because I haven't had to chop my own wood in a few years doesn't mean I've forgotten how. Didn't I chop down the attic door?"

Out of the corner of her eye she spotted a couple of ladies from town, strolling by and staring. She wanted to make the town like her, not give them reasons to justify Quinn's suspicions about her. She was a good person, who'd ended up here by chance. If the people would give her a chance, she could be a good neighbor. But first, they had to meet her halfway, and with Quinn lurking about ready to post more rules, they weren't going to meet anyone halfway. Quinn had them too afraid.

"Please step aside . . ." She hurried inside and changed her dress.

She was standing over the stove a while later, watching the coffeepot boil, when he came up behind her like an invisible shadow. He reached around and handed her yet another button—a blue button. "I found a spare, in case you want it."

"Your blue-button rule is ridiculous and I shall always think so."

He chuckled low in her ear. "Ah, but were it not for my blue-button rule, you would not have discovered a way to earn money at the expense of my bachelors."

"I hardly call them *your* bachelors. You don't care about them at all, except for the profits they bring you."

"Nevertheless, I employ them. You merely provide them with a roof and button sewing."

"It's honest work." This conversation seemed to have no point, unless he was toying with her. Truth be told, she was growing warm, his husky voice was wearing down her defenses. Quinn Montgomery was too attractive for his own good.

His body touched hers at strategic places.

She was caught between the stove and Quinn Montgomery. She scarcely breathed.

"Next time," he said in a low voice close to her ear, "put your body into the swing."

"Will that give the ax more force?" she asked.

"Not necessarily, but it might save you having to sew you bodice together again."

She was dying to touch his hand, his arm. But she'd never be able to stop with that. She had to get away from him.

"This place just doesn't know what to make of a woman like you, Morna. You don't fit in, and—and I—heck, I'm starting to feel like I need to protect you."

"You're only protecting Sarah's ghost. Your past. That's why you're cutting down the woods, isn't it? To try and destroy your past."

He went very white.

She'd hit a nerve. "Why, Quinn?"

When he didn't answer, she went on. "You should be protecting the entire town. The other people. The ones you plan to turn out. I can take care of myself. Your intentions are good, but misguided."

"Oh." He didn't move.

"They're good, though. I mean—there's hope for you as a human being. It's just—that I didn't come to America looking for a man to look out for me. I came here to show a woman needs no one but herself."

"Then maybe you're as big a fool as you say I am, Morna."

He was gone then, just the fire crackling and the whisper of his words on her skin. Her neck still tingled where those words had touched. Darn him and his blue buttons.

"I bet you can't split a toothpick. What do you bet?"

She turned. He was still uncomfortably close. A lot of things. But she wasn't going to play games. That's how he kept things going his way—by hiding behind a rule, a game.

Anyway, the men were calling for him. "Mr. Montgomery. Hey, Quinn Montgomery, it's your turn."

He shed his jacket and unbuttoned his shirt and stripped to the waist.

She averted her eyes.

"Oh, now, don't be shy, Morna. We're in business together in this town. You want to compete on my level. Surely, you can watch something as innocent as men chopping wood without any harm. After all, you lack the sensibilities of other women."

She had thought she had. Now she wasn't so sure.

His stomach was flat and well muscled. She'd never

seen a man's bare stomach before. The bachelors all wore long underwear.

He strode out to the yard and took ax in hand. While she stood transfixed by the window, he cut a log into kindling and bested everyone. The bachelors' mouths dropped in surprise.

Then putting down the ax, Quinn gathered up the wood and carried it in to the stove.

"Cold?" he asked. "Maybe this will help."

And then he dumped it all in the box and shrugged into his shirt again.

Morna was awash in desire.

Quinn was good. But he was also an enigma.

Like the woods, he had many untested dark places to him.

"Come on, Morna," the bachelors called. "You can't miss this."

She came to the door and peered through the screen. For a minute she watched Quinn prove his strength with an ax. But it was too painful to watch. Her desire was too painful.

And so instead she stared over at the dark woods. Why, she wondered, were they forbidden? Was the ghost of Sarah there, too?

She shook off the thought. The sooner this wager ended the better. But she had a feeling it was going to drag on and on. She might as well write a letter to Ireland with her new address.

13

QUINN WAS FURIOUS. He'd spent all morning examining the account books left behind by his cousin Theodore. It was a disaster. Clearly, he made a mistake by entrusting his affairs to a relative. He trusted people close to him too much, a lesson he should have learned from Sarah. He telegraphed Theodore, who declined to come. He was escorting the lovely Louise to a ball that evening. So much for Louise's loyalty as well.

All right, if Quinn could learn to put up chicken coops and dicker over the cost of painting houses and inspire the town to clean up its yards, surely he could sort out his own accounts. He had to, or else Morna would laugh at him. He didn't want her laughing at him. He wanted her kissing him, embracing him. All dangerous thoughts . . . and they had nothing to do with putting his town in financial order. So he gathered up the account books, shut the door on his attic room, and headed for the company store. Otis might know something. Otis might have the prices jacked up, but he wasn't capable of skimming profits. The man didn't have access to the account books.

Maybe, Quinn pondered, maybe he ought to tell Otis to back off a bit on the prices. Since Morna had come, sales were down. She'd discovered the Montgomery Ward catalog, and the slack in buying at his company store coincided with the arrival of that catalog into Morna's hands. He should have run back to Mackinac Island the first time he laid eyes on her, and he might have if he hadn't been so dumbstruck at her beauty. Now it was more than her beauty. . . .

But he had work to do.

He ignored all the bachelors, bent his head to avoid a pair of drying red underwear, and slammed the door. Women. Their social status made them no different. They were all the same, whether high-born or poor and fresh off an immigrant boat. Morna was proof of that.

He started to turn toward the boardwalk leading up to the main street when a movement far across the stumps caught his eye. It was the woods. He stopped and watched. It was one of those cool early-spring days when the world was—well, Morna said it best. The land was like an emerald. Quinn had a more mundane view— there was no wind, no breeze even. So the movement in the woods could not be branches gusting about.

As he changed directions and strode over, he called, "Conor!" Morna encouraged the boy's fantasies about his treasure map and magic blue buttons and all. Which was not a bad thing in itself. Quinn hadn't forgotten being an idealistic boy himself before the cruelty began later— cruelty about his too rugged face, his height. . . .

Just one stump away from the edge of his woods, he pulled up short. It was not Conor at all. He caught a glimpse of dark hair, and a woman in a shawl. For a crazy moment, his heart went to his throat. Was it Morna out here with Pierre?

As he drew closer he saw he was half-right. It was Pierre. He actually breathed a sigh of relief that it wasn't red hair Pierre caressed. If Morna was going to become enamored of anyone . . .

Quinn had been negotiating through stumps. Now a twig crackled beneath his boot, and the couple started. The woman came around from the darkness, familiar and defiant of expression.

"Nellie? Nellie Hargrove?"

"Hello, Mr. Montgomery . . . Pierre and me, we were talking."

"You know the woods are forbidden."

Strangely he felt envious. These woods were his. They held his memories, they were for *his* lovers' trysts. He shook himself. That was a long time ago, and he'd buried the images. He was turning into a sentimental fool. He wished Pierre were gone and this was Morna standing here. He'd go on kissing her, and he'd not be apologizing for it.

He looked at Nellie closer. Her hair was mussed, her lips slightly swollen. Quinn knew how a woman looked when she'd been thoroughly kissed.

Pierre stepped toward him. "It's my fault, sir. I took her for a walk, and well, we like the woods. There's no rule agin that, is there? Walking with a lady?"

Quinn shook his head. "Walking in town—no. But there are rules against trespassing in this part of the woods . . . and Otis and Edith might have their own kinds of rules set for Nellie."

Nellie let out a sigh. "I'm getting tired of rules, Mr. Montgomery. Pierre and I weren't hurting anyone."

Quinn looked over their shoulders to the tree trunk where initials had been freshly carved in the bark of a white pine. "I'm afraid I'll have to fine you for that."

"How much?"

"It might cost you most of your stake."

"I thought you wanted the trees cut and gone."

Pierre was not afraid to speak up. Quinn liked that in a man. If he was going to hire any new men to help him, he might just consider Pierre. Move him up a notch in the estimation of the town. Then it wouldn't go so hard for Nellie. But that would be later.

"I'll settle with you later, Pierre," he said. "For now, maybe I'd better walk Nellie back to her house."

"You aiming to steal her?"

Quinn smiled. He did like this man. No wonder Nellie was attracted to him. And Morna, too. She was his landlady and had danced with him, laughed and talked with him all the time. Morna had eyes. She'd be attracted to a strapping handsome man like this.

"Come work for me," Quinn said impulsively.

"But—but, I'm the sawyer. Besides, I already work for you."

"Can't someone else do that?"

"Not just anyone. It takes a special man to juggle all them logs through the saws."

"It's the top job at the mill," Nellie said.

Pierre colored as if embarrassed at her solicitude. "Well, almost. The saw sharpener is mighty important, too. . . . Still, I'm not the only one in the place. Maybe Dogger's ready."

"Start training him."

Nellie beamed. "Oh, Pierre."

"What do you want me for?" Pierre asked, suspicion in his voice.

"I could use a man who knows this town better than me."

Nellie beamed brighter.

All right, Quinn conceded. He was admitting to less than perfection. But this town took more running than he'd ever realized. It had been a mistake trusting The-odore with it. Well, maybe trust never was the word. Somehow, because Quinn despised Theodore, he had thought exiling him to this little one-horse town was a fitting punishment for all the ways his cousin had irked him. But it was the town that had suffered at Theodore's hands, not the other way around.

Quinn had another idea. "I could use a guard. Some-one to guard the woods. Keep children like Conor out of danger."

A baffled expression briefly crossed Pierre's face.

"The pay is double what you earn as a sawyer. Are you interested?"

Pierre exchanged a quick look with Nellie. Quinn made nothing of it. Men like Pierre were always kissing a pretty girl. Nellie was pretty enough. Not as pretty as Morna. Quinn tensed, worrying about whether the hand-some Pierre had taken Morna for a walk. "Come on, man, decide. You surely can't want to spend your life living in that bachelor house."

"Well, sir, if I marry, I get a town house, don't I?"

The man was smart indeed. "Yes, but if you work for me, you get a bigger town house, and you can earn your stake much faster."

"I need time to train Dogger."

"One week."

Pierre thrust out his hand and Quinn shook it.

Then Quinn reached out a hand for Nellie. "Come on, then. I'll take you home, and your parents won't be alarmed."

Pierre and Nellie exchanged longing looks. Pierre nod-ded, as if to say it was all right. Then Nellie walked off with Quinn.

It was pleasant walking with a woman. Quinn rarely

walked with the matrons of Emerald Island, rarely saw them outside the elegant salons and boudoirs of the resort hotels.

Nellie was silent, and as their footsteps echoed on the wooden boardwalk, Quinn's thoughts went to Morna. It ought to be a simple thing to walk with a woman, but Morna made nothing simple. Quinn wanted Morna. What was so difficult about saying so? Pierre obviously had no trouble wooing Nellie, and he was a mere sawyer.

Outside the Hargrove house, Quinn bade Nellie good night. The lace curtain at the window fell. Edith Hargrove was no doubt watching and speculating. She probably had Nellie and him married before Nellie was in the door. Edith's ambitions for Nellie were amusing. But Quinn didn't feel like setting her straight. He wasn't perfect. He had just enough vanity to like being seen with a woman. The alternative—having a woman reject him—was hell on earth.

Nellie was barely in the door when her mother rushed up, gushing. "Mr. Quinn Montgomery walked you home, didn't he?"

With a shrug, Nellie slipped off her shawl. It was Pierre she wanted to talk about. "Mama, I need to confess something."

But her mother had always been too busy worrying about the impression she was making on people to listen close. "I can see you were out unchaperoned, but you're tetched in the head, child, if you think your father and I won't bend a rule for Quinn Montgomery."

"He's very nice."

But not Pierre.

"He's very rich. Oh, I should get to baking tomorrow

in case he comes calling on you. That'll be next, you know. For him to come calling."

"What if one of the bachelors came calling?"

"You mean the blue-button bachelors?"

Nellie nodded, puzzled. "What other kind are there?"

Her mother waved a dismissive hand. "They won't call. They know their place."

Nellie saw her chance. "There's going to be a social at the boardinghouse."

"Is Mr. Montgomery going to be there?"

"I don't know."

"Well, never mind, because you can't consort with those—those filthy uncouth men."

"Mama—"

"Go to bed now. I've got to look through my recipes. Oh, I may have to borrow sugar from the company store if I'm low, and I'll need those hens to lay lots of eggs, so don't disturb them—"

"Mama, you're not letting me talk."

"The chickens, child. Now go to bed. When we're rich, with you wed to Mr. Montgomery, then we won't need to coddle the chickens. It's your duty to wed well, so don't give me any backtalking sass about love and nonsense."

Nellie didn't. She didn't want to spoil her feelings for Pierre by sharing them. She'd figure out a way to see him again, and she'd marry for love or die an old maid. Oh, how she envied Morna, under the same roof as Pierre.

Morna gave Conor a hug and handed him back his precious treasure map. "No, Conor, it's far too late to go treasure hunting, and you can't go where this map says."

"But Pa wrote that there was treasure in Bunyan. He saw it himself. Not just trees, but treasure."

"Now, if he'd have seen it, don't you think he'd have scooped it up and made your mama rich?"

Conor pondered that. "He never wanted to be rich. He wanted Ma to have pretty things. And a pony for me. Is that being rich?"

She smiled. "Maybe, but you still can't chase after that map tonight. It's bedtime."

Reluctantly, Conor went upstairs, and in a few minutes Morna went up to tuck him in. He slept with the map under his cheek, wearing crease marks on his face. Gently, she pulled the map out and set it on the floor. At the same time she picked up Conor's overalls and shirt. A blue button, one of Conor's shirt buttons, fell onto the floor.

Deciding she'd sew on this last button and then go to bed herself, she returned downstairs for her needle and thread. She sank onto the bench nearest the stove and, while she sewed, allowed her thoughts to wander down secret paths. Wherever her mind turned, she saw Quinn.

Oh, how she envied Nellie walking with Quinn. She'd watched from her window and the envy had been keen as the bitter wind that came up this evening. It began mere minutes after Pierre returned to the boardinghouse, looking glum.

"What's wrong, Pierre?" she asked, giving him a smile.

"Quinn is walking Nellie home." That's all. He slumped down across the plank table and stared into a cup of cold tea. That's when the wind came up, blowing so hard down the stovepipe it nearly put out the fire. Morna felt it clear to her bones. No matter how close to the fire she sat, she couldn't seem to warm up.

The bachelors, even Pierre, straggled in to bed, and still Morna sat, like an anxious hen. One button turned into two and then three. The bachelors' shirts needed buttons, too. She sewed on blue buttons without counting. The pile reached past her ankles. The fire was ebbing. Her fingers were numb and a blister was forming.

That's when Quinn came in.

She looked up to see him staring at her. There was a kind of longing in his eyes, but she thought maybe it was her imagination. Any second now, he'd turn away and head upstairs.

But he didn't. He walked over toward her, and she stood.

"You walked Nellie home."

"I thought it would save her a nasty scene with her folks."

At those reassuring words, Pierre nodded his good night and headed for the bunk room.

Morna and Quinn were suddenly alone.

"The Hargroves will be hoping you marry Nellie next." It was more a question than a statement. More a need for reassurance of her own. He wasn't courting Nellie, was he?

"Only because they want a rich husband for her. I've done that once."

"Why don't you talk about her? Your wife, I mean."

"She's dead."

"I'm sorry." Only she wasn't. She envied the woman who seemed to haunt Quinn still. And she wished she could see inside Quinn's thoughts, especially when he stared off at the untouched woods, like now. It was dusk, and he was staring out the window at the same spot she'd noticed before.

"You must have loved her very much."

"Everyone tells me that."

"I'm sorry—I mean, I—"

He reached for the shirt in her lap and then her. "I'm sorry, too. It doesn't make me much of a suitor."

Morna wanted so much to know. Maybe later, he'd trust her, though it was hard competing with a ghost.

He looked like he was going to kiss her. Instead he handed her a letter. From Ireland. The lace factory; her ambitions all seemed so far away when Quinn was so close.

She expected it was another letter from her brother complaining about the trials of running the factory, while telling her she was lucky to be female and not have responsibility. If it was like his earlier letter, he'd inquire about her boardinghouse.

All the time she thought this, Quinn stood over the stove, pretending to warm his hands. She kept her eyes on her sewing. He, too, avoided looking at her.

"What are you planning now?" he asked at last.

"A social . . . you know, dancing for the men. Music. Food. The usual."

"And you'll dance with them. With millworkers."

She shrugged. Why didn't he care? "Who else will?"

"Nellie."

"I expect so. But there are a dozen bachelors in need of a dance."

"Including me . . . will you dance with me, Morna?" he asked suddenly.

The question was so abrupt she pricked her finger. Looking up, she saw he'd turned to face her. Blue eyes were studying her face.

"Of course. I think you can dance with any woman you want that night."

"Dance with me now, Morna."

She had no will to refuse. Not alone like this in her

own house. "There's no music." It wasn't an objection so much as an observation. Her heart was pounding so loudly she couldn't have heard anything else anyway.

She moved into his arms. Automatically, their hands met and his other came around her waist. It was the first time she really appreciated how tall he was, how she fit against his shoulder. That's when she realized they weren't really dancing, but swaying to some invisible music . . . no, real music. In the bunk room, one of the bachelors was playing his harmonica, "When Johnny Comes Marching Home Again . . ."

The music was gentle and lulled her into relaxation. Morna leaned closer to Quinn until her cheek was rubbing against the nubby grain of his coat. She lifted her head, and that was an even greater mistake. Their eyes locked; his gaze fell first, and it was her lips he was staring at.

She broke away. "Well, that was lovely practice for our social. Good night, Quinn." She dared not say another word.

But she heard his soft reply. "Good night, Morna."

14

"*NELLIE, WHAT ON* earth has gotten into you?"
Edith didn't look up from polishing the silverware.

Nellie, on the other hand, stopped stirring the lemon
sauce. "Nothing, Mama."

"Nonsense," her mother countered, brushing her forehead with the back of her hand. "First you suggest we invite
the bachelors to our social. It ought to be enough that they
participate in the logrolling and such, but to think of
them—those unshaven, smelly ruffians—actually eating
off the same plates as the ladies of town . . ."

Nellie made no reply.

Her mother looked over. "Nellie, you're burning the
sauce. You know my gingerbread is no good without
lemon sauce."

With a sigh, Nellie resumed stirring.

"Mama, please. The social is no fun anymore. There
aren't any single men for the single ladies. You know that's
so."

"Oh, pshaw, what about the Polinski boys?"

"They're still boys."

"Nellie, watch your tongue—"

"Well, they are. All they care about is baseball, and
when they do try to dance, they step on our toes, and they

smell, too. Like too much pomade. So I don't think you should criticize the bachelors. They don't smell, and it's not nice to say so." Actually, Pierre smelled of wood chips. Always of fresh pine. She liked to rub her face close to his shirt to catch the scent of him.

"Nellie, this conversation is unbecoming a well-brought-up young lady, and it's disloyal to your parents."

Nellie didn't care if she was well brought up or disloyal. She cared about Pierre. But she couldn't talk about him—unless she did it in a roundabout way.

"Did you invite Morna to tea? You don't seem to mind if she gossips about Quinn Montgomery." Morna would be candid. Nellie liked that about Morna. As long as she didn't take a fancy to Pierre.

"You don't think I'd invite someone just to hear their gossip?"

All the ladies wanted to know about Quinn Montgomery and what it was like living under the same roof as him. They only allowed Morna Patterson to get away with it because she owned the boardinghouse and because Quinn Montgomery could do whatever he wanted.

"Are you, Mama?"

Her mother denied it. "Keep stirring now and mind your business. We're inviting her to make sure her behavior is respectable. One hint that it's otherwise, and we'll have her gone. But that's not the same as gossip. Not at all."

Oh, but Mama didn't fool Nellie one bit. Why else did ladies invent tea parties if not to gossip?

"Well, I like Morna. And I'm quite certain she's respectable. Look how she cares for that little orphan boy and for the bachelors. . . . Sewing on buttons . . ." Even Pierre's. But Nellie was going to take over his buttons.

"Nellie, I want you to forget those bachelors and at the social smile at Quinn Montgomery so he'll dance with you."

"Oh, Mama, he'll think I'm being forward."

"Aren't you interested in dancing with him?"

No. But she knew the reply that would please. "Every girl is, Mama," she hedged.

"Exactly. He's rich and would make an excellent catch."

"He's not very handsome, what you can see behind that beard."

"He has fine eyes."

"He's so big."

"Then he's strong. Do you want a small man like your papa?"

She wanted Pierre, who was just right.

"I don't know, Mama." She had to fib, which was a sin. But she was so close to saying Pierre's name. "I don't know what I want." Another fib.

Her mother took the lemon sauce and stirred it herself. "Well, you'd best not be too choosy. Eligible men don't come around this town that often, and you're comely but no raving beauty, nor was I. We make the best match we can."

Nellie turned to the back door, which was open. The view was of the back of another row of houses, every one identical.

She pressed her face against the screen of the door. Spring was well upon them, and though it was a cool day, the trees were in bud. She could have screamed at the slowness of this place.

If she didn't change her life, her mother was going to keep her tied here forever, working in that monotonous company store. Oh, she didn't mind staying in the town now that she'd met Pierre, but she couldn't live here without love.

Why didn't Mama understand that?

She and Papa both were too obsessed with money. Why, they'd even taught her how to mark up the prices in the store. Her papa thought it fun to mark them up and watch the customers squirm. Nellie used to think it was fun, too—when she was bored. But after seeing Pierre walk out without buying any blue buttons—well, ever since, she'd secretly been marking some of the prices back down for the bachelors. She ought to feel guilty, for such behavior *was* disloyal.

"You're quiet, Nellie," her mother said. "I don't like it when you sulk."

"I'm not sulking. I'm thinking."

"I know what you're thinking . . . that a man like Quinn Montgomery will never notice you."

Nellie agreed, but said nothing. Her mother would finish her thought while she poured the lemon sauce into a bowl.

She turned and watched her scraping the pot.

"Oh, yes, Nellie, you'd be surprised what a man like him will want in a second wife. Oh, be may go about with those fancy society types on Emerald Island, but you don't see him wedding one. No, he's been burned, and if he's smart, he'll want an entirely different sort the second time. Someone who appreciates his accomplishments. You must flatter him on his brilliance, Nellie."

"Yes, Mama." There was nothing brilliant about Quinn or his town, unless it was Pierre. "But you know what? I think it's Morna he likes."

"Nonsense. He wouldn't stoop so low. She's nothing but a shanty Irish immigrant. Now put such thoughts out of your head, and don't mention it again. Now at tea today you will sit beside me and we will try our best to discuss edifying subjects—if Miss Patterson doesn't bring up the subject of the bachelors again."

"I don't believe she's as uncouth as you think, Mama. She has a more refined air about her than some of the other ladies."

"You're only taken with that red hair. Don't be drawn in by her sort, Nellie. They'll lead you down the wrong paths. Why, when I think of you setting foot in that boardinghouse, never mind owning it . . . well, it does boggle the mind, especially your wild speculation about her and Quinn Montgomery. As I live and breathe, he'd never stoop so low."

Upstairs, Quinn stared out the attic window, frowning at the woods. From this front view, the house looked out on nothing but woods. The town and mill were to the back. He'd planned it that way when he'd laid out the town. His goal was to forget this house, and he was as surprised as anyone to be living in it again.

He missed his luxurious island hotel. Horseback riding. Lazing about on lawns that rolled down to blue waters. Sipping lemonade and dallying with wealthy women on holiday. It was pleasant. It was safe. Those women were not in the marriage market.

The mill whistle shrieked a second time. He watched from his window as the bachelors trooped off to the mill.

The house was silent, then from the other side of the door came Morna's voice, telling Conor to hurry for school. He liked listening to the soft lilt of it. Suddenly he didn't miss his luxurious island life at all. He wanted to gaze into Morna's eyes. He wanted to kiss her, but he was afraid she'd turn into Sarah in his arms.

He waited until Conor's footsteps sounded, and until

he saw him from the window, running out the house and off to school.

Then he counted to ten.

It was Morna he saw, not the lazy lawns and blue waters of his island. It was her hair, hair the color of an island sunset, her eyes the color of green agates. Her face, so like Sarah's. But she was soft where Sarah had been brittle. Gentle where Sarah had been cynical. Intelligent where Sarah had been flighty.

He had to get out of here. Ghosts were too close.

Then Morna opened the door and walked in.

She stopped dead in her tracks.

Quinn sucked in his breath hard. Framed as she was in the morning light, he now saw no resemblance—only a beautiful woman he desired.

"I was going to . . . well, I thought you were gone, and I'd sweep and dust and—"

"Snoop?"

"I'd rather you tell me about the past."

"I don't want to talk about it. It was ten years ago. That's a long time ago. Too long to think about it or dream about it, I suppose."

"Yes. I've had a dream that long."

"About a man?"

"Of course not. About owning something of my own. This is it—unless Ireland calls me back."

One tendril of hair was badly in need of touching. The curl right by one ear.

"I think I'll go down to breakfast," he said.

"You don't seem to want this house very badly."

"I don't like an unfair contest, Morna. When a woman walks into a man's bedroom, that's no contest at all."

She blushed, and looked utterly vulnerable. He didn't want the house that badly. He never had.

Downstairs Cookee waited on them while Widow-maker began preparations on his supper stew. Cookee slid a plate of pancakes toward Quinn.

"Are there any potatoes left?" Morna asked. "Not for me. I've eaten. For Mr. Montgomery."

"They're cold," Widowmaker called out from the kitchen. "Cold potatoes are bad luck. They mean the river will freeze."

"You tell too many tall tales around here," Quinn said.

"They have nothing much else to do," Morna said softly.

"I could think of plenty of things besides spreading tales about ghosts." He looked at Cookee. "Heat them, please."

Morna did not sit with him, but pulled the single chair over near the stove and settled down to sew.

Quinn ate and made small talk with Cookee, who kept coming back and forth with silverware and syrup and coffee.

"It'll be turning real spring soon," said Cookee. "Warming up."

"Yes."

"But whatever the weather, that won't stop us having fun at the Lumber Days."

"Good."

Cookee went back to the kitchen. Quinn stared at the stove and sipped his coffee. "Morna, are you going to sit there all day and sew on buttons?"

"If I have to."

"Are you going to be at the social tomorrow?"

"Yes, of course, and I wish the bachelors were invited, too."

"I can't change the rules now."

"No, I suppose rules are carved in permanence the way initials are carved in trees."

From out of the corner of his eye, he watched her. She dropped her sewing. "I think I'll go do that dusting after all. Have a nice day."

Have a nice day . . . is that all she could say to him? Oh, she assumed he wasn't going to touch her. Assumed the wager meant nothing. Assumed he was so wrapped up in the ghost of Sarah that he'd never dare touch her.

Cookee came out. "More?"

"I'm done."

He was done with ghosts. He wanted a flesh-and-blood woman in his arms. With long strides, he headed up the stairs, not his stairs, but the stairs to Morna's room.

She was at the top, and he stopped on the bottom step.

"Morna, come back here," he said.

Slowly, she turned and looked at him.

Slowly, she did as he bid.

Desire was pulsating between them.

When she got two steps above him, she stopped.

"You're trembling," he said.

"You are, too."

"No, I'm not." He climbed the last step until he stood one below her, his face even with hers.

Then he reached out and touched her chin, slid his hand up to her hair, and threaded his fingers through it. His mouth came down on hers, tentatively, and then as she responded, he deepened the kiss. She moaned against him and wrapped her arms about his neck. He could, if he wanted, have swept her up into his arms and carried her upstairs. But he didn't want that—not yet. He wanted to know the feel of her against him, the scent of her hair, of her skin, the taste of her lips. It had been so long since he'd held a woman like this. Affectionately. So long.

"Sarah . . ." he murmured, and too late caught himself.

Morna pulled away, then pushed him away. He staggered back down a step. "I'm not your private ghost, Quinn Montgomery."

"It isn't what you think. This was our home. She and I lived here and—"

"And you still wish you did. Don't you? Well, don't touch me again. You'll never get this house back. You'll never get her back, whoever she was. And if I were you, Quinn, I'd rather live for today than yesterday."

She picked up her skirts and, turning, ran up the stairs and slammed her door.

He stood there a few minutes, waiting for the desire to subside. It wasn't Sarah he'd kissed. It was Morna. And he did want her. But not for this house. For herself. But she'd never believe him now.

Maybe at the social. Yes, he'd dance with her, and it would be all right. There wasn't a woman who said no to Quinn Montgomery.

15

$\mathcal{E}$DITH DIDN'T REALLY want the bachelors to come to the town social. It was breaking with all precedents. Then again, with the most eligible bachelor in three states now in town—namely Quinn Montgomery—she guessed she could bend her ways. After all, even cucumbers turned into pickles and no one suffered. Berries turned into jam. Maybe the bachelors could be turned into dancers. Not that she cared if they danced. But she was wise enough to know that inviting those scruffy bachelors was the only way she could justify inviting Quinn Montgomery.

And that's who she hoped Nellie would dance with.

So she fluffed up her parasol and snapped it open to shade herself from the pale spring sunshine. And off she went for a walk to the company store. She'd pretend to go visit Otis on a household matter, but she timed her jaunt to coincide with Quinn Montgomery's daily visit to the office upstairs.

Sure enough, her timing was impeccable. She was at the door when he approached the steps. "Mr. Montgomery," she said, lingering out on the store veranda. "I have a favor to ask of you."

He waited quietly. Such a big, almost homely man.

Maybe if he shaved off his beard . . . or smiled. . . .
She plunged ahead. "The ladies and I talked it over and
we'd be most pleased if you could attend our Lumber
Days Social."

He looked at her a minute, and she rushed on.

"Of course, if you think the other bachelors would like
to be included, then that's all right, too, I suppose. I
mean, if that makes you feel the town's being more fair
in including them."

"We've never included them before."

"That's why I'm seeking out your opinion."

"Is your daughter sweet on any of them?"

Aha, so Quinn Montgomery did have his eye on
Nellie. So much the better. She pressed on. "Nellie would
never stoop to wed one, but she's friendly with them. She
has to wait on them in the store, you know. If anything,
they behave around her, so she'd be a good influence at
the social. . . ." Maybe he'd come out of jealousy.

He looked off up the street, eyes thoughtful. "Have
you invited that Irishwoman?"

Edith didn't know the meaning of the question. "Do
you think we should?"

"She's on a crusade to make the bachelors a part of the
town. Maybe you ought to and then she'd see for herself
how they don't fit in."

An excellent idea, and Edith was reassured by his
reply. He didn't want the Irishwoman around either; he
was merely being practical.

"Very well. . . . And of course you'll come to ensure
everything runs smoothly. As the owner, your very presence would ensure good behavior."

"I'll come. I'd like to see the bachelors handle
themselves . . . and of course your lovely daughter as
well."

Edith glowed for an hour. "Nellie," she called when she arrived back home. "Stoke up the stove and get the iron heating. I want you to wear your best gown for the social."

Quinn paused in the doorway of the town hall. His town hall, come to think on it. Everything about it appalled him—from the sawdust in the air to the wood chips under his feet. The people dancing were family men, but they didn't look much different from the bachelors at the boardinghouse. No, now that he looked at them for himself, he had to admit he didn't see the logic of the rule barring bachelors. Well, sure they weren't married, but they dressed the same and talked the same—and spat the same. He was suddenly glad he broke his own rule and that he was not the only bachelor here tonight.

He hated it. Everyone was staring like he was big Paul Bunyan suddenly emerged from the woods. They stared as if they'd never seen him before.

They were all simple, humble people, celebrating a day of logging competitions. They had chopped wood, sawed branches, rammed peaveys into logs, stacked lumber. They'd all competed like lumberjacks and saw-mill hands, married and single alike. He'd handed out the prizes. He was out of his element. He wanted to laugh at the feeling.

He owned this town, dammit.

He owned it, from its wooden walls to its every last nail.

There was only one small thing he didn't own.

The affection of the people. Their respect maybe. But he wasn't one of them.

For the first time, he saw that, and he didn't like the feeling one bit.

But that wasn't all. There were too many women staring at him, and for the first time in his life, Quinn was ill at ease over that, too.

They weren't his sort of women, none of them.

All day long Nellie Hargrove had found excuses to saunter by and ask about Pierre.

Likewise her mother had hinted Nellie would love to dance tonight.

Of course he knew Nellie's game. Quinn could read a woman's motives a mile away, and Nellie's motives were all too clear. If she was flirting with him, it was only to get to Pierre.

Likewise, Edith Hargrove was pushing Nellie toward him only because she wanted him to raise her status in town. Mother-in-law to the richest man in town. Edith would relish a title like that.

Every other woman in the state and three islands wanted him for his money.

And then there was Morna.

The one exception.

The one woman he wanted to possess but who practically laughed at the notion. The one woman who didn't want any man, especially him. Fate had never been kind to Quinn when it came to women.

Morna was standing alone.

He headed over to her.

Morna was going to dance with him. He was going to hold her in his arms and not have her squirm away.

She didn't see him approach. Her back was turned, and all he could see was that rich reddish hair piled on her head. A few stray tendrils floated down her neck. Below that, buttons, shiny blue buttons marched down her back in a straight row, but the dress flared at her hips. He wanted to span her waist with his hands, feel the flare of her body with his bare skin.

On the crowded dance floor, people jostled and bumped him. He was pushed against her back.

She turned suddenly and he knew the exact moment when she realized who had bumped her. Her eyes grew wider. Or maybe it was the quick intake of breath.

"I came to dance with you. I thought we'd be suitable for each other."

Her expression froze. He thought maybe she hadn't heard.

"You don't look like an immigrant in that dress. You look like you belong in a ballroom."

She glared. "I don't want to dance because I look suitable."

He half smiled. There she was, taking his words the wrong way again. As fiery as that red hair. She probably wanted him to ask all proper like.

"All right, then," he said. "May I have this dance?" The words came out in a rush, and right away he knew he'd made a mistake. "May I?" he asked more politely.

Morna only paused a moment. In that moment, she saw Horace accosting her with wet kisses before he stomped off in a fury to have his way with her maid. She wasn't suitable. Morna didn't want any man to find her merely suitable.

"I don't care to dance," she said.

"You what?" His jaw dropped with incredulity.

"I find us totally unsuitable for a dance."

Quinn was flabbergasted. It had been years since he'd been turned down for a dance. For anything. Not since he was a boy had the female population rejected him. Once he'd learned how money attracted them, no one said no.

No stubborn Irish immigrant was going to humiliate him publicly. Especially not after the way she'd kissed him last night. She had him whipsawing like a tree in a gale.

But he'd show her. He'd dance with Nellie first. He'd play her little game of flirtation, despite all his rules about dancing with his own employees.

Maybe to keep sane, he'd have to bend a few rules. It wouldn't hurt that much. When he invited Nellie to dance, Edith practically pushed her daughter into Quinn's arms. So he danced with Nellie. She never said no. Women never did. And with Nellie he felt safe enough, for he'd been watching her make eyes at Pierre, the French-Canadian bachelor, the one he'd pegged as intelligent.

At the close of the dance, they did what came naturally at high-society balls. He passed Nellie off to Pierre and took Pierre's partner, a nondescript schoolmarm who blushed shyly. Nellie blushed, too, as she looked at Pierre. Quinn felt a stab of envy then caught a look at Edith Hargrove's face. Poor Nellie. Her mother wasn't going to make this easy.

Nellie glowed. She'd had three dances in a row with Pierre, and now at the end of the dance, she floated off the dance floor. This was how all the dances should be— with lots and lots of bachelors to dance with. Especially Pierre. Even if only one bachelor could come, Pierre would be enough.

And then she saw her mother. Glowering. Arms folded. Maybe she should have just danced once with Pierre. Then her mother might not have noticed.

Too late.

Already Edith had her by the elbow and was pulling

and pushing her off the floor. She felt like a child. But she was a grown woman of eighteen. A woman who loved Pierre. Panicking, she looked back over her shoulder. Pierre was swirling Morna around the dance floor. The landlady with the pretty red hair. Nellie's heart sank. She was going to lose Pierre to that—that woman, and worse, her mother was going to treat her like a child.

They were out on the veranda. "You made a spectacle of yourself, child."

"I'm not a child."

"As long as you cavort about the dance with the same bachelor for three dances, you are."

"Pierre is a gentleman."

"He's a common mill worker."

"He's the sawyer."

"That's still common. Good heavens, child, you're not smitten? Oh, but I should have sent you to join your sister long before this."

Nellie had obeyed her mother since childhood. She'd been the dutiful daughter. She'd worked for no pay in the company store. She'd never asked for anything special. She'd never dreamed of anything much beyond this town. She'd never desired the impossible.

Until she laid eyes on Pierre. From that moment on, she could never be the same. She ached for something else in her life. Not a different place or money or prestige. Only the love of one man. "I like Pierre," she said.

Her mother gave a sharp laugh. "You'll end up poor if you allow your heart to lead you."

Her mother had led a practical life, a company-town life. Nellie was raised to be practical. But love was not a practical thing. It blossomed unexpectedly and had no price.

"Poor and impoverished forever." Her mother wagged a finger in her face. "Do you hear me, Nellie? I declare, you are not the same. Did one of those bachelor sneak some liquor into your punch? Is that why you danced with Pierre so much?"

She shook her head. "I like Pierre," she said again. On this subject she would stand her ground.

Her mother's mouth dropped open, then she found her tongue. "Like. Love. Romantic nonsense. Oh, if the man were Quinn, then you could talk romance, but with a poor man, it's a frivolous proposition."

"Mama, there are no other bachelors in this town. How do you expect me to marry?"

"There's Quinn."

"Mama, be practical. He'll never wed a company-town girl."

"You never know. You should have flirted with him more while you danced. And as for the others, I'm sorry now I saw fit to bend the rules and invite them. A sorry lot, every one of them, and no good for a woman. They'll never amount to a hill of beans. Never save up a stake. Goodness, Nellie, why they never even wash, or . . . or . . ."

On she sputtered, listing the faults of the bachelor sawmill workers.

"Stop it, Mama," Nellie said softly.

"They're filthy, smelly, rough talking—why, even deaf. Some are no better than animals, wearing their underwear till it falls off from rot and . . . well, they're not first-class proper people. Why do you think we've tried to keep them separated from the God-fearing family people in town—"

"Mama." Nellie covered her ears. "They're people like you and me."

"Of course they're people, child, but not our kind of people."

"Oh, Mama, that's old-fashioned and mean. You shouldn't say it."

"It's true. I rue the moment I let down my standards and allowed those—those beasts access to our social—"

On her mother went. As Edith ranted, one by one the bachelors sauntered out to see what the feminine commotion was about. First Widowmaker. Then Cleatface. One by one they came and formed a circle around Edith and Nellie. Their expressions were wary.

Digger pushed his way forward and joined the group.

"I think we maybe ought to leave," Cleatface said. For once, his tone was humble.

Nellie looked around at them. "Is Pierre here?"

"He's dancing."

With Morna. Oh, Nellie was heartsick and humiliated both.

And then two more figures pushed into the circle.

It was Pierre and Morna.

"What's wrong?" Morna asked.

Widowmaker thrust out his chin and pointed at Edith Hargrove. "She called us names, said we don't belong."

"Why, Mrs. Hargrove, I'm truly surprised. When you gave your word about inviting the bachelors to the social, I assumed you'd be gracious and polite."

Edith pulled a hanky from her sleeve and dabbed at her forehead. "Now, now, the town is trying to look out for everyone's best interests. It's—it's Quinn Montgomery's rule, after all."

Cleatface snorted, as if in disgust. With one quick jab, Widowmaker poked him in the ribs.

"We don't seem to be welcome." Widowmaker turned away.

Cleatface was right behind him, calling over his shoulder, "Yeah, and we're tired of it. Told ya we should never have trusted the folks in their uppity wooden houses."

Nellie started after them. "Ma didn't mean it that way. Ma's tired. You wouldn't walk out on a lady, would you?"

Morna stood in mute shock. They'd promised to have the bachelors to their social, but they had not promised to treat them like gentlemen. She'd made a mistake in not assuring in advance that the bachelors, her bachelors, would be accorded the same respect as Quinn.

She watched the bachelors file away, one by one, until there was only one man left on the veranda.

It was Quinn.

He was calmly lighting a cigar.

"This is all your fault," she said.

He shrugged. "I tried to tell you those men would never fit. They're a different kind."

"How many kinds of people are there?"

"Two. Socially acceptable and socially unacceptable."

"That's your opinion." Picking up the hem of her skirt, she hurried down the wooden steps to where the bachelors were clustered, grumbling while they hitched up their suspenders. They pulled their hats down over their ears, and she wasn't sure they'd hear a word she was going to say, but she'd say her piece and, if necessary, back at the boardinghouse.

Already Pierre was sauntering off, so it was him she ran after.

"Don't let them disturb you. Don't. You're only different if you let them treat you different."

Pierre was gentlemanly and stopped to give her a smile. "We're lucky to have you, landlady, but this is not your fault. It was this way in the town before you came and it'll be the same as long as the place stands. We're not welcome. I don't stay where I'm not wanted."

"Nellie cares for you." She blurted it out without thinking.

He appeared uncomfortable. "That doesn't endear me to Mrs. Hargrove, I reckon."

Widowmaker grabbed him by the suspenders. "Leave the ladies, Pierre. Let's go home."

One by one they filed away, and left Morna, their landlady, standing there in the middle of Main Street.

Tears filled her eyes. It wasn't right. This town had entirely too many rules. Ridiculous rules. And the one about the bachelors' buttons was the most ridiculous of all.

Temper flaring, she turned on Quinn, who was calmly smoking his cigar. He was dressed in a stiff white collar and fancy tie with stickpin. Clothes like no one in this town could ever hope to afford, certainly not her bachelors. She'd begun to think of them as her bachelors because as their landlady she felt a responsibility to them.

"This is all your fault, you and your rules."

She was annoyed at him, but it wasn't for the reason she gave. All day she hadn't been able to banish last night's kiss from her mind, and now, to compound her agony, she kept seeing him holding Nellie in his arms on the dance floor.

Nellie might be smitten with Pierre, but it was Quinn on whom the Hargroves had set their sights for a son-in-law. The town owner. Edith had beamed like a shiny kettle during that entire dance. Morna had felt only envy. She couldn't let Quinn know of her feelings, though. Never would she allow another man to touch her heart, and she suspected in that respect she and Quinn were equals.

"What's wrong with my rules now?" Quinn said lazily.

"Everything. They lack dignity. The people are over-charged. The town is no fun to live in. The mill can't function without blue and white buttons. No wonder your cousin—Theodore—no wonder he couldn't keep it all in order. I'm surprised you hung on to him as long as you did."

"You don't know anything about Theodore. There's a reason I kept him here as long as I did. And as for the town going bankrupt, you don't really want that. The bachelors would have to leave and you'd be left with an empty house. Your business would fail, Morna."

"Well, if it does, at least I'd have the satisfaction of knowing I cared for them and they respected me, which is more than anyone will ever say of you."

He flinched. He actually flinched. He was human after all. But then she knew that. Flesh and blood and sinewy with a man's strength. She couldn't erase the memory of his warmth when he'd pushed against her in the crowd. Of course she couldn't let him know, so she forced a stern look on her face.

"For a rich man, you certainly are poor in spirit."

"And you, Morna, are lacking in logic. I fail to see the connection between business and feelings. Caring and liking are no ways to make a profit, Morna."

"Is that all you think about?" She wanted to scream.

He paused and gave her a long look. "I have many things on my mind besides feelings."

"You have nothing on your mind except profit." *And Sarah.*

"Morna," he said gently, "I could have predicted they'd walk out if they pushed for too much. The town is set in its way. Company towns are like that. That's all this place will ever be."

"Why?"

"Because that's all I want it to be. In ten years the place won't even exist. Don't tinker with the way of the place too much, with anything too much. You never know what tomorrow might bring. That goes for boardinghouses, company towns, and even people. Even you. How do you know you might not change your mind and want to move on?"

She pressed her lips tightly together. She didn't know. Any day her brother could write begging for her help back in Ireland. It would be Morna's dream come true. But since meeting Quinn, she was beginning not to watch so closely for the mail, for fear she would have to make the choice—between here, a place of her own—no, a man she was attracted to, and who she felt was attracted to her without knowing of her wealth. Between all of that and going back to Ireland to a lace factory. A bittersweet choice. Meanwhile, she hadn't worn her lace in days. It all seemed far away and out of place with her new life.

Nevertheless, her new life demanded one quality she'd brought from her old, a quality her father had ingrained in her—duty. She could not do less.

"Morna," Quinn said softly, and she stopped, letting his voice wash over her.

"If it makes you feel better, I've decided to change that rule. The bachelors, I realize, need something to do. Something apart from the families, of course. Something on their own."

Spoken like a man with a grudge or a wall about his heart. Morna longed to know the secrets of his past, the paths he'd walked that had led him to such cynicism. But like the real forest outside her boardinghouse, it was a dark, forbidden place. And now was not the time.

She decided to change the subject back to her bachelors, to her duties as a landlady.

"Your gesture is magnaminous," she said, "but too late."

She could almost see him tense in surprise.

She rushed on, uneasy at his silence. "I've thought it over and after tonight I'm going ahead with it. A social at my boardinghouse. And if you mean it about changing the rules, if you want the town to mingle with the bachelors, then everyone is invited to the boardinghouse."

"How can you have a social with all men?"

"I'm a woman," she said, and set off for the boardinghouse. The men would need cheering up.

With his long strides, it only took Quinn a minute to catch up.

"Why, are you actually walking me home?" she asked. "I thought you'd be avoiding me, like usual."

Quinn didn't know if she was flirting or being sarcastic. But he was more aware of her as a woman than he cared to admit. "I live there, too. We may as well share the same piece of boardwalk."

She shrugged. "I suppose."

"You've turned this town upside down already. Don't make it more confused."

"This town needs a good shaking out, like spring housecleaning. Do it good."

"It won't do me good."

"What does that mean?"

"I'm more than the owner."

"You're the most egotistical man I've ever met."

"But a man. A man."

She slowed and stopped, facing him. "What are you saying?"

"You've spurned me publicly, Morna."

"It was only a dance."

"No one refuses to dance with the owner of the town."

"Except the owner of the boardinghouse. You may own the others, Quinn, but you don't own me. And as for dancing, I dance when I want to, not when I'm commanded."

"You're a hardheaded woman, Morna."

That was too much for Morna. "And as for my own social, I'll dance with every single one of the men—any man who's wearing a blue button."

His low chuckle unnerved her, but she kept silent and stared up into his eyes.

"You're asking for trouble, Morna, I hope you realize that."

"Trouble's better than boring rules."

"You've turned me upside down, too."

"How?"

"I want you."

"You're only saying that to win the wager."

"I wish I were."

"You still think I'm a loose woman. I'm not, but I guess last night I gave that impression. I'm sorry I got carried away."

"I'm the one who got carried away. And I know you're not a loose woman."

"Then don't make bold suggestions. They only embarrass me and remind me all over again how I lost my virtue to you."

"We only kissed. You haven't yet lost your virtue."

They had stopped walking. Morna fought to keep her heart from hammering. Quinn wanted and got every woman he laid eyes on. Telling them sweet words, provocative words, meant nothing.

But her heart would not obey her. For she wanted him, too. As he leaned down to kiss her, she knew she'd be helpless to push him away. She didn't want to push him away. For he made her feel completely different than Horace had. She wanted Quinn, too.

Already his lips were melding with hers. Warm and firm and tender all at once. Her legs turned even weaker, and her arms came up around his neck. He held her close about the waist and kissed her deeper. Right there on the main street of his town, they kissed. Right in the shadow of the company store. Oh, mercy, it was sweet.

At length she pulled away, her hands to her face. She was so ashamed. She'd behaved no better than her own maid with Horace. "I'm sorry. . . . I—I don't know why I let you do that."

He smiled sardonically. "Don't you? Because you want me."

Oh, he was infuriating in his confidence with women. "That's not so. I don't want any man."

Once again, she was running. Oh, sure and she was only running to the boardinghouse, but she felt the coward. Never again was she going to run away from the consequences of a man's lust. Never.

She stopped on the boardinghouse veranda to catch her breath. Inside, the bachelors were talking loudly, still complaining. Quinn was out in the dark somewhere, lost to her as surely as if he'd taken another path in his woods.

It would be best if he did sell off this town and cut down his trees and move on. Oh, aye, the sooner the better. Best he left, for she was falling in love with him.

Wouldn't he gloat over that—if he found out?

16

THE NEXT MORNING, Quinn was already downstairs when Morna entered the dining room.

She stopped in the doorway leading from her room. He didn't see her at first, and she had a chance to watch him unobserved. He was, she decided, a lot like a tree, tall and straight and someone to lean on—the way she had last night. It was a wonder she hadn't thought of it before this.

He was a tree set apart from the forest and the town both. Alone. Trees weren't meant to grow alone. That was what made her heart reach out. Only he was inpenetrable. Whatever bitter blow had struck him, he'd grown a protective bark around himself.

The door squeaked or else Widowmaker came out and glanced at her. Whatever, Quinn glanced over his shoulder and saw her.

His gaze narrowed on her, and she was unable to do anything but stare back, caught in the spell of his eyes, remembering.

Widowmaker cleared his throat. "Tea anyone?"

Morna, spell broken, managed to nod. No one was about. She hadn't heard the whistle on the mill. Then the shrill sound split the air. "I didn't realize I'd slept so late. Is Conor off to school?" She was trying to avoid Quinn.

He likewise was trying to catch her eye. She walked to the table and sat down on the same side as him. It was easier to avoid meeting his gaze that way. Widowmaker left.

Quinn and Morna sat in silence, a foot between them. After last night's passionate kiss she wished it were a chasm.

"About last night—" Quinn paused.

"It was my fault. You don't have to say a thing. You warned me it would be hard living in a house full of bachelors. And I guess last night you proved me right."

"I'm not sorry."

Her heart thudded in her ears.

He was only saying that because he was used to having his way with any woman he wanted. She didn't want to be any woman to him. "I'm sorry."

Widowmaker returned and plopped down two mugs, one tea, one coffee. She stared at hers, at the thin swirl of steam rising up like mist from a wintry millpond.

She wrapped her hands around it. "Where's Conor? Gone to school already?"

"There's no school today. The teacher canceled it. Conor left and came back."

Morna *had* overslept.

"Why didn't he awaken me" A suspicion nagged at her. "He's not out with that treasure map, is he?"

Widowmaker shuffled his feet uneasily. "Heck, I didn't know there was rules about being a boy, too."

Quinn shot him a look, and Widowmaker held his chin up. "Mr. Montgomery, meaning no disrespect, but I think a boy ought to run about."

Quinn wrapped his own hands around his mug so tightly his knuckles whitened. "I told you last night I was going to make some changes."

Widowmaker half smiled. "I thought you was just saying that to keep us from brawling."

"I never say what I don't mean."

Morna half glanced at him and paused. He was turned to her as he said the words. Last night he'd said sweet words. A few. Did he mean them?

Widowmaker stood, a frown etched in his face. "But where is Conor? I gave him one rule and that was to never go in the woods. That's following orders from Quinn, of course."

Now Quinn stood and stalked over to the front window of the dining room, the one that looked out on the stand of trees that were off-limits. He stared out.

"Where is the boy?"

Morna stayed where she was, concern moving across her mind like an onrushing cloud, growing in size the closer it came to her question. "Where is he?" she repeated.

"I don't know."

Quinn turned. "Someone should know. Boys can play, but there's danger in not knowing what they're walking into. And those woods are not safe. The branches have been sawed off for trimming before the trees are felled."

"Then there's no danger."

Quinn swiveled. "If only one branch got overlooked, it doesn't take much wind to bring it down." He let that sink in. "And you don't know what a branch from a tree that size can do to a boy that small—or anyone, for that matter. Do you want to add anything, Widowmaker?"

The cook stood silent. "I seen a man die from a widowmaker once. . . . I quit going in the woods and took up cooking then. Sometimes I been accused of having no respect for the woods, with my nickname and all, but I figure if people ask how I got the name, they'll know to look out."

They were all three silent.

Morna moved first, heading to retrieve her cloak from the row of pegs. "I think I'll have a quick walk outside and call for him. That makes more sense than us standing around in here questioning each other."

"I'll come, too," Quinn said.

She looked up from buttoning her cloak. She didn't object.

They walked up the boardwalk of Main Street. This morning, the little town was quiet, its plainness a welcome sight. Familiar and homey. It felt all the more so with this tall strong man beside her. A tree against which to lean.

The townspeople smiled.

At their questions about Conor, the answer was over and over the same. "We haven't seen him."

Then they came to the livery. The doctor was there, handing his horse and buggy over to the livery hand for a checkup. He looked weary, as if he'd been up all night.

Morna asked him the same question.

"I rode into town through the woods. Had to attend an injury out in the woods."

Quinn stepped closer. "What is it?"

"Oh, nothing but a bellyache and a nightmare. A waste of a drive except for the pleasant chat I had with the little orphan boy."

"Conor?"

"Sure."

"Where?"

The doctor gave Quinn a look of chagrin. "Now, I ain't supposed to tattle on my patients."

"What do you mean?"

"He needed a splinter taken from his finger."

"Tell us. You know he can get hurt in the woods."

"There's no logging going on there."

The doctor was new and naive. Quinn had said so.

"But he's disobeying my orders."

"Rules don't help a boy grow—"

Already Morna was running down the street back toward the boardinghouse. Some rules had to be obeyed. Quinn caught up with her at the veranda. "You can't go out in those woods."

"I'm going to get Conor. And there's no need getting angry. I know what he's looking for. He has a map from his father."

Quinn looked over at the dark woods, dark because the sun had not yet risen above the trees. But rays were slanting through the trees, sparkling, beguiling. A small boy on a quest would find that light beckoning.

"A map to what?"

Morna shrugged. "Please, Quinn. It doesn't matter. It's only some fancy of his about a secret letter his father sent to Ireland. It's not really a treasure. It's a boy's fancy. But he has so few things left from his family, I didn't want to discourage him in this one adventure—"

Quinn's face darkened. "I know the paths in there."

Had he once strolled there with Sarah? Maybe.

But she also knew from everyone in this town how long it had been since he'd gone in those woods. What was in there? Some secret to his past?

The questions intrigued her.

But more pressing now was finding Conor. Later she'd worry about Quinn and his town. Unless, of course, in finding Conor she found the mysteries to Quinn as well.

She quickened her steps.

Quinn matched her, outpaced her.

A bird hiding in shady branches flew up from a tree. Twigs snapped where she did not step. Instinctively she reached out for Quinn's arm. They were at the edge of the forbidden woods. The woods about which the town had so many tall tales.

"He's probably playing," she said.

A breeze blew through the branches. The air was scented with pine and dirt. "Conor," she called.

No answer. No small boy's voice.

"Did you read the letter, the treasure map?" Quinn asked.

"No, he only told me."

"What?"

"Why does it matter? You're acting more worried over a boy out playing than about the entire town and mill."

"He might be lost. He might have run away."

She laughed sharply. "What do you know?"

"Strange as it may be for you to believe this, Morna, but I started out as a boy, too."

Indeed he had. His masculinity was one thing Morna could never ignore, any more than she could ignore the woods.

"He's off playing. Not in the logging area, but in the woods by the boardinghouse. The woods you said you'd never cut down . . . so you see he's perfectly safe, after all."

"In my woods?"

She slanted a glance at him. His forbidden woods. Forbidden because these woods had something to do with Sarah. "Surely he's not the first little boy who's wandered off into the woods to follow a bird to its nest, to chase a windblown twig, to carve his initials in a tree trunk. . . ."

"The townspeople know the rules, and they carefully instruct their youngsters in the rule about the woods."

"What's so secretive about them? Maybe there really is a treasure hidden in them."

Quinn's face was averted, so she could not read the expression on it.

Quietly, he spoke. "Widowmaker and I explained it, Morna. Rules and danger."

Rules.

Always, no matter what they discussed, always their talk came full circle back to his rules. He guarded himself with his rules as if they were a suit of armor. Rules. Rules. Rules. So many that a body would have to be dumb not to suspect a secret. Like a man protesting too much, he surrounded himself with too many rules about these woods. Like rings around the core of a tree, they were endless. Years and years of them.

"Wait here," he said, and by the time the words got through to her, he was tramping off ahead of her.

She would not wait.

She pulled her cloak close about her to protect her skirt from the undergrowth and with a determined stride set off after him.

Into the dark, dense forbidden forest.

There was only one path, and Quinn walked it. So fast she could not keep up.

She rounded a bend in the path and he was completely out of sight. She could hear the sound of footsteps in the woods, birds taking wing. Then no sound at all. All she had to guide her was the imprint of his foot.

Morna followed for a few minutes and then pulled up short at the sight of tiny footprints in the mud. They were child size, like Conor's, and they led off away from the path, off in a totally different direction from Quinn, whose prints went on straight ahead.

She took off after the footprints, over low-growing brush and ankle-high mud.

"Conor," she called.

There was no sound except the breeze in the trees.

This deep in the woods, it was impossible even to hear the familiar whine of saws at the mill, the sound that seemed as much a part of Bunyan as air and water. Instead, it was still and dark. She swallowed back her fear and walked on.

Soon she'd come to a clearing. Perhaps a house, some sort of refuge. But instead just trees, so many trees, she could barely see blue sky filtered through the canopy of evergreen.

Maybe she should have done it Quinn's way, followed him.

Then it happened.

The trees did thin out. Only there was no fairy-tale cottage.

Instead, in the small clearing was the stump of a tree. A big tree. And it was hollow.

And sleeping in the hollow was a small boy.

Her heart leaped with relief. Conor.

He was curled up in the hollow stump.

"Conor." She whispered his name.

He opened his eyes. "Hello, Morna. How did you know about the hollow log?"

"I didn't. I thought you were lost."

"I'm not. I'm hiding."

She assumed he was playing and so went along with the spirit. She was so glad to see him she felt like a child again. "Did you find your da's treasure?" If he wanted to believe in it, she didn't care. Just so he was safe.

He was shaking his head. "It wasn't a treasure. Just a lot of papers." He reached down into the hollow and pulled one up. "See."

She reached for one. Spidery black ink stretched across the pages. Pages and pages of numbers. Columns of numbers. They were account sheets, and at the head of the first page were the words *Profits of the Company Store*.

Her heart beat faster. From the day she'd arrived and seen for herself how the bachelors were fleeced with exorbitant prices, she'd not felt right about that store. But it was Quinn's store, and there was no evidence that anything was wrong other than greed.

Now perhaps there was more than greed proven here. Perhaps someone was stealing from that store. That would explain the whispers about town, the secretiveness. It might even explain all the ridiculous rules. Rules could keep the truth hidden.

But was it Quinn who was dishonest?

Morna felt sad. If he was dishonest, it was only with his heart and soul. She wanted to believe that was so. In business he was honest. He had to be. Business was his shield from emotion. No, Quinn couldn't know about this.

But he would.

Morna was going to stand this town on its head if that's what it took to awaken Quinn Montgomery to the heartache his ways were causing.

She might never penetrate his hardened heart, but at least she'd have the satisfaction of having done right by the bachelors. They had befriended her when no one else trusted her honor, and they deserved her loyalty in return.

"Morna, what's wrong?" Conor asked.

The little boy, thoroughly awake now, had climbed out of the hollow log. He was holding a blue velvet book.

"What's that? Something else of your da's?"

He shook his head. "I found it in the log, under the papers."

"May I see it?"

He shrugged. "I suppose so. I can't read it."

She smiled. "You keep going to school, and you'll read before you know it. What else have you found in this hideaway?"

"A bird's nest. You want to see?"

"Of course. There aren't eggs in it?"

"No, wait here. I've saved it in a safe place."

He ran to a nearby tree, another hollow hideaway, and while he was retrieving another treasure, Morna opened the velvet book and thumbed slowly through the pages. It was a diary.

And the frontispiece again had spidery black writing in it. A woman's name.

Sarah. Sarah Montgomery.

She couldn't resist. Quickly, she thumbed through the pages, randomly stopping here and there to read. It was private, but her curiosity won out over guilt. The entries were dated ten years ago. They were love letters in diary form. But they were not written to Quinn. They were written to Theodore.

She didn't want to know any more.

Unless Quinn told her. And she didn't even know if he knew about this diary.

Theodore! But why, why would Quinn have kept him on in his employ? Did he not know about this? Then what had happened to Sarah?

She tucked the diary in a pocket under her shawl and went to find him.

His voice carried through the trees; he was talking to someone.

She hurried to find him. He was along the path, deeper in the woods.

She rounded a bend and pulled up short. He was with a woman, deep in conversation.

A familiar dark-haired woman. She turned. It was Nellie, and her eyes were red from weeping.

When she saw Morna, she picked up her skirts and ran off.

Quinn stood still.

Morna, stunned, turned to retreat down the path.

These woods were heartbreaking, that was clear. They held more secrets than trees.

"Morna! Wait."

She began to run.

Quinn caught up with her and reached out to take her by the arm. Instead he grabbed her shawl. Morna lost her balance and stumbled against Quinn. He caught her by the arm and straightened her but never let go. She was aware of his touch burning through her.

"About Nellie . . ."

"Let me go, Quinn."

"It wasn't what you think."

"Pierre is sweet on her. Are you trying to steal everything from the bachelors?"

Now he grabbed her by both shoulders. "I was talking with her about Pierre. Nothing more."

They were close enough to kiss. This time she didn't stumble against him; she leaned. All around them was the scent of pine and longing.

"Morna," he whispered, his lips touching hers.

Then another voice shouted her name also. "Morna!"

It was one of the bachelors, and by the sound of his

voice, he was coming closer. Already she had slipped out of Quinn's embrace.

She rushed out to meet Cleatface, who brandished a telegram.

"Good news for you," the man said.

"How do you know?"

"Aw, everyone knows what's in everyone's telegram. Ain't no secrets in this town."

"Except for Sarah," Morna noted. She glanced back at Quinn, who stood expressionless, hands thrust into his jacket pockets. He looked as if Sarah was on his mind again.

"Yeah, Sarah. But she's who started this town."

Morna didn't want to hear him sing the praises of a dead woman. "Did you need me for something in particular?"

Proudly, Cleatface brandished a telegram. "It's from Ireland."

With a resigned sigh, Morna took it and ripped it open. This wasn't the first time she'd heard from her brother about his woes with the lace factory. She expected more of the same.

Dear Morna, the factory is yours—if you fancy coming back.

It was hers? After giving up on the dream, it had come true, only now she had a new dream in life. Quinn Montgomery.

Faced with the stark choice of a lace factory or Quinn, it wasn't hard to decide. Dreams changed. She'd fallen in love.

The only problem was Quinn. He didn't love her. And a woman couldn't very well compete with a ghost.

17

ONCE AGAIN, QUINN found himself on the side-
lines in Morna's boardinghouse. Here he stood, alone by
the table with his coffee, while Morna sat by the stove,
surrounded by the bachelors. Adoring bachelors. He
clenched his coffee mug tighter. Inside, his emotions
churned uncontrollably.

He hated the way those scruffy millworkers clustered
around Morna. They were entirely too familiar, telling
her their heartbreaking life stories. Worse, she was
actually consoling them. Her voice was soft and concerned.

Widowmaker needed a new apron.

Cleatface shouldn't worry about being handsome. It
was the measure of his heart that counted.

Cookee didn't have to feel ashamed of getting sick in
the mill. Every man had his calling.

Finn made a good brew, but he must remember
temperance.

Arne was so busy pleasing everyone else. Didn't he
take time to smell the trees?

As as for Pierre, well, the other men could josh him all
they wanted, but if he liked a town lass, that was fine. A
man could dream as big as he wanted.

On and on she went. Quinn gritted his teeth, clenched his fists until his knuckles were white, and then when that didn't lessen the impact of her voice, he gulped his coffee. It burned.

Down went the mug with a crash.

Suddenly everyone turned around and was staring. A gaggle of plaid-shirted mill hands in scruffy beards was smiling at him. At him. The owner of this town. The most eligible man on Emerald Isle and Mackinac Island both.

Then Morna stood and took a couple of steps toward him. "Are you all right, Quinn?"

The bachelors faded into the background, and he had her all to himself, her smiling green eyes looking into his, concern on her face.

"I think I burned my hand," he replied in a voice that sounded more like Conor's than that of a millionaire lumber mogul's.

"Let me see it."

She held out her hand to him, and with no hesitation he walked toward her. The bachelors spread out even farther while Quinn basked in the undivided attention of Morna, who took his hand in hers and examined it.

"Widowmaker," she said, "get me some butter."

There was a scurrying movement, but Quinn could not take his gaze off of Morna—her face, her hair. She smelled of fresh soap and pine. She felt soft. He would endure pain forever to have her this close. He would walk through coals to have her touching him like this.

Then she was rubbing butter on his burn, her fingers caressing his own from the knuckle on down to the juncture. Around and around her fingers rolled, sensual and intoxicating.

"Is that better?" she asked.

"It still hurts," he said.

She looked up and smiled at him. "Then we'll dunk your fingers in something cold."

Conor pressed close and peered at his hand. "I had a burn like that once. It didn't hurt much at all."

"Hush, Conor," she said. "Everyone hurts in different ways."

And with that she plunged Quinn's hand into a bowl of cold water and held it.

"How long are you gonna hold his hand?" Conor asked.

Cleatface snickered. "Hush up, boy. Us menfolks like it when pretty women hold our hands, so don't be in a rush."

Quinn's face burned with embarrassment. Was he that easy to read? Was he that desperate to have this woman's attention?

Never in his life had he competed with mill hands, and he'd be damned if he'd stoop to doing so now. Morna might be pretty, but she was a woman, and all women did was lead men down bleak paths.

With a jerk he pulled his hand out and shook it dry. Water droplets splattered on Morna's face and apron.

She reached up and wiped one off her cheek, another from her forehead.

"You can soak your hand some more at bedtime."

Someone snickered.

"Thank you," he managed, and beat a hasty retreat to his attic.

He sank onto his bed, and buried his head in his hands. This place was getting to him. Maybe Sarah's ghost haunted the place after all.

He stood and paced back and forth. This was not passion. Nor did he feel any jealousy for those mangy men downstairs. Impossible. Or, if he did, it was misplaced jealousy. Any normal male of his social standing would naturally want to show up the bachelors.

Wouldn't they? Why then did he resent them crowding around Morna, commanding her attention? Because he felt left out. He wanted her for himself.

But Quinn wasn't going to let any woman arouse feelings of possession . . . no one. There was a simple solution to this. He stopped pacing and stared out his window at the dark woods, pondering the obvious solution.

If she didn't sew on buttons for the men, then they wouldn't have any need to cluster around her so.

So all he had to do was banish the blue-button rule.

He was the owner. He made the rules and he could end the rules. Of course, he'd need some plausible reason. After all, it was because of the blue-button rule that Morna was living here. And she might be annoyed at losing her little button-sewing business. She might miss all those bachelors clustered around, adoring her.

Laughter drifted up from downstairs. Morna's laugh was included. She laughed the way a woman did when too many men were adoring her. She was enjoying this house. Quinn hated the place, and she liked it.

Conor appeared in his doorway.

"What is it?" Quinn snapped, then caught himself. He held up his sore hand. "I'm sorry. It—uh, hurts, so I'm a bit grouchy."

"That's all right," Conor said. "I brought you some more cold water. Morna said for you to soak your finger in it for the next hour."

"Did she?" He arched a brow as the boy came closer. "Where shall I put it?"

Quinn gestured to a trunk near the bed.

"Is that all?" he growled when Conor stood there.

"Morna said to ask you if it feels better."

"Yes. Tell her yes." And leave. Morna should have come herself instead of sending this—this child.

No, she was having a better time with those mill hands.

Well, that was too bad. It was indecent for one woman to have so many men gawking at her. Ignoring the water, he shrugged into his coat and headed for the company store. The sooner Otis posted the new regulation, the better.

When Morna heard the news, she pricked her thumb with the needle.

She half stood. Buttons slid off her apron and rolled about the wooden floor. The shirt she'd been sewing followed, landing in a puddle at her feet. She sat down so suddenly the back of the rocker came up and bumped her in the back of the head.

Briefly, she shut her eyes, then sighed and looked straight at Arne. "You can't mean that about the blue-button rule."

Arne stood his ground. "It's true, Miss Morna. It's posted on the vall outside the company store, written in black and white for the whole town to see. Bachelors are exempted from the blue-button requirement."

Morna pressed her lips together. Her mouth felt like cotton, and she swallowed a couple of times while she fought for composure. Quinn was up to something, only she didn't know what.

"Do you have any idea why this change has occurred?"

"No, miss."

"Well, what about the people in town—you know, at the company store. What are they saying?"

Arne shrugged. "There's some talk that maybe because Nellie is sweet on Pierre, the town people don't vant the bachelors to stand out so."

"Is that what you think?"

"Me?" Arne blushed to the roots of his hair and knelt to pick up the buttons. "Vhat I think doesn't count. Otis, now, though, he is mumbling some about the profits he'll lose."

"Yes, well, the profits belong to Quinn Montgomery in the end. Now, why would Quinn willingly give up the profit from selling blue buttons to the bachelors?"

Arne picked up the last of the buttons, stood, and held them out in his cupped hands. "Here you go. . . ."

Morna stared at them. A handful of blue buttons. They reminded her of the proverbial nail. For want of a nail the shoe was lost.

"For want of a button, the town was lost. . . ."

"Huh?" This was Arne, standing now, scratching his head.

One by one the other bachelors came tiptoeing in from outside. Finn sat on the bench and played a few notes on his harmonica, then the tune died away. Everyone was quiet.

Widowmaker stepped forward. "You heard the news, then?"

Morna nodded.

"He don't like us around you. He even hates it when you sew on buttons for us."

"Nonsense. He doesn't notice what any of us do. He's too busy trying to manage the town."

"He notices you." Arne said this, then looked away.

Widowmaker punched Arne in the arm, a teasing gesture. "Aw, you're noticing too much. Heck, we're all sweet on you, Morna. If he's doing this to put you out of business, we'd give you the shirts off our backs to help you get back to Ireland . . . assuming that's where you want to go."

They were all quiet.

Finn played a few notes of an Irish jig, then stopped.

"Do ya want to leave us?" Cleatface asked.

Morna looked from one to the other, her heart touched by their earnest, endearing expressions of affection. "I'm not sure what I want," she said.

Well, that was a fib, but it was to spare the bachelors' tender feelings. No, of course, she didn't want to go, but it was Quinn's face she saw. And Quinn didn't care if she stayed or went. In fact, he'd probably changed the rule to force her out. He was that determined to have his way . . . and preserve his memories of Sarah.

"I can't fight the ghosts of this town," she said quietly. "Maybe it'd be best if I did go back. After Conor finds a home, of course."

Arne perked up. "Heck, Quinn forgot all about Conor. You can't leave an orphan boy here. That's in the town rules, too. No orphans allowed."

"I can take Conor with me," she said. This was not the kind of town she had in mind for him when she came to America. The bachelors didn't know it, Quinn didn't know it, but she could give Conor a rich life back in Ireland.

"Vell, you better ask Quinn."

"What for?"

"Because he's the owner. No one does anything like that vithout clearing it vith him."

No, she supposed not. And probably the ghost of Sarah didn't dare walk the woods without his permission. Oh, what an impossible man she'd fallen in love with.

Once out, the thought would not be bound back inside.

She had fallen in love with Quinn, and there was no denying it. She could hide it from the others, but not herself.

And in the end, that's the only reason she had the courage to confront him about his blue-button rule and Conor—because she wanted to see him alone one more time.

18

*E*VEN AFTER EVERYONE went to the bunk room, Morna sat alone by the stove, reading and rereading the telegram from Ireland. It was her dream come true; it was what she'd wanted from the beginning. The lace mill. She'd be wealthier than she'd ever be in this company town. Aye, she'd leave behind this sawdust-filled place. She'd leave behind rules and regulations.

She'd leave behind Quinn Montgomery.

There. She'd allowed the thought to pop up again. Not that it mattered, really. Quinn wished she would vanish. Whenever he looked at her, she could feel him measuring her against the ghost of Sarah. She felt less beautiful. Less everything. Loving without love in return was harder, she realized, then anything Horace had done.

Footsteps sounded above her, and Morna glanced up at the ceiling. Quinn was pacing . . . pacing . . . pacing.

And so were her thoughts. Pacing in measure with his footsteps. Pacing as far as his doorway. Pacing into his arms. Then breaking and running back into her room where everywhere Sarah's ghost watched her, laughing, telling her she was a fool to think she could compete with a memory.

Well, there was still the matter of little Conor, and she might as well get it over with.

Minutes later she stood at the door separating their rooms. She put her hand up to knock, then pulled back.

Then, without warning, the door opened.

Quinn stood there, wearing only trousers and his white shirt, tieless and, in fact, unbuttoned.

"How did you know I was here?" Morna asked.

He looked her up and down and smiled. "Footsteps."

"Does Sarah's ghost have footsteps?"

His expression froze. "No, nor is this house haunted. You've been listening to too many tall tales."

"I'm sorry. I know it's a painful subject."

"You don't know."

"No . . . I came for another reason. I'm needed back in Ireland, so it looks as if you'll get your wish and have me gone."

"Is that my wish?"

"I assumed so. . . . You've not exactly proclaimed me welcome, and then when you changed the blue-button rule, well, naturally, everyone thinks it's a way to force me out."

"Since I can't win our wager, is that it?"

She gulped. She was hoping he'd forget about the wager.

"I can afford to give you the house. It's Conor I came to discuss. I want to take him back to Ireland."

Quinn leaned against the doorjamb. "To what? A hovel? What's this sudden inheritance? A diamond turned over in a potato field?"

"I'm not who you think. I never was."

"I always wondered if you were Sarah come to life."

She'd never played second fiddle to anyone, and it hurt. "What do you mean?"

"I told you, you look remarkably like her. That's why

I thought you were the ghost of her that night when you came tiptoeing in looking for Conor's toy."

"Not a toy. His pa's blue button, his most precious possession . . . Why do you mention Sarah still?"

His jaw tensed.

She backed away. "Why did you give me her room?"

"I didn't give it to you. You own it. I only showed it to you."

She licked her lips, nervous at the turn of this conversation.

"When you kissed me, was it her you wanted?"

He reached out and, taking her by the hand, pulled her toward him. She had no will to resist, especially when he touched the curl by her ear.

"When I first laid eyes on you," he said softly, "I thought she'd come back to life." He tightened his hold on her, and Morna melted into his arms.

"Your hair is hers . . . but nothing else. And when I kissed you, I knew it was you and not her."

"You've never gotten over her?" Morna couldn't help the tremble in her voice.

He pulled her more tightly against him. The room swam dizzily.

"Quinn, answer me."

"I made the wager with you not for this house, but because I wanted you. I want you now, Morna."

"You can't want me. It's Sarah—"

He placed a finger to her lips. "Stop it. If you think I'm pining away for Sarah, you're wrong. No one knows the truth. I brought Sarah here long before I built this town. She deceived me, do you hear? I never cared if I loved another woman. Never trusted another woman. And then you came to town."

"And I reminded you of her."

"Only at first . . . not now. You're the opposite of her in every way—except for the red hair. You're gentle, kind . . . aw, hell, Morna, I'm out of practice at saying all the fancy words. But I can't stand watching you with the bachelors, and that's admitting a lot for me."

"You're jealous of them?"

"Sometimes."

"Now?"

He cracked a slow smile. "Now you're in my arms."

So she was, and loving every minute of it. Desire pulsed between them, and his lips were too close to her. "I want to kiss you," he murmured.

He didn't have to ask twice. He didn't get to ask twice. Morna had fought back her longings too long. And so apparently had he.

Neither spoke another word. Their lips said it all. For long moments, the only sound was his heart pounding against her breasts, her own heart pounding in her ears, and the sound of breath coming too fast. In the silent room, kissing became a precious sound. A tiny moan, another and another. A sigh. The rustle of clothing. The sounds of desire were many, none more intoxicating than the blessed silence created by two people for whom an embrace and kiss said more than words ever could.

Quinn suddenly let her go and took a step backward. "Leave, Morna."

Morna made up her mind quickly. Desire made up her mind. Yes, she was leaving. She'd never love another man like she loved Quinn. She wanted to know all of his loving. Even if it was only once. That would be enough to last forever. And if it wasn't, well, she'd cross that bridge and those tears later.

"You win the wager," she said. "But you have to win

it by our agreement." It wasn't poetry, but she suspected it was the only terms under which he'd take her. Business terms. Anything emotional and he'd shut the door on her.

"You don't want me to ruin you."

No, she wanted him to love her, but that would never happen. "I want you to win the wager. I'm strong enough to deal with later, Quinn. Don't worry. There'll be no obligation on your part, except to let me go. Me and Conor. Life here will be just like it was before I ever came."

She moved against him and put her arms about his neck, buried her face in his neck, breathed in the piney masculine scent of him.

With a shudder, his arms came up around her, and his hands were fumbling with the buttons at the back of her dress.

She stood trembling while one by one he slipped each button out of its loop, and when he slipped the gown down over her shoulders, she stood perfectly still as if watching from a great distance. It fell to her hips, and she reached up and pushed it the rest of the way. He backed away, as if shaken at the sight of her standing there in camisole and slip.

He backed away another step, but she reached for him this time, took his hand—the burned one—and lifting it to her face, held it against her cheek.

"Morna, don't torture me. This making love is not as drawn out as a business negotiation."

She smiled. All these years she'd feared her wedding night, heard horror stories. And now she was giving herself to a man she loved, it wasn't even her wedding night, and she was not at all afraid, only overjoyed.

"I have only request."

"What?"

"Let me unbutton your shirt."

"You know a thing or two about unfastening buttons, I guess."

"Enough that it won't take me forever."

He smiled briefly, then as her hand slid inside the middle button on his chest, his face darkened with passion. "Hurry up, then. I wish now I'd made a rule forbidding all buttons in the town."

"Your oversight." Now she deliberately took her time, prolonging the agony for him. With each button she allowed her hand to linger on his flesh. Finally, he pulled his shirt out of his trousers and undid the last button himself—so quickly, it tore off and hit the floor.

"Now look what you've done, Quinn. Shall we postpone this while I sew it back on?"

"You're not sewing any buttons on for me—ever."

Briefly, pain shot across her heart. No, she'd have to mean something to him to do that. That was too intimate. This was simply a man and a woman fulfilling a contract.

"Are you a virgin?" he asked.

She nodded, feeling the color rise up her cheeks.

He cupped her face in both his hands. "Are you sure, Morna? Are you sure you want this?"

"Do you?"

He moaned and swept her up into his arms and deposited her on the bed. His trousers came off, and then gently he slipped off her undergarments. It was pure joy having him look at her body, feeling his hand sweep up her skin. Wherever he touched, she turned to fire, then ice.

He bent and planted a trail of kisses on her face, starting with her mouth, moving to her cheek, her temple, her hair, and then suddenly her upturned throat. She moaned softly, and his body covered hers. For the first time she felt the hardness of his desire.

He rolled her sideways and continued to stroke her skin from shoulder on down to her thighs. "Touch me, Morna," he pleaded.

With a tentative gesture, she placed the flat of her hand on his chest, then caressed his skin slowly. He buried his head against her hair. "You are so beautiful, Morna."

Pretty words. She could listen to them forever. Stay with me, Quinn. Let me stay with you. . . . But she dared not say it out loud.

They kissed and caressed until she cried out for mercy. "Sure and you drive a hard bargain, Quinn. Now take your prize. Show me."

He spread her legs, gently, ever so gently, and his hand was in her, inside the most secret part of her, again caressing her to an ecstasy she'd never known.

Then he positioned himself over her and he entered her. They were joined, spiraling together to the ultimate desire. She ran her hands along his back, threaded her fingers through his hair, and then clung to keep from crying out I love you. She bit back the words with such force her inner lips bled.

When it was over, they lay together and dozed. She woke first, looked at him sleeping in her arms, and memorized the moment. When she was old and love but a memory, she'd have this. This one moment. It would be enough. Life, she'd learned, was just a string of moments, like beautiful buttons on a thread. And some moments were meant to be cherished more than others.

He lifted his head, eyes at once alert, and cautious. She doubted Quinn fell asleep on many of the women he knew.

At once, they turned formal. He got up and retreated

behind a screen with his clothing. She picked up her garments and, wrapped in a sheet, headed for the door to Sarah's room.

"Now you do look like a ghost," Quinn called after her.

Her heart sank. It had been so beautiful. But even now, despite his words to the contrary, it was Sarah, always Sarah. He might hate Sarah for her betrayal, but he still loved her. Sarah haunted him even in lovemaking.

Quietly, she let herself out.

19

$\mathscr{A}$FTER THE FIASCO at the town social, Morna was determined this first annual bachelor social would go smoothly. She'd even clued in Nellie and her friends so they could "happen" to stroll by on the boardwalk when the social got going, and then Morna could "happen" to invite her in for a visit, and Pierre could dance with her without the censoring eyes of the town.

It was rather fun playing Cupid for someone else, if only to prove love still came true for some people.

The bachelors and Morna had together planned everything—from punch to violinist. The thorniest question concerned whether Quinn should be invited. "He is a bachelor," Widowmaker pointed out.

"Aw, he's too fancy for the likes of us."

"We'll see," Morna said. "We'll invite him and let him decide. After all, he is one of my boarders."

And so the day arrived, with a perfect still spring glow in the air.

All day long Widowmaker and Cookee fussed in the kitchen over cakes and pies. Outside, Finn stirred his brew. And everyone, absolutely everyone, had their long red underwear hanging outside in the sun. Red flannel was draped off the porch, hanging out of windowsills, and when the best hanging places were gone, the men strung up a clothesline from the porch to a tree.

Conor was almost forgotten in the excitement. But late in the afternoon, Morna found him digging near the tree.

"Conor! You'll be all muddy, and tonight's the bachelor party!"

"I don't care."

But Morna did. The townspeople knew about this social—Morna had posted an open invitation at the company store—and though she did not expect many except the very brave single lasses to show up, she did want everything to go well. If word got back that the bachelors were keeping Conor up to his nose in mud, it would only fuel the speculation about Morna.

"Come in now and take a bath."

"I'm looking for the treasure."

Morna sighed. "Not now, Conor."

"He said I could find it."

"We'll find it later. Now come along. All the men are cleaning up for the party."

"You aren't going to let me come. I'll have to go to bed."

"Conor, I promise you may stay up late tonight. Not as late as the grown-ups, but long enough to eat Widowmaker's cake and pie."

"Both?"

"Both." How nice it was to see Conor smile.

Quinn Montgomery was another matter. Ten minutes before the appointed hour, he strode downstairs from his room. Unlike the bachelors, who had dressed up in shirts with brand-new blue buttons, Quinn was unusually casual—open-neck shirt, tall boots pulled up over his calves.

He walked straight over to Morna, who was arranging

little glass jars of wildflowers. In her surprise, she even tipped one over, and she swiped up the water with her apron. When she righted the vase and had dried her hands, she looked up. Quinn was smiling at her. And she felt the silliest urge to smile back. She was trembling. Happy and desperate both.

Their eyes met.

His smile faded.

"You're staying, aren't you?" she asked.

He shook his head.

Disappointment coursed through her. She wanted very much for him to stay. Yet she should have known he'd think himself too good. Only the high society of Mackinac Island would be suitable for him. Or maybe it was the ghost of Sarah driving him away.

"Well, since you officially gave me permission for this event, you can at least stay for one drink. This is a special event for the men, you know. And I'm sure you'd like to know they appreciate it. As they appreciate you."

"I've never been worried about appreciation."

"Well, then it's time you did. That's what owning a town is about. It's what caring is about."

"I've never thought those two were mutually dependent."

She reached for a mug and handed it to Finn. "A drink for Mr. Montgomery, please, and a quick toast to our social. Then he has to leave."

Quinn took the mug, and when everyone was clustered around, they toasted him. "To the most wonderful owner ever."

"Aw, don't get mushy, Finn. You been drinking too much of your own brew."

Morna lifted her mug and toasted Quinn. "To the

owner. May the road rise up to meet you, and may you never meet another rule except the Golden Rule."

She touched her mug to his, then sipped.

He nodded and took a sip, never once taking his gaze off her.

Then he set it down. "Have a good time."

And then he was gone without a backward glance. Morna stared after him. Why could he not have stayed—just for a little while?

Quinn wanted to stay but only because of Morna. It was hell sharing her with a houseful of scruffy bachelors. He wanted her to himself, and the thought scared him. So instead he headed up the street to the hotel to while away the evening in the lobby. It might be lonely, but it was easier than watching Morna hold court with all those adoring bachelors.

Nellie passed him. She was walking with Pierre.

"Evening, Nellie."

After greeting him, the couple paused. "Heck, Mr. Montgomery, aren't you going to the bachelor social?"

"I stayed for one toast. I have other plans this evening."

They exchanged a look that made Quinn wince. It was almost painful to look upon Nellie gazing in adoration at Pierre. Pierre had desire on his face.

Quinn was envious and disgusted with himself. He was beginning to notice things only a woman would.

He needed no woman. He wanted no woman. And to prove it, he'd have a good time alone in the hotel lobby if it killed him.

"You know," Morna said, "it wouldn't kill any of you to dance with me."

Pierre was first to take her up on the offer. Such a gentleman. She could see why Nellie was so smitten.

The social was almost over, the men had eaten, drunk, played harmonica, and told tall tales. When it appeared Paul Bunyan could not grow any taller, Arne pulled out a harmonica, and while Nellie watched anxiously, Morna and Pierre danced. Nellie need not worry, for as friendly as Pierre was, in her thoughts Morna was dancing with Quinn. Her imagination served her well.

The music was sweet, and after that Morna gave each bachelor a dance. But she had to force herself to keep on smiling. The bachelors' social was a grand success; even the brave townspeople who had come had enjoyed themselves.

Morna felt alone in the crowd. What irony. She had worked so hard to convince Quinn why he should allow this social, and now the one person she wanted was him. Him alone.

It hurt most to watch Nellie and Pierre. They could dance together, laugh together, talk together. At least until Edith found out her daughter had come here on the sly.

Nellie waited outside on the veranda for Pierre to steal away from the social and walk her home. At last the door opened, and it was him. He saw her and at once came toward her. Her heart thrilled. She didn't care what Mama said. This was the man she wanted.

Pierre walked up to her and leaned over and kissed her in that dark corner in which she waited. Nellie's arms stole up about his neck, and she kissed him back.

"I don't take liberties with men," she murmured. "Mama says I must not until—"

"Until when?" He pulled her close, so close her face pressed against his chest.

"Until I wed."

With a gentle hand, he tipped up her chin and caressed her face. "Then perhaps I should wed you so I can have more liberties."

They kissed again. Mama would be so mad. And yet they kissed again. And then at last they tore themselves away from each other. He took her hand, and they headed to her home, quiet, content to be with each other. On the way, as before, they passed Quinn Montgomery. This time he crossed the street before they met.

Morna was still in the dining room when Quinn came in. At first he did not see her, and she could watch him. He looked lonely. Such a big tall man, and friendless. She longed to be the one to love him. But he seemed to walk with ghosts still.

She moved, a bench scraped against the floor, and he turned. Slowly, it registered that he was coming toward her. She stood frozen in place, unable to move, not wanting to.

"Was it a success, then?" he asked.

She nodded.

Before she could move he pulled her into his arms and after kissing her hair, lifted up her chin and kissed her on the lips. It was the most natural, wonderful thing in the world to put her own arms up about him and lean into him, to kiss him back, to accept his kiss. They broke away, but still he clasped her close.

"I wanted you alone, you see."

"You have me now," she murmured.

"But now is a short time," he said. "And I've learned not to count on tomorrows."

"You live in yesterday," she said sadly. "Why, Quinn? Why?"

"I can't explain it, Morna. I wish I'd met you years ago, but it's too late for me now."

"Oh, Quinn . . . I'm not sorry about how I feel. But I am sorry for you."

"I don't believe in feelings," he said softly. "But if I did, I think I might love you. Only a new love is not what I want. It is too late for me."

"Yes." She knew what he wanted. Sarah. He wanted a ghost. Suddenly she wrenched herself away and fled upstairs. She threw herself on the bed that had once been Sarah's and buried her face in the pillow so that he could not hear her sobs.

A few minutes later the storm subsided. But still she was too limp to move. She lay on her side on Sarah's quilt and she stared at the gilt-framed wedding photo. She had not removed it from the room or hidden it. Instead she kept it propped up on a little shelf, a reminder that another woman consumed Quinn's thoughts, occupied his heart.

Footsteps sounded on the secret staircase, and she sat up.

"Conor?" Her voice was shakier than she would wish the little boy to hear. He needed her for strength, not the other way around. And she hadn't even noticed he wasn't in his bed. Quinn was becoming an obsession. If he were a tree, she could cut him down, saw up all the memories, and burn him. But it wasn't that easy. She actually felt a bit of empathy for his memories of Sarah. She must have been very special for Quinn to still love her so.

Conor tiptoed in.

"Where were you?"

"I left when you were crying."

"You mean, you were here?" That was even worse. She'd not seen him leave. "Well, you shouldn't be wandering the house at night. You'll catch your death. I know how your ma worried about you on the boat."

She rolled over onto her back.

Conor stood in the doorway. "Why were you crying? Is it because you want to go back to Ireland?"

She half smiled. "A little bit of me wants to go back, but now I've got the boardinghouse to care for."

"If I find the treasure Da wrote about, I'll share it with you."

A half smile for Conor. How simple children made life's problems seem.

"Now, don't tell me you went searching at night for more blue buttons. You might run into the man next door, you know, and remember how scared you were last time?"

"I'm not scared of him anymore. He's been telling me about the woods. About the animals and birds."

"Well, that's very nice of him." She didn't think Quinn had it in him. "Will you please come to bed now."

"First I want to get my book."

"What book?"

"The one he loaned me."

So Quinn was softening, turning into someone human after all. But then Conor was endearing.

"All right, but hurry." She never asked where the book was.

She sank back on the pillows, utterly exhausted, shut her eyes, and half dozed.

In her half sleep, she heard Conor return. His footsteps were louder than usual, and brought her fully awake.

He sat on the edge of her bed.

At once her eyes opened. Wide.

Quinn sat there.

"What are you doing here?"

"Why are you crying?"

"I wasn't."

"Don't lie, Morna. I know the sound of tears better than you do."

"You shouldn't be in here. Conor might come back."

"I left his book with Finn, so by the time Conor finds it in the bunkroom, I'll be gone."

"Well, don't think you're going to have your way. You've won the wager."

"I have other things on my mind than our wager."

"You mean you don't care that you won back this house?"

"I like to win wagers, and this one is especially worthwhile, but not because of the house. I hate this house and have ever since Sarah left it. But I'd like to kiss you again. . . ."

"Why?"

The light from a lamp shone behind him like a halo. Only he was no angel. He was a devil sending little Conor off on a wild-goose chase. And yet she yearned to kiss Quinn, too.

"Shall we call a brief truce?" he said, his voice soft.

"Yes, then."

"You don't fight very hard, Morna."

"You make it hard to resist."

He was silent. "Make sure you understand what I said downstairs. I have no room—no permanent room in my life for a woman. Only temporary women."

She thought that over. It doesn't matter."

He bent down and kissed her lightly. "This is a truce. No wagers—"

"And no kissing. Conor might come back."

"I can solve that."

He scooped her up in his arms and carried her from Sarah's bed to the dividing door, kicked it open, and took her into his part of the attic. He set her down, deliberately close so that she slid against his body. Before her toes touched the ground they were kissing. Desperately touching. With his hands he caressed her hair, stroked her arms, dispensed with buttons and corset laces. Her breasts sprang alive. He kissed the rosy tips, slowly lingering over her. He lay waste to all her inhibitions, except for the last one.

When she was limp with desire, begging for release, it was he who released her. "Go away, Morna. I don't want the house. But if I take you, if I make love to you, I'll have a lot more on my hands than a house. I don't want to deal with it."

"But, Quinn, please. I won't ask anything. I don't know what Sarah did, but—"

"Don't mention her name." He moved away. His eyes were dark with passion, his hair tousled.

She looked up at him, so tall, so big, and so alone. His beard made him more forbidding.

He tossed a robe at her. "Conor's back in the room. Put this on, and tell him anything."

"I'm not telling him you kissed me."

Quickly, he closed the space between them. "Then you'd best fix your hair. Even children have a sense about these things." He reached up and slid a strand of reddish gold between his fingers, bent to put his face in it, then drew in a deep breath and pushed it behind her ear. "Leave now. I wish you'd never come to town."

He might as well have shoved her away. She felt utterly rejected and didn't know why.

"Whatever Sarah did, I'm sorry, Quinn. More for myself than you." And on that stark admission, she left, quietly closing the door behind her.

20

$\mathcal{T}$HE DAY AFTER the boardinghouse social, Quinn couldn't go anywhere without hearing talk about the bachelors. He hadn't realized so many people in the town even knew the bachelor's names, let alone would stoop to attend their party. But to hear people talk—and talk they did—you'd have thought the town had never seen a decent social before. Moreover, to his surprise, everyone seemed to think the bachelors were the friendliest people in town.

The liveryman said it first. "You missed a good party, Mr. Montgomery."

Quinn frowned. Party? Then the light dawned. "You mean that social at the boardinghouse?"

"Yep. They're right nice fellows. I'm glad you decided to let them mingle more."

"I haven't decided that yet. . . . Now, where did you want the roof patched?"

"Oh, no worry now. One of the bachelors fixed it for me this morning. Arne, I think. Nice fellows. They'd do anything for the town."

Quinn proceeded on.

He stopped at the saw sharpener's house. "I came to see where your clothesline is broken."

The lady of the house beamed. "Oh, no need, Mr. Montgomery. One of the bachelors already restrung it."

"Which one?"

She crossed her arms, as if in defense. "I don't rightly know. Bill and I only met some of them for the first time last night. He never sees them at work. They wanted to thank us for coming to their social . . . you know, do something neighborly. I hope that wasn't against the rules."

Quinn felt deflated. Beat to the punch by one the town's lowest citizens on the totem pole. "Of course it's not against the rules." At least he didn't think so. Actually, he was getting tired of worrying about all the rules. When had the strict company-town rules gotten started anyway? But of course he knew: when Sarah ran off and he turned their haven into a sawmill town. That's when. With rules, Quinn had always thought he could control people. He needed to control things. He still did, and today, he felt he wasn't quite in control of his own town.

But he'd regain control. No Irishwoman was going to take over his domain. The bachelors? How could it be? He'd been ready to evict them. He had fired them. He allowed them to be second-class citizens. Until Morna arrived and dusted them off and polished them up. It flew in the face of all Quinn's rules. And he just bet Morna Patterson—who'd plotted the event—was feeling smug. A quick stab of desire shot through him. She felt like a lot of things he'd nearly forgotten. Soft. Vulnerable. Feisty. Desirable. But he didn't want to feel that way. So he did something he'd never done before: he stood about on the veranda of the company store mingling with the towns-people. Where every matron of Bunyan was congregated. They stopped chattering as he passed by them, but he heard enough to know the topic they were discussing. The bachelors.

"Morning, Mr. Montgomery," Otis said politely when Quinn entered the store to head for his office. Even in here, more women than usual were milling about, doing more gossiping than buying.

Edith separated herself from the group and blocked his path. "This is my greatest humiliation, and it's all your fault."

"What did I do?"

"Nellie has accepted a proposal to wed Pierre. Can't you make up a rule to forbid it?"

"Well, now, I can't seem to please everyone. Half the town seems to suddenly like the bachelors, and now you want them controlled."

"Well, you're the owner. Can't you do something?"

Short of marrying Nellie himself, Quinn couldn't, and he had no intention of wedding Nellie. Suddenly he wished Morna were here. She could handle anything in this town.

"There are no rules against single women marrying bachelors."

"Then make one." Edith practically wagged her finger in his face. "Nellie never would have looked at those bachelors if they hadn't been allowed to become familiar."

Quinn did not like women wagging fingers near his face. Sarah had done that once. Once too often.

"Well, do something. We need a new rule."

Quinn was not about to be told what to do by Edith Hargrove, and the entire room knew it. On the other hand, Quinn was also tired of trying to control a houseful of bachelors, tired of being outwitted at every turn.

The solution was so obvious he almost laughed out loud.

"A new rule it is, then," he said. "I'm abolishing the rule that forbids bachelors to mingle. Furthermore, they no longer are the first fired at the mill."

Edith's mouth opened and shut. Ladies all about gasped, then bent to whisper.

"Well," huffed Edith, "I can see you aren't at all loyal to this town, but then we all suspected it meant nothing to you. Not it and not the families. Now, thanks to you my Nellie is going to insist on wedding that sawmill hand."

Quinn actually had grown to respect Pierre. Of all the bachelors he seemed to have the most ambition, which of course was why he'd offered him a job. "Maybe it'll turn out to be a good match."

"He's got nothing."

"He's a good man. It takes more than money to make a marriage, Edith."

"And you should know, I suppose."

Everyone gasped at once.

Quinn fell silent. He'd never told anyone about Sarah, and yet somehow he was sure they knew. At least bits and pieces.

Nellie swooned against the button and notion counter then pulled herself upright. "Mama," she pleaded, hand-kerchief to her mother's mouth to silence her.

Quinn started to smile, then checked himself.

Edith sputtered, words muffled. Finally she pushed her daughter's hand away.

"Don't be impertinent, young lady."

"And don't tell me who I can marry, Mama. If I don't marry Pierre, I shall leave this place forever with him. Either way I'll have him."

"Your pa won't approve."

Otis appeared out of a dark corner. "I do approve, Edith. Now quit bullying the girl."

"You'd defy me on this, Otis?"

"I'd see our daughter happy, that's what. If Quinn Montgomery can do away with town rules, then we can do away with our rigid thinking. So what if the fellow's a mill hand? It's honest labor, he's a fine upright fellow, and money can't buy happiness."

"What do you know?" his wife sniffed.

Otis shrugged, a sheepish look on his face.

"Well, then ask Mr. Quinn Montgomery." As one, the crowd turned to the owner.

Quinn wanted to evade them all and hide out in his office, but he was tired of hiding out. Again, he wished Morna were here, and that thought hit him like white lightning splitting open his heart.

"I guess I can talk about that all right, Edith. I've had money and I've had a wife. And there's no guarantee that either is going to last."

"Hmmph. And no guarantees this town is going to last either, isn't that right?" huffed Edith, hands on hips. "So what if we watch our Nellie marry Pierre? You're going to leave this town high and dry as soon as Pierre and his workers finish logging the place."

"No, I'm not."

"Prove it."

"Mama!" Nellie was shocked.

Actually, Quinn was shocked, too. No one in town had ever talked back to him before. They were all too afraid of him for that. It actually felt good to be mingling with them, talking on an equal level with them, and yes, caring about them. Not just Morna, but the entire town. What indeed would happen to all these people if he shut his mill and moved on? Morna had taunted him with such questions, and now he knew the answer.

"Edith Hargrove," he replied, "if you and Otis consent to Nellie here wedding Pierre, I give you—and everyone in town—my vow never to shut down the town."

"Well, heck," Otis said. "Someday the trees'll be all felled. Any fool can see that."

"The town will stay." He didn't know how, but he hadn't grown rich for lack of imagination. That was all he had to say on the subject for now. He had work to do, and he was for the first time eager to get at it. Somewhere in that stack of paperwork would be a way to make this town work besides with trees. He'd figure it out, because if he didn't he had a feeling Morna would.

Morna. Morna and the hair of reddish gold.

She was always on his mind.

And that's why he had to find a way to keep this town going. That's why he cared so much. Because he wanted her to stay. He'd do whatever he had to do to keep her here.

Morna had helped clean up the boardinghouse from the social and, finally exhausted, propped the broom by the door and collapsed into the rocker on the veranda. She was satisfied with last night's event, but still torn over Quinn's refusal to attend.

She reread her brother's message. None of the bachelors had an inkling of the choice she faced. Her own business, or an unexpected love. Wealth? Love? Independence? Love? It should have been an easy choice for a lady.

To give up this boardinghouse and return to Ireland for the lace mill or stay here for the rest of her life. Watching Quinn from afar. Loving him from afar while he mourned the ghost of another woman. She didn't think she could bear it.

Naturally, she'd said nothing of her dilemma to the bachelors.

She didn't want them to know, for she feared they'd be disappointed. And she felt if she returned to Ireland, she'd be doing exactly what she herself had accused Quinn of doing—walking out on people.

Someone called out to her.

She looked up. With a wave for her, Pierre came running across the stump-filled yard. He took the steps two at a time and stopped in front of her, out of breath but with a big smile on his face.

"It is settled. The Hargroves have given their consent."

Morna sank back a bit deeper in her chair and smiled back, truly delighted. Pierre would be a fine husband for Nellie.

"Oh, that's wonderful, Pierre. Nellie will make you a fine bride. A lovely bride." She tried to put as much enthusiasm as possible into her words. She was happy for Nellie and Pierre, yet a twinge of envy swept through her. Why couldn't this happiness be hers?

Pierre stood beaming. "And that's not all. Mr. Montgomery is giving the entire town a wedding present!"

Morna listened. "Changing the rules!" Why, she thought the Rome River would freeze over before he'd give up any of his precious rules.

"And there's even more . . ."

Morna could scarcely believe the next part.

A vow from Quinn Montgomery? Why, it actually sounded like he was starting to care about something in this world, and high time. Yet it sounded too good to be true; no man changed that fast.

"I think I'll find out for myself if he means to keep his word."

"You don't think he will?"

"I think there's got to be a reason for this sudden change of heart."

"Maybe he's lived here long enough that he likes the town a little bit."

"Mmm . . ." Or maybe he was planning to sell it and so could say anything they wanted to hear. Which probably was not the case. But she was curious enough to seek him out.

And very much in love. But that would remain her secret. She'd take it back to Ireland with her if need be. It'd be as easy as packing up Conor and taking him back. Love was easy to bundle up and lock away in a valise.

Wasn't it?

21

CONOR HAD NO place left to search for the buried treasure of his da's letters. The trouble was it was the forbidden part of the woods—the place that big gruff Quinn was always trying to keep him away from. The place where Quinn and Morna had found him with the velvet diary and chased him out. Ever since, Conor had wanted nothing more than to come back.

But today everyone was in town talking about the boardinghouse party or else slapping Pierre on the back about getting married. Conor didn't know what all the excitement was about. But he did feel temptation coming on. If everyone—even Morna—was away for a while, he could peek into those secret woods across the stumpy field and see if the velvet book had been put back into the hollow stump.

A row of ants marched around the stump. A black beetle scurried across a root and burrowed under some moss.

Since he couldn't read yet, he didn't care about the velvet book like Morna had last time he came here. But if a velvet book was hiding out here, then chances were good that the treasure was, too. He quickly found the book. Blue velvet, right where it had been dropped. Last time, Conor hadn't had time to examine it before Morna found him and chased him back to the boardinghouse. But if there was any sort of treasure map, it would be in here.

Eagerly, he opened it, looking first at the front cover, then the back. Nothing. Just blank paper, yellowed and water-stained and mildewy. He thumbed through page after page of handwriting he could not read. Disappointment filled him. It wasn't a map at all, but just a book.

Then something fell out from the middle. It landed right on his lap. Reaching down, he touched a brittle stem. Carefully, he picked it up and examined it. It was a flower. A dried flower. The poor thing was all squished from having to lie inside that book so long. Its color was faded blue edged in brown. Conor didn't think it was very pretty, but it reminded him of some other flowers he'd seen this spring.

Blue flowers crowded his memories. Little fuzzy-topped blue flowers. A patch of them in another sunny place. Behind the company store. That's where.

He pressed the flower back into the book and, taking it with him, ran out of the woods and back up the main street and around the back of the company store. Little shoots of green were coming up. The beginnings of flowers. He knelt and dug around the dirt, hoping to find treasure.

"Conor!" Morna was standing out on the boardwalk. "Come here. That isn't your yard to play in."

Reluctantly, he left the flower patch and headed to her. "I was looking for the treasure."

She eyed the blue velvet diary. "You've also been out in the secret woods again, haven't you? I think you'd best leave well enough alone. And give me the diary. It belongs indoors."

"But—but, you mean, there is no treasure?"

"I don't think so," she said as gently as she could.

"Then why did Da write about it?"

"Maybe he meant another kind of treasure. Not the kind pirates have. Not gold, but maybe just the place itself. Maybe he saw this town as a place to bring you and find happiness."

Conor was silent, and Morna feared she might have talked over his head.

"Happiness is a treasure? How can it be if you can't count it?"

"Lots of treasures can't be counted."

"I thought he meant gold. Or else a giant stack of logs."

"Maybe he loved you and your ma very much. That would be the best kind of treasure to hang on to of all."

Conor thought about that. "I miss Ma."

"We always miss the people we love."

He handed her the diary. "There's a flower in there. You can have it."

She looked at the flower. "Cornflower. Somebody was partial to them." Probably Sarah. Blue cornflowers. Bachelor's buttons. They obviously meant something to Quinn. "I'll give this back to Quinn. It's his. Maybe we can plant the little seeds around the boardinghouse and someday more flowers will spring up. That's another kind of treasure, too. Pretty things to care for."

"I wanted pirate treasure." With a boyish sigh, Conor ran off to play. Morna straightened her shoulders and with a tight throat continued on to her boardinghouse. She wanted so much to see Quinn, to talk to him without betraying her feelings, above all to keep her dignity. Her own father had taught her that it was best to leave with your dignity intact.

Moments later, she knocked at the door separating their two attic rooms.

Quinn opened the door immediately, almost as if he'd been waiting for her.

Their eyes met and locked in a gaze of longing. It took a minute before she realized what was different about him.

"You're shaving off your beard."

"It's time for a change."

"Yes, I agree. Since you won the wager with the boardinghouse—"

He grabbed at a towel and wiped his face, first one cheek then the other. "There was a truce on, Morna," he said, voice muffled.

"You won, Quinn. I honor my wagers."

He let the towel drop to the washbasin and kept on staring at her, gaze fixed on her hair, then her face, then her dress, and back to her face. She was melting under his look. Without his beard his face was square-jawed, his features kind. His blue eyes stood out even more, if that was possible. She envied Sarah, envied her with a raw agony. The woman was dead, and that made it worse. A live woman she could compete with. Her heart ached with longing, and suddenly she knew exactly what she had to do. There was no more indecision.

"I'm leaving."

Now his gaze bored into hers. Blue into green. "Why?"

"As you said, it's time for a change."

"Where?"

"Back to Ireland. My brother needs me to take over the lace factory."

He took in a sharp breath. "You own a factory? I thought you were an immigrant."

"Someone else asked the same thing. Your cousin, I believe. We immigrants are not all poor, and I had other reasons to come. Where did you think I got the money to buy this house?"

"I was never certain."

"The entire town thought I'd stolen it or earned it by ill-gotten means, but it wasn't so. It was my dowry."

Quickly, she told him about her fiancé. "And so," she finished, "I think it's safe to go back now."

She handed him the diary. "Conor found this. I thought you'd want it. There's a flower pressed inside."

He nodded. "I'll burn it."

"I thought you'd like to have it."

"You think I'm the grieving widower still, don't you?"

She gulped, trying to swallow back the knot that was growing tighter in her throat. She was so close to Quinn and so far away. If she wasn't in his arms, they might as well be in separate rooms. She couldn't bear this.

"Sit down, Morna, and I'll tell you my secret past. Then at least we'll part on equal terms."

"You don't have to, Quinn." She wasn't sure she could bear to know. "I know you've changed the rule about the bachelors, and I know you've vowed to keep the town intact. I wanted you to know that if I helped change your mind about that even a little bit, I'm glad."

"Maybe you helped me start to live in the present, not the past. But still, I want to tell you. Will you listen?"

Nodding, she sat down on the trunk nearest the door. She knew, of course, because she'd read the diary, but she longed to hear the story from Quinn himself.

Quinn paced. "It's very simple. Sarah ran off with another man, and when she did, I no longer cared about this place. This house was where I brought her to live. When she left, so did I . . . and that's why I decided to cut down the trees. It's because of Sarah I was destroying this place, tree by tree . . . at least I was."

She yearned to touch him. So that explained his moods, the rigid rules.

"I'm sorry," she said softly.

"What for? You're leaving."

"I care about you. I care more than you realize."

"Why?" Blue eyes studied her intently.

"Because . . . because—" She turned and stood and headed for the door. If she didn't leave, she'd surely break down.

She got no farther. One step across the threshold into her room—Sarah's room—and he caught up with her. He pulled her close to him, and they stood like that, her back to his front, his heart thudding against her spine, his chin resting on the crown of her hair. Time stopped.

"Morna, don't go."

"I have to, Quinn."

He kissed the nape of her neck then, and she turned and melted in his arms. He asked for no surrender; he didn't have to. Some force beat between them, pulled them together. She had no willpower, no conscience. They kissed urgently, tongues meeting, dancing, taunting. His hands caressed her body, and wherever he touched her, she went feverish, until, moaning, she begged for release. He took his time unbuttoning her dress and then suddenly a new urgency returned. Desire was all they had in common, all they wanted to have in common. Passion was the center of their universe.

This time it was Sarah's bed he took her to, after leaving her dress on the trunk. He paused long enough to lock the door and shed his own clothes and then he joined her. He unpinned her hair until it spread over the pillow and he kissed the stray tendrils, kissed her throat, her breasts, until she moaned in agony, begging for release. He sank down upon her and once again they were one. Ecstatically one.

A few minutes later she asked quietly, "Sarah had hair like mine, didn't she?"

He was still, as if pondering his choice of words. He rolled off her and kissed her temple again. "Do you mean the color? That's all. Her hair was not at all like yours.

Nothing about her resembled you. She's in the past now, Morna. Can we leave her there?"

She stroked his clean-shaven chin, savoring the smooth feel of it. Love welled up in her breast, and when she bent to kiss him on the lips, he took her in his arms again, long and lingering. And that time, Sarah's name was never mentioned.

A while later, when Morna was dressing, he came over to button her dress. "When are you leaving?"

She felt heavy, leaden. She wanted nothing more than to lie in this man's arms forever, to have his arms about her always. But life, she knew too well, did not turn out perfect. If she stayed, she'd be no more than his mistress. He'd become the very thing she hated about Horace. A man unable to commit.

They would end up hating each other.

He asked her a second time, and she said, "I'll wait for Pierre and Nellie's wedding." She lingered at the mirror, piling her hair up and hastily jabbing pins in. "It's part of caring. I'd disappoint them if I didn't wait at least that long."

When she let herself out, he was staring at the rumbled bed. Sarah's bed? Or the bed in which he'd had made love to her? She'd never know, she supposed.

Normally, the wedding service would be over. Today, on this shining spring day, there was more.

At the altar, Nellie shyly pulled a white button out of her hanky. Then to the surprise of everyone but Morna, she also reached into the breast pocket of Pierre's brand-new suit and pulled out a pair of scissors.

From the guests in the church, an audible gasp went up. This, Morna knew, was not in keeping with custom or rule or tradition.

Morna glanced over at Quinn, partly to see his reaction, partly to look at his face in profile one more time. If he were a poor sawmill worker, maybe then it would have worked. Maybe then he would have loved her the way she loved him—if only money weren't in the way. She wished now she'd never bought the boarding-house, but it was too late to cry over tangled yarn. Lace collars didn't get made in a day any more than forests grew in a decade. Time would not make him love her when he loved another.

He glanced at her, expression inscrutable. How she wished he would smile at her the way Pierre smiled at Nellie, but it was not meant to be. Even here, especially here in church, the ghost of Sarah, the legend of Sarah, would stand between them.

She turned away to watch the bridal couple. Still, out of the corner of her eye, she could feel Quinn's gaze on her, and she grew warm—with longing. The warmth of her longing enveloped her, and she snuggled closer into it. That was the one nice thing about a secret desire—no one in the world could know. If Morna had any pride left, she'd have shrugged it off, thought of something else, but she couldn't. She loved Quinn, but he could not let go of the past, and that was that.

He had sacrificed his past.

She could give up all pride and savor little memories.

"Morna." Widowmaker touched the top of her hand as if to awaken her. "This is the part you have been waiting for. Watch."

After exchanging a grateful smile with her favorite cook, Morna turned her attention to the altar. Nellie snipped off the blue button Pierre wore to his wedding ceremony and then left Pierre standing at the altar while she came toward Morna.

Everyone sat there buzzing in bewilderment, except Morna, who knew exactly what would happen next, for she had planned this part with Nellie and Pierre. She reached into her bag and pulled out an envelope, which she handed to Nellie.

Nellie beamed with joy and ripped it open while she turned to Pierre's side. Her new husband smiled broadly.

Nellie held up the contents of the envelope for all to see—a needle and thread—white, of course. And then, as part of the wedding ceremony, she stitched a white button onto Pierre's shirt. In moments she was done, and buttoned her new husband's collar for him. Of course, Quinn had done away with the blue-button rule, so strictly speaking this little ritual wasn't necessary. But it was a charming touch.

"There you are, Pierre. Let that be a sign to all the other eligible ladies in this town that you're no longer a bachelor. You're a married man."

Pierre pulled her close for a kiss.

The congregation sighed in unison.

Her mother handed her back her bouquet, and before they headed down the aisle, Nellie held back. "Wait, Pierre."

"Bossing him already," Dogger whispered in the pew ahead of Morna.

Widowmaker elbowed him. "Hush up. We're going to miss the best part."

"What's that?"

"Getting out of here and being first to the vittles."

"You saying it'll be better'n your usual cookin'?"

"Maybe. I went all out for Pierre. Now hush up. Next thing we know you'll be crying like a woman at a wedding."

Morna reached forward and tapped Dogger on the

shoulder. "Don't leave too fast. Watch what Nellie's going to do next."

Nellie held up the blue button—Pierre's bachelor button—in her right hand. "Get ready, ladies. Bachelor ladies, that is. Get ready to catch."

She flung back her arm as hard as if she were about to take an ax to a log and then threw the button out into the congregation.

Ladies squealed and hands came up to catch it. It landed in the aisle near Morna, who made no move for it. Instead, one of the single girls from town swooped down on it and grabbed it up with a triumphant smile. "It's mine."

"That means you're next to marry," Nellie crowed, and as the young lady clutched the button to her breast in rapture, Nellie and Pierre walked down the aisle hand in hand.

Widowmaker stood and wiped a tear from his cheek.

"You ain't gonna drip tears into the punch, are you, Widowmaker?" Dogger harrumphed. "Too bad you didn't get that button, Morna," he added. "What d'ya think, Arne? Morna should have caught that button."

"I think you should shut up, Dogger."

Arne herded the bachelors out of the pews. Cleatface. Dogger. Widowmaker. Cookee. And last of all, Finn, with a warning. "Don't you be sneaking any of that brew of yours into the punch now, you hear. Vidowmaker's orders . . . C'mon, Vidowmaker, quit crying, or ve'll all be bawling."

Morna couldn't help but smile at them all. They'd become so dear to her.

It was going to hurt to leave them here. Yet not even for them could she stay.

When she got outside, she decided it was as good a

time to tell them as any. Before the reception, so they had time to let the news soak in. Then while they partied with Pierre and Nellie, she could slip back to the boarding-house and pack her belongings. She hadn't collected all that much. A few clothes and toiletries. A letter from her brother.

And a shadow. The shadow of woman named Sarah. She supposed she'd pack that with her wherever she went, too.

The bachelors stood in a cluster, waiting for her. She walked up to them. "I think you'd better go ahead to the reception."

"Why, don't you want to come? Someday you'll get married and we'll throw you a party, too. . . . A bigger one than this. Heck, Morna, any one of us would marry you tomorrow if you'd have us."

She gave them a grateful smile. So dear to her heart. Oh, yes. Now came the hard part. "I have never known better friends than you, and you will always be a part of me. But . . . I think I'll be selling out and heading back to Ireland."

"Leave?" Cleatface's face fell.

"Since when?" Widowmaker said with genuine sur-prise.

Arne gave him another poke. "Maybe she doesn't vant to talk about it."

Quinn came down the church steps then, and as one, the bachelors stared at him.

"It's him, ain't it?" Cleatface whispered to Arne.

"Hush up. She's got a letter from Ireland."

"She left there."

"But not her family. Someone needs her."

The wrong someone.

Morna did not turn around, nor even glance sideways

at Quinn. Instead, she pulled the letter out of her pocket. "Arne's right. I heard from my brother in Kilkenny, asking for me, so you see, I am needed." A lump welled in her throat and a giant weight seemed to be pressing in on her chest. She wouldn't be able to stand here talking much longer.

"But I thought you wanted to be a . . . a independent gal, a woman with a boardinghouse business."

"My family owns a business." Briefly, she explained about the lace factory. "So you see I'll have a different business to tend to, and actually it's what I've always wanted." To her own ears, her voice held a hollow ring, but maybe the men wouldn't notice.

"But—but, wait," Cleatface stammered. "Wait until after the reception, so we can talk about this. You won't go without saying good-bye, will you?"

"I'll say good-bye," she promised. "Now off with you before all the wedding cake is eaten up."

By now the people of Bunyan were filing out and heading for the reception at the Hargrove house. With crepe paper and silver bells decorating the door and windows, it stood out from all the identical houses. And of course when the usual things were said, everyone talked about the cutting of the blue button. What a strange thing and kind of romantic, too, in its way. Maybe the next bride to wed a blue-button bachelor could do the same thing. It would be nice for Bunyan to start a new custom, be known for something besides lumber.

Morna didn't linger at the reception. Her heart wasn't in it. Watching people in love hurt when your own feelings of love weren't returned—worse with Quinn there. It was an agonizing half hour just going through the receiving line and trying not to meet his eye.

She hurried home to pack. Her brother needed her. He was conceding defeat in the lace mill, begging her to come take half ownership. It should have been Morna's dream come true, and it would have been, if only she hadn't fallen in love with Quinn.

Half an hour later, the trunk was half-filled with her dresses, but it still was slow going. Everything she packed had a memory of Quinn attached to it. The dress she'd been wearing when she'd met him. The dress she'd had on when he'd first kissed her, thinking her a loose woman. She smiled at the memory of his chagrin. . . .

"Morna, where are you going?"

She stiffened.

It was Quinn, and slowly she turned.

"We always knew we'd leave this town eventually. You said so yourself, as soon as the trees were all cut down. . . ." Her throat clogged with emotion.

"The trees aren't all cut down," he said softly, voice husky.

He was perfectly logical, and totally mistaken about her.

"My brother needs me. I have to leave."

"You mean, go back to Ireland?" He sounded incredulous. The only immigrants who went back were the sick ones. He said so.

"I'm not sick. I haven't got scurvy or typhoid."

"What's there for you, then?"

"Family." It was better to leave it at that. If he didn't love her thinking she was poor, she didn't want him to love her at all.

He was silent, and the only sound was the insistent pounding of her heart. His footsteps crossed the room and he moved up behind her. He reached to touch her arms, drew back, then touched her again, finally pulled her around to face him.

Tears swam in his eyes.

"Quinn, please. Don't make this hard on me. I have no regrets, you see."

"I do," he said in a voice like granite. "I regret almost letting you walk out on me. You're the best thing that's happened to me since . . . since . . . Well, the best."

"What do you mean?"

"I love you, Morna."

She stared up at him. "Go on with you now, Quinn Montgomery. What are you saying sweet things for now? Hoping to buy the boardinghouse for a good price? You won the wager. So there's no need to negotiate over it. I'll find some other occupation."

"Is that all you want, Morna?"

"A lady has to support herself."

"Stop it. You don't mean that. Haven't you ever known what it is to want love? To want it so bad you couldn't sleep for the yearning?"

She looked at him. "What are you suggesting?"

"I'm not suggesting. I'm telling you something. I don't want the boardinghouse. I want you. I love you."

"Go on with you. Me, an immigrant from County Kilkenny?"

"I can and I do. Don't go, Morna. What do I have to do to keep you from going back? What's your brother got that I don't?"

She allowed herself a sad smile. Only her dreams.

"A lace factory," she said so softly she wasn't sure he'd hear.

"What?"

She could have told him the truth, but held back. If he didn't love her, he didn't love her, and telling him of her past would not change things. She only wished he understood that.

"My God, Morna, but I never thought I'd love again, never mind to a stubborn woman like you."

"I'm not stubborn. This hasn't been an easy choice for me—choosing between my family and my . . . what did you say?" Had she heard right?

He was smiling at her.

"You argue too much, Morna."

"No, that's not what you said."

"I love you. I've been saying it for five minutes now."

She caught her breath. Her heartbeat quickened, and everything around her became muted or paled against the larger thing—her spinning senses.

Love? Quinn Montgomery didn't love anything except this town and his possessions. Money.

He touched a hand to her chin, tipped her face up to his, and leaned down to touch her lips with his own. He kissed her, pulled her closer, and wrapped her in his sigh.

"Morna, Morna," he whispered against her cheek while he was stroking her hair.

"Quinn, you don't need to say sweet things if—"

He laughed and hugged her closer. "I don't want your damn boardinghouse. Oh, I should have known you'd never believe me. I know what you think—you despise me."

She pulled back and looked into his eyes. "Oh, no, Quinn, that's the last thing I think."

"You don't."

"Far from it. I've loved you for the longest time."

He stared at her. "Then why are you leaving?"

"Because I thought you didn't love me, and I couldn't stay anymore, having you ignore me because of Sarah's ghost."

He looked at her for a minute. "What do you mean, Sarah's ghost?"

"Your wife. The tall tales. The photo. Her room. You still love her, despite what she did to you."

"I used to love her," he corrected her. "At least, it was some infatuation that I thought was love. I've learned different since then. It's you I love, Morna. True and deep and forever."

She gazed up at him, wanting so much to believe his words, but afraid she was hearing things. "When did you decide you love me?"

He smiled at her. "When? A hundred different times. Probably I knew for sure when you waved that blue button at me and told me I was being cruel to the bachelors. I was jealous of them for the first time, and that's when I demanded I move into the boardinghouse for you to have your way. That was the first time. Do you want the other ninety-nine?"

"Mmm. Do we have time?"

"What do you mean, time? You're not going to leave now?"

"Everyone leaves Bunyan. You said so."

"Well, I changed my mind. The trees can be planted again. We can spend the rest of our lives watching them grow. We can make this place a bigger one, one with a fancy hotel for travelers, something to compete with the hotels on Emerald Isle, and—"

"Stop, Quinn. You do what you want. I told you—"

He grabbed her by the arms, gently stroked her wrists, then kissed one palm. "Marry me, Morna. Be my life partner, not my business rival."

She thought she'd gone deaf like Dogger and was hearing her own wish in her imagination.

"Didn't you hear me?"

"The sawmill is loud," she said. "Ask again." She was teasing, but this was a moment to remember. Quinn asking her to marry him. Well, sure and the leprechauns had done their work.

"Marry me?" It was a plea from a man uncertain of his future.

"Yes."

"Yes?"

She nodded, too happy for words.

"Yes!" He held her so close she could scarcely breathe, then whirled her off her feet and around. Then he set her down. "I've been the fool, Morna, living in the past, afraid to live again. I see that now. You made me see that."

"We could go over and visit the lace factory, or I could write and tell my brother that I'll be delayed."

"I spent too long in the past, now I don't want to talk about the future. Only now. Marry me now."

"Will you wear a blue button?"

"As God is my witness, I'll go to the altar decked out in nothing but blue buttons if you'll have me."

And she loved him the more for trusting his heart.

"Let me tell you who I am, for I want no more misunderstandings between us, and if when I'm done with the telling you want to leave, I'll understand. You see, Quinn, I deceived you, too."

He drew in his breath, as if expecting an ax to swing against his heart.

"There's not another man in Ireland, is there?"

Dear Quinn. "No, not in the way you mean. Just my brother."

"And your brother wants you home. What for? To keep house for him? I don't want you to leave. Tell him I'll send him a housekeeper."

She couldn't resist a smile. Oh, she had deceived him, but he'd forgive her.

"He wants me to come help him run our father's lace factory."

"Your what?" Quinn's mouth hung open in surprise. He wasn't an easy man to surprise, she knew.

She gave a little laugh, a laugh of joy overflowing. "Well, sure and you didn't think all this time I was poor, did you? You didn't fall in love with a poor lass, did you?"

"I don't know."

"Well, of course, I came here wanting to compete with you, to be more successful than any man, and, well . . . bide my time until my brother . . . until he failed. And now he has and needs me. I've got what I wanted when I came here. Except now, of course, as irony would have it, I don't want the same thing anymore." Morna choked out the last words.

Quinn's face was wet with tears. She touched her hand to his cheek. Then her lips. She tasted the saltiness of his tears.

Pressing her hand against his lips, he kissed her hand, her wrist, pulled her tight into his arms. "I need you, Morna. I've never needed anyone like I need you. Please stay. I'll give you anything—"

She was weeping, too. "Oh, Quinn, there's not a thing you own I want beyond what I have this moment. Your words, your heart. Things that have no price."

"If everything I owned vanished, I would still be the richest man in the world."

She replied with a kiss to match his own.

From a turn-of-the-century guidebook to Bunyan, Michigan

Bunyan was founded as a company town, which for many years employed workers in the Bunyan Sawmill. But the town is more famous for the legend that grew up in its midst, a legend that has led to numerous Bunyan traditions.

A grand tourist hotel was built there by Mr. Quinn Montgomery, onetime lumber mogul, as a wedding gift to the aristocratic Irishwoman he married, and around the same time, a unique custom began that has continued to this day: Bridal couples wed in Bunyan traditionally exchange blue buttons for white ones as part of the ceremony. Bachelor's-button flowers grow all over town, and blue buttons are popular tourist souvenirs.

The original bachelor boardinghouse where the Montgomerys met is now a museum. Quinn and Morna live with their family in a secluded home in the wooded grove. These woods continue to be off-limits to lumbering, but not to nature enthusiasts.

The town of Bunyan welcomes visitors. Have a pleasant stay.

Our Town

...where love is always right around the corner!

__Harbor Lights__ by Linda Kreisel
> 0-515-11899-0/$5.99

On Maryland's Silchester Island...the perfect summer holiday sparks a perfect summer fling.

__Humble Pie__ by Deborah Lawrence
> 0-515-11900-8/$5.99

In Moose Gulch, Montana...a waitress with a secret meets a stranger with a heart.

__Candy Kiss__ by Ginny Aiken
> 0-515-11941-5/$5.99

In Everleigh, Pennsylvania...a sweet country girl finds the love of a city lawyer with kisses sweeter than candy.

__Cedar Creek__ by Willa Hix
> 0-515-11958-X/$5.99

In Cedarburg, Wisconsin...a young widow falls in love with the local saloon owner, but she has promised her hand to a family friend—and she has to keep her word.

__Sugar and Spice__ by DeWanna Pace
> 0-515-11970-9/$5.99

In Valiant, Texas...an eligible bachelor pines for his first love.